bad for you

ALSO BY ABBI GLINES

The Vincent Boys
The Vincent Brothers

The Sea Breeze Series
Breathe
Because of Low
While it Lasts
Just for Now
Sometimes it Lasts
Misbehaving

The Rosemary Beach Series
Fallen Too Far
Never Too Far
Forever Too Far
Rush Too Far
Twisted Perfection
Simple Perfection
Take a Chance

Abbi Glines

bad for you

A Sea Breeze novel

SIMON AND SCHUSTER

First published in Great Britain in 2014 by Simon & Schuster UK Ltd
A CBS COMPANY

Published in the USA in ebook in 2014 by Simon Pulse,
an imprint of Simon & Schuster Children's Division

1 3 5 7 9 10 8 6 4 2

Simon & Schuster UK Ltd
1st Floor
222 Gray's Inn Road
London WC1X 8HB

Simon & Schuster Australia, Sydney
Simon & Schuster India, New Delhi

A CIP catalogue copy for this book is available
from the British Library.

ISBN: 978-1-4711-2206-4
Ebook ISBN: 978-1-4711-2207-1

*This book is a work of fiction. Names, characters,
places and incidents are either a product of the author's imagination or
are used fictitiously. Any resemblance to actual people, living
or dead, events or locales, is entirely coincidental.*

Printed and bound by CPI Group (UK) Ltd, Croydon, CR0 4YY

www.simonandschuster.co.uk
www.simonandschuster.com.au

Abbi loves to hear from her readers. You can connect with her on
Facebook: Abbi Glines (Official Author Page)
Twitter: @abbiglines
Website: www.abbiglines.com

To Colleen Hoover and Jamie McGuire.
I wouldn't want to travel this road with anyone else.
Knowing I have the both of you to talk to is priceless.
I love your faces.

Acknowledgments

I need to start by thanking my agent, Jane Dystel, who is beyond brilliant. The moment I signed with her was one of the smartest things I've ever done. Thank you, Jane, for helping me navigate through the waters of the publishing world. You are truly a badass.

My amazing editor, Bethany Buck. She makes my stories better with her insight and always seems as excited about the Sea Breeze stories as I am. That makes it so much easier to create. Anna McKean, Paul Crichton, Mara Anastas, Carolyn Swerdloff, and the rest of the Simon Pulse team for all your hard work in getting my books out there.

The friends that listen to me and understand me the way no one else in my life can: Colleen Hoover, Jamie McGuire, and Tammara Webber. You three have listened to me and supported me more than anyone I know. Thanks for everything.

Natasha Tomic for always reading my books the moment I type "The End" even when it requires she stay up all night to do it. She always knows the scenes that need that extra something to make them a quality "peanut-butter-sandwich scene."

Autumn Hull for always listening to me rant and worry. And she still beta reads my books for me. I can't figure out how she puts up with my moodiness. I'm just glad she does.

Last by certainly not least: My family. Without their support I wouldn't be here. My husband, Keith, makes sure I have my coffee and the kids are all taken care of when I need to lock myself away and meet a deadline. My three kids are so understanding, although once I walk out of that writing cave they expect my full attention, and they get it. My parents, who have supported me all along. Even when I decided to write steamier stuff. My friends, who don't hate me because I can't spend time with them for weeks at a time because my writing is taking over. They are my ultimate support group and I love them dearly.

My readers. I never expected to have so many of you. Thank you for reading my books. For loving them and telling others about them. Without you I wouldn't be here. It's that simple.

Prologue

BLYTHE

"Go to bed, Blythe. And don't forget to say your prayers," Mrs. Williams's voice broke into my thoughts. I turned around from the window I was perched next to and looked at the woman who was my guardian. I didn't refer to her as "Mother" because I had made that mistake once and she had hit me with a belt.

"Yes, ma'am," I replied, and climbed down from the window seat I loved so much. It was the only thing that I felt was truly mine. I had asked for a window seat like this when I saw one in a movie once. Mrs. Williams had called me selfish and materialistic. I had been beaten for making a request such as that one.

But her husband, Pastor Williams, had surprised me with one on Christmas morning. It was worth the secret punishments I later received from Mrs. Williams for making her husband sin by giving me a gift.

Mrs. Williams continued as I stood by that seat. "Remember to thank God that you're alive and not dead like your mother," she snapped. The tone in her voice was especially nasty tonight. She was angry about something. I hated it when she was angry. That meant she was going to punish me if I wasn't extra good. Even though I was not the cause of her anger.

"Yes, ma'am," I replied again. I cringed when she spoke of the mother I had never really known, and of her death. I hated hearing the sordid details of how my mother suffered because of her sins. It made me hate God even more. Why he was so mean and full of vengeance, I didn't understand. But then over the years, I realized that the kind heart I saw in Pastor Williams was what God must really be like.

"And," Mrs. Williams went on, "thank him for the roof over your head that you do not deserve," she spit.

She often reminded me of how I didn't deserve the goodness extended to me by her and Pastor Williams. I was used to this as well. They were the closest things to parents I had ever known all my thirteen years here on Earth. My mother had died giving birth to me. She was sick with pneumonia, and it was a miracle I had lived. I had been born six weeks early.

"Yes, ma'am," I replied again, walking slowly over to my bed. I wanted her to step out of my room before I got too close to her. She liked to strike me, but I didn't like to be hit.

She stood with her shoulders straight and her nose tilted up so that she had to look down at me. Her red hair was long and pulled back in a tight bun. The black-rimmed glasses she wore made her squinty brown eyes seem even more sinister.

"And, of course, thank the good Lord for your health. Even though you are exceptionally ugly and have no hope for any beauty, you should be thankful that you are alive. That you are healthy. Because you do not deserve it—"

"That's enough, Margaret." Pastor Williams voice interrupted her. It wasn't the first time she had told me how ugly I was. How the sin of my mother had made me unappealing in looks. How no one would ever love me because I was too hard to even look at. I had accepted my life a long time ago. I didn't look in a mirror if I could help it. I hated seeing that face stare back at me. The one that made Mrs. Williams hate me, and Pastor Williams pity me.

"She needs to know."

"No. She doesn't. You're just angry and taking it out on Blythe. Leave her alone. I'm not warning you another time. This has to stop," he whispered to his wife, but I could still hear his deep voice.

Whenever he caught her telling me how ugly I was or reminding me of the sin that would forever haunt my life, he would correct her and send her away. I let the relief come because

I knew for the next day or so he would be watching her. She wouldn't come near me. She would pout and stay tucked away in her room.

I didn't thank him because I knew that he would ignore me and turn and walk away like he always did. He didn't like looking at me either. The few times in my life he actually looked at me, I could see him wince. Especially lately. I was getting uglier. I had to be.

One day I would be old enough to leave this place. I wouldn't have to go to church and listen about the loving God these people served. The one who made me so ugly. The one who took my mother away. I wanted to escape all this and hide away in a small town where no one knew me. A place where I could just be alone and write. In my stories I could be beautiful. The prince would love me, and I would know how it felt to belong. I loved my stories. Even if right now they were all in my head.

"Go to bed, Blythe," Pastor Williams said as he turned to follow his wife down the hallway.

"Yes, sir. Good night, sir," I replied.

He stopped, and I waited to see if he would say more. If he would turn around and smile at me. Or if he would just look at me. Maybe assure me that my mother's sin wasn't going to control my life forever. But he never did. He just stood there with his back to me for a moment before his shoulders sagged as he walked away.

One day ... I would be free.

Chapter One

BLYTHE

I was as ugly inside as I was outside. It was the only explanation for the fact I hadn't been able to cry one single tear. I hadn't even squeezed out one fake tear at Mrs. Williams's funeral. I knew the church people thought I was evil. I could see it when they looked at me. But they had all gotten to witness it firsthand when they'd watched me not show one small streak of emotion when I'd stood beside Pastor Williams as they'd lowered his wife into the ground. She had been diagnosed with a brain tumor only five months ago. It had been stage five, and there had been nothing they could have done.

The congregation had stopped by to check on her daily, and the parsonage had been flooded with casseroles, pies, and flowers. I had been told to stay out of sight. I'd only upset her. Pastor

Williams had been kind when he'd instructed me to keep to my room when I'd come home from school, but it'd still stung. I'd waited until I was sure they were asleep most nights to sneak downstairs and fix myself something to eat for dinner. The endless supply of food had made it easy.

When she had finally taken her last breath, the hospice nurse had come and knocked on my door to inform me. I had been asked to call Pastor Williams at the church and have him come home. I hadn't felt anything. Not one emotion from the news. I'd realized then that she had been right all those years. I was evil. Only someone truly evil could be so indifferent to death. Mrs. Williams had been only fifty-four. But then, that was much older than my mother had been when she'd died—she had been only twenty.

That was all behind me now. That life was over and in my past.

I stood outside the apartment building that overlooked the Alabama gulf coast and let it sink in that this was now my home. I was far away from the life I'd lived in South Carolina. I would have a new life here. One where I could sit and write my stories and attend the community college.

Pastor Williams had wanted to get rid of me. I was thankful for that because I needed a way to get free from that place. He had called a friend of his and had gotten me into a community college ten hours away from the town full of people who hated me. He had bought me an apartment on the beach and even managed to get me a job working as a church secretary. He had a friend who pastored a church in Sea Breeze, Alabama. It was one of the reasons he had sent me here. He had had someone help set me up while he remained in South Carolina.

I had heard Pastor Williams on the phone explaining to the man who would be my boss that I wasn't good with people and I was sheltered. Which wasn't exactly true. I had gone to an all-girl Christian academy, and everyone there had pretended that I hadn't existed. It wasn't my fault their mommas had told them about the evil inside me. I had never had a chance to actually be around people who wanted anything to do with me.

Before I took my boxes out of the truck, I wanted to check out the apartment. Pastor Williams had given me a truck, too. Grabbing my purse and the keys he had placed in an envelope, along with one thousand dollars in cash, I jumped down out of the old truck and headed for the stairs. None of the apartments were on the street level. They were all on stilts above the ground. I figured this was for times when the water got high … or during hurricanes. I wasn't going to think about hurricanes. Not now.

I slipped the key into the lock and turned before pushing the door open. It swung wide, and I took in the pretty pale yellow walls and white wicker furniture. It was all very coastal. I loved it.

Smiling, I walked inside and spun around in a circle with my arms opened wide. I tilted my head back and closed my eyes and let myself bask in the solitude. No one knew me here. I wasn't the evil girl who the pastor was stuck taking care of. I was just me. Blythe Denton. And I was a writer. A recluse eccentric writer who didn't care what she looked like. It didn't matter. She was free.

Loud male voices laughing and throwing insults in the hallway interrupted my quiet moment of joy. I dropped my arms to turn and lock gazes with ... with ... a guy. Blue. Like the sky on a clear sunny day. That was all I could focus on. I had never seen eyes so blue. They were so startling, they were almost breathtaking. His friends' voices were fading away, but he was still standing there. Then I noticed it. ... Was he wearing black eyeliner? I dropped my eyes to take in the rest of him.

The pierced eyebrow and colorful tattooed skin I saw covering his arms had me jerking my gaze back up to his face. Seemingly windblown platinum-blond hair finished the wild look.

"You done, love? Or is it my turn?" The teasing lilt to his low husky voice reminded me of warm chocolate. It made me feel almost giddy.

Not sure what he was talking about, I looked back at his amused eyes. "I, uh ..." I what? I didn't know what to say. "I don't know what you mean," I finally told him honestly. Should I apologize for staring at him? Had I been?

"Are you done checking me out? Because I'd hate to interrupt you."

Oh. My face heated, and I knew my cheeks were bright red. What was I thinking, leaving my door open for the world to see me? I wasn't used to this. Keeping my distance from men in general made me extremely inept at talking to one. However, this one didn't stare at me with that leer that made me nervous. I was used to the look men gave me because they thought I would do bad things with them. The ugly they saw didn't seem to deter them from wanting to see if I was as evil as they had heard.

"It's just some tattoos and a couple piercings, love. I promise I'm harmless," he said, this time with a smile on his face.

I managed to nod. I should say something. I just wasn't sure what to say. He was waiting on me to speak. "I like them," I blurted out nervously. That sounded stupid. He raised an eyebrow, and a smirk touched his lips. "The tattoos—they're nice. Colorful. Uh ... I ..." I sounded like an idiot. There was no saving myself from this disaster. Closing my eyes so I didn't have to see those blue eyes watching me, I took a deep breath. "I'm not good at talking to people—guys, people, anyone really." Had I really just told him that?

If he would just turn and leave, then we could forget this moment forever. I forced my eyes open and caught him studying me with that grin still on his lips. He was going to think I was nuts. Maybe he was visiting someone here and didn't live in this complex. I really didn't want to face him again. Ever.

He pressed the pad of his thumb to his bottom lip and bit the tip of it before chuckling and shaking his head. "Not sure I've met anyone quite like you," he said before letting his hand fall back down to his side.

I was positive he hadn't.

"Krit, dude." A male voice called down loudly from what sounded like the second floor. "We got, like, thirty minutes until we gotta be there. Go fucking shower and change."

"Shit," he muttered, glancing down at his phone as he pulled it out of his pocket. "Gotta go. But I'll see you around, little dancer," he said with a wink, then stepped back out of the doorway and walked down the hall.

Little dancer? Oh. I covered my face with both hands. He had seen me spinning around like an idiot. I sure hoped I didn't see him again. I just wanted to live life without drawing attention to myself. I was leaving that life—the one where people saw me and huddled together while laughing and glancing at me—behind. I didn't want to give anyone here ammunition to make fun of me. Being invisible couldn't be that hard.

Unless you try to talk to guys, genius, I thought to myself. Walking over to the door, I closed and locked it. Next time I wanted to do something like spin in circles, I needed to close my door first.

KRIT

Tonight we had a gig at Live Bay. It was a club in town that drew both tourists and locals. We had become a crowd favorite over the past two years, so the three nights a week we played at the club equaled four hundred and fifty dollars for each of us. Live Bay, along with the bar we played at an hour away in Florida, and another club in Mobile, Alabama, both weekly gigs, allowed each of us to clear over a grand a week just performing.

Green, my best friend and bass guitar in our band, Jackdown, and I shared an apartment. However, we always had people crashing there. We were a family. We had been since we started this thing. Other than my older sister, Trisha, I hadn't had family, really. Our home life had sucked growing up. Now Trisha had her husband, Rock, and the three kids they'd adopted. She managed to make it most Thursday nights to listen to me play, but that was it now. Used to be that she wouldn't miss a single one of my shows.

I got it though. I was good with it. She finally had the family she'd always wanted, and she was happy. That was enough. She was a damn good mom, and those kids were lucky she was theirs now.

We had a good show even though Trish wasn't there. But the redhead I'd decided to bring home that night was tugging on my arm, needing attention. I hadn't had enough to drink, and I was lost in my thoughts instead of focusing on her tits, she so wanted me to notice her. I'd noticed already. It was one of the reasons she was going back to my place.

"You're ignoring me," the girl pouted, sticking out her lips, which were painted a deep red. I liked red lips. Another reason she was with me.

"Easy there. He has an easy trigger after a gig," Green called back to us from the driver's seat. He knew how annoyed I could get with clingy needy girls. I just wanted them willing and easy.

"I'm just making sure he hasn't changed his mind," the girl replied.

"When I change my mind, love, you'll know it," I told her, then leaned down to take a taste of her red lips. They had the flavor of the candy she had been sucking on earlier, and beer. It was a good taste. I wanted a little more.

Green chuckled from the front seat as the car came to a stop. "See, he's all fun and games if you just let him be," he said.

I broke the kiss and got out of the car. I was ready for a drink and some music. And a lot of people. I needed the crowd. "They all coming?" I asked Green as I held out my hand for the girl to take. She quickly scrambled out of the car and clung to me.

"Probably already here," he replied. The band liked crashing at our place on nights we played at Live Bay. We kept an open door for any neighbors. Seeing as they were all college students, they never complained. They came and joined the party.

"What's your name?" I asked the girl on my arm.

I glanced down at her to see the pinched frown on her lips. She'd told me earlier, but I hadn't cared then. I hadn't been sure I'd be spending the night with her yet. Now I wanted to know. I didn't fuck a girl if I didn't know her name.

"Jasmine," she replied, then flipped her red hair over her shoulder.

Jasmine seemed to have a bit of a temper with that red hair of hers. Normally, I was amused but not tonight. I was moody.

The music was already going when we started up the stairs. There was no doubt it was coming from our apartment. Matty, our drummer, always grabbed a girl or three quickly and left the club after we finished our gig. But most of the time he got to the apartment first if his females didn't slow him down.

"Looks like the party has already started. I'm gonna step out early and go find somewhere to study," Green said as he slowed to walk beside me.

Green was almost done with law school. He would be taking the bar exam in six months. I was proud of him, but I also knew things would be changing soon. He wasn't going to be able to pursue law and live like we were living. He rarely stayed for the parties. He always escaped to go study. Eventually I would lose him, but I wanted him to succeed.

"We should move the parties to Matty's from now on," I said, feeling guilty that Green had to leave his place to be able to study.

Green shook his head. "Hell, no. The dipshit doesn't ever clean up, and his apartment is tiny as fuck. Besides, let's not mess with a good thing. I've made it this far doing it this way. It works."

Since we'd been kids, Green had been the smart one. The one who always sacrificed. He made things happen. But somehow I had always been the one in the spotlight. Didn't really seem fair.

"Just say the word when you want to change that," I told him, then glanced over at the closed apartment door we were passing.

A smile tugged on the corner of my lips. Damn, that girl had been adorable twirling around her apartment. I had never seen such long thick hair that was so dark, it was almost black. Then those eyes of hers had been fucking amazing. I wasn't even sure what color they were exactly. They looked like they were hazel, but they reminded me of jewels. They'd been startling at first.

Although she had been wearing baggy-ass sweats and an even larger T-shirt, I could see the curves underneath. Sucked that I was only going to have to imagine what they actually looked like because I wasn't touching that. The innocence pouring off that girl was thick. She had barely been able to form words to talk to me.

Fucking adorable was what it had been. And I didn't do adorable. Ever.

Jasmine's hand slid down over my jeans and cupped my balls. "I like to suck," she whispered in my ear.

"Good. You can show me how much as soon as we get in the room," I told her, and reached around to cup her ass.

That had been all the reassurance she needed apparently, because she started unbuttoning my jeans before we reached the door to my apartment. Green turned back to say something to me and saw her hand busy at work with my jeans. He laughed and rolled his eyes then walked into our apartment, which was already full of several of the guys who lived around us, and a few locals who we partied with regularly. Of course, there were plenty of girls. Just in case Jasmine didn't work out.

Chapter Two

BLYTHE

The sun broke through the blinds on the windows, waking me up much sooner than I'd wanted to. I reached for my pillow and covered my face with a groan. It had been sometime after three before the noise upstairs had ended and I had been able to fall asleep. I kept waiting for the cops to show up and shut the party down. Surely there had been other people in this complex who had been trying to sleep.

But the cops never came. The music continued blaring, and the banging on my ceiling had only gotten worse. I hoped they enjoyed themselves, celebrating whatever it was they were celebrating, but I hoped they never did it again. I still had a week before my classes started. Which meant I had a week to get the things I needed and get settled in my apartment.

Even exhaustion couldn't keep the smile from creeping across my face. Wearing panties and a tank top, I was about to get up and go fix myself breakfast. Then I was going to sit and eat it in on the sofa and not worry about anyone making me feel unwelcomed. I was free. I was finally alone, and there was no one to disapprove of me.

Kicking off my covers, I got out of bed and looked down. Normally, the first thing I did when I got up was make the bed or suffer punishment. Now I wasn't sure if I would ever make my bed again. With a spring in my step I headed for the kitchen to make coffee and toast a bagel.

Then I would make a list of things I needed for school and my apartment. Although it had come with furniture that Pastor Williams had said was part of the monthly payment, it didn't have things like curtains or a can opener. The shower curtain was also a plain white. I wanted to add some color, and because I wasn't supposed to paint the walls, I had to add color elsewhere. Maybe I could find some pillows for the sofa and some pictures for the walls. I didn't have an unlimited budget, so I needed to be careful.

I also didn't start my job for another week, and then it would be another week before I received my first check. Some things would have to wait until later. But I could get started today.

Clothes. I needed a few outfits that weren't oversize hand-me-downs or had come from the thrift store. I really needed to buy a few basic things to get me through the next few months of school and work. I couldn't go to work in what I owned right now. I knew that clothes wouldn't change the way I looked, but they would at least help me appear more presentable. I decided to keep the pillows that came with the sofa. And the pictures for the walls could wait.

It took me a little over an hour to find two pairs of shorts and a denim skirt that all hit above my knees. I had never worn anything that showed off my legs before. It was both terrifying and exhilarating. Even better than leaving my bed unmade. Then I had bought one pair of jeans that actually fit me. Almost too well. Once I had bottoms, I went to look for tops. I had bought four blouses and two tank tops. Finally I picked out a pair of tennis shoes that would work best for work and school. They were all I really needed, but the pretty pink high heels kept drawing my attention. I had never had shoes with heels, or shoes that could be considered pretty, for that matter. These weren't very dressy and could be worn with the skirt and two of my blouses. I could even wear them with the shorts. I had seen girls do that before.

I tried several times to walk away from them, but in the end I picked up the box with my size and walked to the register to pay for them before I could change my mind again. I was going to live differently here. These heels were a symbol of that new life.

Carrying all the shopping bags up to my apartment wasn't exactly fun. I was on the first floor, but I was also on the beach. So I had to walk up a flight of stairs just to get to the first floor. The people above me had even farther to walk. There were no elevators here since it was just the two floors. It took me five trips up and down to get everything into my apartment. But then my energy was renewed with the thrill of getting to put things in their places.

When I turned to close my apartment door my eyes locked with the electric blue ones I'd seen yesterday. That guy was standing there again, leaning against the door casing with his arms crossed over his chest and a smirk on his face.

"Looks like someone went shopping bright and early this morning," he said with that husky voice of his that made my body do funny things.

I nodded, afraid of the stupidity that would come out of my mouth if I tried to talk to him again. I suddenly wished I had put on one of my new outfits and worn it home. Which was silly. I shouldn't care what I looked like for this guy.

"My band plays at Live Bay on Thursday, Friday, and Saturday nights. You should stop in one night and see us. I'll even buy you a drink during my break," he said with that amused grin still on his lips.

Was he teasing me?

I had to respond this time. Nodding again would be rude. "Okay. I'll do that one night ... maybe," I replied. I wasn't sure if I would ever go to Live Bay—wherever that was—but telling him no seemed impossible.

"I'll look out for you then." He straightened up from his relaxed stance. "I never got your name."

My name. He wanted to know my name. I could answer that easily enough. "Blythe?" I replied, wishing it hadn't sounded like I was asking him instead of telling him.

He winked. "Fits you," he replied, then sauntered off without another word. He hadn't told me his name, but I remembered it from yesterday when his friend had called for him. Krit. It was an unusual name. I wondered what it was short for. Walking over to my door, I closed it and forced all thoughts of how sexy Krit's eyes had looked without black eyeliner far from my mind.

KRIT

"I need something more than shitty beer," Legend, our keyboard player, grumbled, sinking down into an overstuffed chair that belonged to Green.

I leaned forward and kissed the ear of the girl who was in my lap, and I relaxed on the couch. "Why don't you go fix Legend some whiskey on the rocks, love." It wasn't a question, and she knew it. Britt was one of the girls I saw off and on. I didn't see most girls more than once, but there were a few who were good with no attachments. The fact that Britt was nice and flexible, she was one who I got in the mood for every few weeks or so. Sometimes we saw each other more regularly. Just depended on how things were going in life.

Legend was busy watching television that couldn't be heard over the music and voices. There were over thirty people in my apartment. Several were watching the football game on my flat-screen. It was an early night for us. I hadn't planned on a party tonight, but the guys had shown up, and Green had been free of studying for once. So it happened.

Britt sashayed over to Legend and bent over while she handed him his drink to make sure I got a good view of her ass. It was barely covered up with the skirt she was wearing. Chuckling at her attempts, I took a drink of my beer and lifted my eyes to see Green standing and talking to someone at our open door.

Normally, people just came on in, but whoever it was wasn't coming in. They were just talking to Green. He waved his hand and stepped back in invitation. It was Blythe. Her eyes scanned the room of people nervously, but she didn't step inside. She also didn't seem to notice me. Then Green reached out and took her hand and pulled her into the room.

I only noticed Green's stupid grin before my eyes snapped back to Blythe. Holy shit, she wasn't in baggy clothes tonight.

Those curves I had thought I had seen hiding beneath those awful clothes were right there for the world to see. A pair of black shorts that showcased legs from fucking heaven was only outdone by the tank top that covered an impressive set of tits. Then put that all together with the glasses perched on her cute little nose. She hadn't had those on before, but damn, they were sexy.

I realized Green was walking her over to me. Britt slipped her arm around me, plopped herself back in my lap, and began nibbling on my neck.

"Uh, dude, can you break free long enough to come here a sec?" Green asked, sounding uncomfortable. Blythe's eyes grew wide as she watched Britt. Fuck, that innocence was there, shining like a warning sign. As if I needed it. I knew the girl wasn't my speed. But damn, she was tempting. I wanted to reach up and undo that messy bun she had her hair pulled up in.

I moved Brit off of my lap and stood up. Blythe's eyes went from Britt to me, and then she dropped her gaze to study the floor. I noticed Green's hand resting on her arm as if he was there to jerk her from harm's way if needed. I didn't like that. I wasn't sure why, but I didn't. She was letting him keep his hand on her too.

"Did you decide to come join the party, love?" I asked, keeping my grin in place so I didn't scare her with the snarl I was tempted to give Green. He was a horny bastard. Blythe wasn't his speed either.

"No, that's not why she's here. Can we take this outside where we don't have to talk so loud?" Green asked me with a pointed stare. What was his deal?

Blythe looked back longingly at the door like getting out of there was all she wanted in the world.

"Sure," I replied, and Blythe spun around and hurried for the door.

Green shrugged and turned to follow her.

I glanced back at Britt, who was watching us closely. I motioned to her that I would be right back, then headed toward the door.

Green was standing there asking Blythe her name, and Blythe gave him a shy smile that was more than I had ever gotten from her. What the hell? Green wasn't the charmer. I was.

"What's the problem?" I asked, as I joined them in the hallway. The annoyed tone in my voice didn't go unnoticed by Blythe. Her eyes widened, and she started wringing her hands in front of her nervously.

"Krit, this is our new neighbor, Blythe. She lives directly underneath us," he said in a tone that was obviously trying to make up for mine.

"We've met," I told him, swinging my gaze to hers.

Her cheeks turned bright pink. Why? I hadn't said anything to embarrass her.

"Oh, okay. Well, we are being inconsiderate with our noise level. This is two nights in a row that we've partied, and Blythe isn't getting much sleep."

So she was here to complain. Interesting. No one had ever complained before. This apartment complex was known for parties. Had she not known that when she moved in here?

I studied her face as she bit down on her bottom lip and looked ready to bolt. She thought she was going to make me mad. I was pretty damn sure that a girl who looked like her was incapable of making me mad. She gave off the "I need protecting" vibe in a big way. Add that to the heart-stopping face of hers, and she had a winning package deal to get away with all shit, even from me.

I stepped closer to her, which forced Green to move back some. Reaching down, I pulled one of her hands she was gripping so tightly into mine and ran my finger along the inside of her palm.

"Why don't you come inside with me just for a few minutes? Meet some of your neighbors, and then when you're ready to go, I think I have something that will help with the noise," I told her as I kept my gaze locked with hers.

"I, uh, I'm not good with crowds," she said, with an apologetic tone.

I tugged on her hand until she was almost pressed against me. "I won't leave your side, and I'm fucking amazing with crowds," I replied with a wink to let her know I was serious.

"Don't make her—" Green started to argue, but I cut him off.

"Not your business. Back off," I warned him before sliding my hand around Blythe's waist and walking her to the door.

Chapter Three

BLYTHE

I didn't want to do this. Why had I come up here? Because I was tired and frustrated with the noise. That's why. I had spent hours writing, then, when I got ready for bed, the noise had started up again. Did these people not need sleep? I just wanted to ask them to be a little quieter. I hadn't wanted to be forced into staying at the party. I just wanted to go to bed.

"I really don't want to do this," I told Krit, who had his hand on my back and was firmly guiding me inside.

"Why not? They won't bite you. I promise, because I won't fucking let them." The amusement in his voice bothered me. I wasn't kidding. I didn't want to go into this party.

"Please. I'm sorry I came up here. I will figure out how to sleep through this. Just let me leave." I was ready to beg now.

Whatever I needed to do to get away from this place. I could feel people staring at me. I hated that feeling. I knew what they were thinking. What they saw. I had come up here with my glasses on because I'd needed to see the computer screen, and my hair was in a mess on top of my head. My heart began to race. I had to get out of there.

"Shit, love, you're shaking." Krit's voice was no longer amused. He stopped walking, and slipped his finger under my chin to tilt my head back. The frown on his face as he studied mine was new. He normally looked constantly amused.

"Come with me," he said quietly, and reached down to take my hand. Then he walked down a hallway toward a closed door.

My panic escalated. That was a bedroom. I wasn't going into a bedroom with him. I had to get away. I tried to tug my hand loose from his hold, but he threaded his fingers through mine and tightened his grip. No one had ever held my hand before. I stared down at his hand in mine and lost my train of thought for a moment.

It was a warm feeling having someone's palm pressed against yours. His fingers laced with mine made me feel like I wasn't alone. Like I was connected to someone. Had I ever felt that before? I wasn't sure.

A door swung open, and Krit pulled me inside before closing it behind me.

"Don't look so terrified. I'm not going to do anything you don't want me to. Just wanted to get you away from the noise a minute so we could be alone and talk."

"Talk?" I asked, as his hand released mine. The cold lonely feeling was back. I clasped my hands in an attempt to hold the warmth there. I had liked that warmth.

"You confuse me. Most girls don't confuse me. But you, little dancer, have me playing guessing games. Why is that?"

He called me little dancer again. I wasn't a dancer. Not even close. But I liked that he had a special name for me. It made me feel like I belonged.

"I didn't really get into a social scene growing up. Not very good at that. I don't fit in." I hated pointing that out to him. For some reason he didn't seem to get that I didn't fit in, and I hadn't wanted to be the one to break the news to him.

Krit cocked an eyebrow. "You say that like it's a bad thing. Most people want to stand out."

Stand out? That wasn't what I meant. I shook my head. "No, that's not … I mean, I don't … I'm not appealing to be around." That probably made less sense. I wasn't about to open up to this guy about what was wrong with me. If he didn't see it, then good. I liked that.

Krit frowned and stared at me like I was insane. Great. Now he saw the real me. Whatever he had been missing, I had just pointed it out to him. Why hadn't I kept my mouth shut?

"You really mean that," he said in a low whisper as he continued to stare at me. "Who the fuck told you that?"

I shrugged and turned my gaze from his to study the bedroom we were in. I wasn't going to answer his question. That was something no one needed to know.

The walls were a smoky gray color, and the ceiling was painted black. I wasn't allowed to paint my walls, yet he had painted his. The large king-size bed in the middle of the room was a rumpled mess. An electric guitar sat in one corner, and in the other far corner was an acoustic guitar. I turned my focus to the posters on the walls. Two of them were of what I assumed were rock bands, and there were signatures on them. Then, of course, the other poster was of a naked blonde with really big—and hopefully fake—boobs, because they looked a lot like bowling balls. They couldn't be real. The blonde was straddling a guitar, and the only thing keeping her private area covered were her hands gripping the guitar between her legs.

"I wonder if she ever wears panties," I mumbled out loud before I could stop myself.

Krit's laughter startled me, and I turned to see two very distinct dimples on his face. He didn't look like the kind of guy who would have dimples, but wow, they did things for me. "I like to believe she doesn't," he replied, once he was through laughing.

"Where are you from?" Krit asked.

"A small town in South Carolina. You wouldn't have heard of

it," I replied, feeling the sick knot in my stomach forming, the one that always came with memories of my life there.

"Are they blind in that small town I wouldn't have heard of?" he asked with a softer tone to his voice.

I swung my gaze back to his and studied his expression. Was he teasing me again? "No," I replied.

Krit frowned then slowly ran his thumb over his bottom lip several times. It was a fascinating thing to watch. He had really nice lips. I wondered how often he used them. I would assume he was very talented with those lips.

His hand fell away, and he took a step toward me. "Will you go in there and meet everyone for me? Maybe have a beer? Just try to relax and enjoy being in a crowd?" His voice had dropped to a smooth thick drawl. It was very hard to tell him no. "I just want you to ease into being social. Here it's safe because I'll make sure it's safe. I won't let anything happen to you or hurt you."

In a few days school was starting, and I would need to be in lots of social situations. This was my new start. I wanted to be able to walk through a crowd without having a panic attack. If Krit could help me, then maybe I should at least try.

"Okay," I blurted, before I could change my mind.

The pleased grin on his face was almost worth the fact I was going to have to face strangers who might not be as blind as he was about me. Someone was bound to see the bad in me. They always had before.

He nodded toward the door and grinned. "Let's go." Then he made his way to the door to walk out of the safety I had found in his room. I couldn't seem to get my legs to follow him.

When he glanced back to see I hadn't made a move to go with him, he chuckled and shook his head. Then he held out his hand to me and waited.

I liked holding his hand. I could do this. I took a step forward and slipped my hand in his. The warmth was back, and I was able to take a deep breath again. Okay. This was good.

"Come on, little dancer," he said gently, then led me out of the room and down the hall.

The music was louder out there and the laughter and voices reminded me of how I didn't fit in to this world. I was a loner. I liked being a loner. As if Krit could read my mind, he squeezed my hand reassuringly. Right. He was with me. This was his crowd, and he wasn't going to let anyone say anything to hurt me.

"Where'd you two go?" Green asked with a frown on his face, but I couldn't hear Krit's response over the noise.

I started to say something to Green, who was really nice and who I had felt comfortable with right away. He had a friendly smile. Before I could speak to him, Krit pulled me over to stand beside him. "Here's a beer," he said, handing me a red plastic cup. I took it, although I wasn't sure I was going to drink it. I didn't like the way alcohol smelled.

"You left me," the blonde I had seen him with when I arrived said as she walked up to him and turned her back to me.

"A friend showed up. Sorry, babe, but I'm going to spend some time with her. I'll find you after she leaves," he replied with a wink, and tugged me closer before walking us toward the sofa.

The girl pouted at him then shot an angry glare at me. She was upset that I was taking her date away. She should be. I wasn't going to make any friends by doing that.

Krit sank onto the sofa, pulling me down beside him. I could feel people staring at us. Were they all mad that he wasn't with the blond girl? I studied the cup in my hand, unable to lift my eyes.

"Who's this?" a curious male voice asked. He didn't sound angry. He sounded nice.

"This"—Krit slipped his finger under my chin and lifted it so that I was now forced to look at the person speaking to him— "is my new neighbor, Blythe. Blythe, this is Matty. He's the drummer in our band."

Matty had bright orange hair that stuck up in all different directions. I wasn't able to focus on much else. I had never seen hair quite like his before.

"Hello, Blythe," Matty said, and I realized he had a warm smile and friendly brown eyes.

"It's nice to meet you," I croaked out. The nerves weren't letting up. Speaking to strangers was hard.

Matty's grin got bigger, and he shifted his gaze back to Krit. "Dude," he replied, and shook his head. I watched him take a long drink of the beer in his hand.

"Matty can be a douche, but we overlook his lack of verbal skills," Krit said so close to my ear that his warm breath tickled the sensitive skin there.

I shivered, and Krit went very still beside me. Before I could start worrying about my reaction, his hand tightened its hold on mine. Again the warmth calmed me.

"Dude," Matty said a second time, now chuckling. "Shitting me," he muttered, then turned his attention to me and smirked. "Careful with him, sweetheart."

"Don't," Krit said in a hard voice that startled me.

Matty's eyebrows shot up, then he walked off. He had seen me. He saw what everyone saw. I wanted to leave. Krit was the most accepting person I had ever met, and I didn't want to meet any more of his friends, because I was sure they would all react like Matty had.

"I need to go," I told Krit as I tried to slip my hand from his.

"No," he said, tightening his grasp. "Ignore him," he said.

I wished I could have ignored him, but I had spent my life dealing with people not wanting to be around me. And there was a beautiful blond woman there who wanted to be with Krit. He was trying to help me fit in, and he was being so kind about it. I couldn't do this to him.

"I am really tired. Thank you for … for sitting with me and talking to me," I said. "But I really am ready to go back to my apartment."

I managed to get my hand free, and I stood up quickly and darted for the door. I kept my head down and my attention focused on not tripping and falling. Once I was free of the apartment, I took a deep breath but kept moving.

"Blythe." Green's voice called out to me, and I wanted to ignore him and get to the safety of my apartment. But he had been nice to me.

I stopped and looked back at him. He was walking out of the apartment and headed toward me. "Are you okay?"

I nodded and forced a smile. "Yeah, just tired."

He didn't look like he believed me. "You sure?"

Krit was moving through the crowd now. His eyes were on me, and he was headed my way. I had to go. "Really, I'm fine. I just want to go back to my place."

"Blythe." Krit's demanding voice stopped me from running. He sounded angry. I hadn't meant to make him angry.

"What did you do?" Green asked him as he scowled at Krit.

"Fuck off," he growled at Green. "I didn't do shit. I need to talk to her, so go," he replied, but his eyes were locked on me.

"She's not one of—" Green started, but Krit was in his face immediately.

"I fucking know that. Not what this is about. Now, go."

Green let out a defeated sigh and nodded before turning to walk back into the party.

"What happened in there?" he asked me.

He still didn't get it, and I couldn't bring myself to break the news to him that I was tainted. "I'm just tired," I told him.

He ran a hand through his blond locks and sighed. "Okay. I get that. If it's the real reason you're leaving." He pointed back at his door. "But if this is about what Matty said, then ignore his stupid ass. He thinks I'm trying to make a move on you." He stopped and grinned at me like he had made a private joke. "He saw you and assumed the wrong thing. I'm not blind, Blythe. I know you're not my kind. He was worried about it. I'm not a bad guy. I would never go there with you. I see you. I get it. I was just trying to be friendly. You seemed like you needed someone to help you deal with shit, and I wanted to help."

Oh. So he did see me. He knew. I was going to be sick. My head started pounding, and the small amount of comfort I had taken from him was ripped away. I had to go. I managed a nod before I took off running. I had to get to my apartment before I threw up. The sick knot in my stomach had exploded.

KRIT

I stood at the window overlooking the gulf as I drank my second cup of coffee. It was fifteen minutes to eleven, but I hadn't been up very long. Britt's snuggling had woken me up. I didn't like it when Britt passed out and stayed the night after sex. She touched me when she slept, and I hated being touched.

It had taken me getting trashed to fuck Britt after my sexy little shy-as-hell neighbor went running off like the bats of hell were chasing her. Shit, that girl was fucked up. It was the only explanation. The girl had head issues. Sure, she was gorgeous, and damn, those eyes were hard not to get lost in. But the head issues were more than I could handle.

Britt was easy. I liked easy.

But Britt didn't have the sweetest smile I'd ever seen. Shit. Shaking my head, I slammed my cup down and turned around to see Green standing in the living room, glaring at me.

"What?" I snarled. I hated it when he had that judgmental look on his face.

"You know what," he replied, annoyed. "You couldn't just leave it alone. I had it under control. She liked me. She was getting comfortable with me. But you had to fucking prove you could get her attention. She isn't like that. She's *innocent*, Krit. Motherfucking innocent. Stay away from her."

It had been a long time since we had fought about a female.

"I know she's innocent. I was being friendly. She was freaking the fuck out, and I was trying to help her. She's shy."

Green threw his hands up into the air. "What the hell did you think I was doing?"

He had been looking at that sweet ass body of hers, was what he had been doing. "I was just trying to help her," I explained. "Not get her to let me in her pants. I was protecting her from you too. *You* stay the fuck away from her," I warned him.

"Unbelievable. You are a selfish shit. That isn't what you were doing. She liked me. I could see it in her eyes. But you came and snatched her away and sent her running off."

"Something is off with her. I don't know what, but she has some issues. She isn't up for getting to know you any more than a friend. You want a helluva lot more than to be her friend. My last warning, Green. Stay the fuck away from her. She's not like that."

"What are y'all going on about?" Britt asked as she rubbed the sleep from her eyes. She was wearing the sheet off my bed. I hated it when she went walking around with my damn sheets.

"Go get clothed and leave," I ordered, before heading for the bathroom to take a shower.

"I don't know why you always treat me like shit the next morning. We had a good time last night," she snapped at me as I walked by her.

"Throw that sheet in with the dirty clothes before you leave," was my only reply. Then I closed the bathroom door and locked it.

"You're an ass!" Britt yelled loud enough for everyone to hear.

"Yet you keep fucking him," Green replied. "Told you before, he'll never treat you like he did Jess. She was different for him. No one else is gonna get that Krit."

Jess. She had been the only woman I had ever let get close enough to me to get me. But we had grown up together. It was easy with Jess. And damn, she was smoking hot. The things she could do with her body. Fuck, I missed her. I reached into the shower and turned on the faucet.

I had put Jess behind me. She was in love and living up north with her Harvard trust-fund boyfriend. She was getting that fairy tale she had always wanted, and I had to admit I was happy for her. A life like that didn't come around for people like Jess and me. If I couldn't have Jess, I was glad the man she wanted adored her. And that fucker worshiped the ground she walked on. It was the only reason I had been able to handle watching her go.

I knew I'd never be what Jess needed. I had addictions, and women was one of them. Lots of women. I loved the way they smelled and how soft they were. I loved how warm and tight they felt when I sank into them. I loved everything about them. When Jess had put a halt to our relationship, I'd run off that night and had a threesome. No problem.

Apparently Jess saw that as me not loving her. I did love her, but she'd pushed me away and I'd gone and gotten me some. I realized later that that had been a bad move. But it had been real. It had been me. Jess knew that deep down I wasn't a one-woman guy, and as much as I wanted her, I couldn't be what she deserved.

Craving touch wasn't a fucking sin. I had gone without it growing up and I liked affection. I liked how good a woman made me feel. My sister wanted me to get counseling because she was sure our childhood had screwed me up. But I was fine. Life was good and I didn't need a psycho shrink telling me why I liked to fuck women.

Chapter Four

BLYTHE

The rest of the week went by without one sighting of Krit. He didn't even have any parties. Although, the day after I had gone upstairs to quiet the last party, I had come home from the library to find an iPod and a set of earbuds by my door. A small note read, *To help with your loud neighbor's noise.—K.*

I had looked for him over the next couple of days to tell him thank you. The iPod had been stocked with more than two thousand songs. It seemed I never ran out of something good to listen to. After I didn't see or hear him for seven full days, I realized that maybe he was avoiding me.

It was what I'd expected, but it still hurt more than I wanted to admit. For a moment I thought maybe he could look past all that was wrong with me, and I could finally have a friend. That, however, wasn't the case.

Today I started college. I had World Literature and Physics 101, and then I had a meeting with my new boss. Pastor Williams had set me up to work with a pastor at a local church. I wasn't sure what Pastor Williams had told this pastor about me, but he seemed sure that I would fit in there just fine. The fear that this new pastor would take one look at me and throw me out had been weighing on my mind. If an eyeliner-wearing tattooed rocker could see the faults in me, then surely a minister of a church could.

But worrying about that wasn't going to fix anything for me. It would only make matters worse. I brushed my hair one more time and stared at myself in the mirror. I had decided to wear a pair of jeans today with the nicer blouse I had purchased, the one that matched my pink heels. I wasn't sure what the church expected me to wear to work, but since I was just meeting with the pastor today, I figured this outfit would do. I made sure I had my glasses in the backpack I had my laptop tucked safely inside of. Once I was sure I hadn't forgotten anything, I headed for my car.

Getting through both of my classes without getting lost and making sure I took good notes had been easier than I'd anticipated. I felt good about my professors. I hadn't spoken to anyone, but that was okay. I didn't have to make friends. I wasn't there for that.

The church I would be working at was a Baptist church much like the one I had grown up in. From what I could tell, it was one of the larger ones in the town. The coastal appearance was something I hadn't been expecting, but I liked it. Something about that made the church feel less like home. I didn't need any reminders of the life I left behind. Walking into a church was literally terrifying for me. I had made many of my worst memories in a church.

But this was the job Pastor Williams had set up for me. They were willing to work around my classes, and the pay was enough for me to get by and live comfortably. If this didn't work out, I was going to have to find another job on my own, and I wasn't sure what I was even qualified to do.

I pulled the backpack strap up higher on one shoulder and walked inside the front doors. The smell of coconut met my nose, which was odd. Our church never smelled like suntan lotion. It smelled like flowers. Lots of flowers. This place even smelled like the beach. I relaxed as I looked around at the casual atmosphere. The church wasn't decorated like any one I had been to.

"Can I help you?" a masculine voice asked, snapping me out of my thoughts, and I spun around to see a guy not much older than I was. I was sure he wasn't the pastor. No pastor I knew was this young and this handsome. His dark brown hair was cut short, and his green eyes sparkled. Wide shoulders and really nice arms were as far as I got in my study of him when he cleared his throat.

Snapping my head up, I met his gaze. His smile was now amused. Crap. I was acting like an idiot. "Uh, yes. I'm here to meet with Pastor Keenan. I have an appointment," I explained without tripping over my words like I normally did when attractive guys spoke to me.

"You're Blythe Denton?" he asked as his eyes went wide in surprise.

I only nodded. How did he know my name?

"Not what I was expecting. Wow. Um, yeah, okay. Uh, I'm pretty sure you aren't what Dad was expecting either. Just, yeah, okay." He stopped and chuckled, then shook his head and rubbed the back of his neck.

I wasn't sure what was wrong, but this could not be Pastor Keenan. Something was bothering him though. "Dad?" I asked him, unable to keep the nervous edge from my voice.

"Dad," he repeated, staring at me blankly. Then he blinked and turned his head, grinning as he looked down the hallway. "Yeah, my dad. Pastor Keenan is my dad, and your meeting is with him."

Okay. "Is he here?" I asked.

He nodded and took a step toward me and held out his hand. "I'm Linc Keenan. It's nice to meet you, Blythe."

I slipped my hand into his for a polite handshake. "Thanks," I replied.

When he let my hand go, he nodded toward the hallway. "This way."

Good. That had been awkward, but I liked Linc's smile. He seemed sincere and kind. I had never actually liked pastors' kids before. I had met many of them when they'd come to visit the church with their parents. They'd always either treated me badly, or given me the creeps. If it hadn't been one of their daughters making fun of me, it had been one of their sons looking at me funny. One had even gone as far as touching me and covering my mouth so that I hadn't been able to scream. He had said he knew I was a dirty slut because he'd heard the gossip. He just hadn't been told how hot I was, and he'd said he wanted a taste of my pussy. I had started crying as he shoved his hand down my pants. Luckily, Pastor Williams had shown up and ordered him to leave. Then he sent me to my room for the rest of the weekend.

It was never discussed. No one ever asked me about it or checked on me. I was just told to stay in my room. I had been terrified and humiliated.

Needless to say, my experiences with pastors' kids hadn't been pleasant. I just really wanted this job to work out.

Linc led me to the room. "Let me go in and speak to my dad and tell him you're here. Have a seat and make yourself comfortable. I won't be but a minute."

I nodded and sank down to wait on the soft tan leather sofa. The decor in the room was also bright and laid-back. A palm tree was in the corner, and bamboo plants adorned the end tables and front desk. The smell of coconut lingered in there as well. I noticed several candles that were in rustic-looking metal tins sitting around. They obviously used them often.

The door to the pastor's office opened, and an older version of Linc stepped out of the room. His eyes locked on mine. A smile lit up his face as he smiled at me. I stood up quickly and nervously fidgeted with my backpack.

"I was at your dedication nineteen years ago, but seeing you standing there all grown-up, it's hard to believe that's you."

This man had been at my baby dedication? Pastor Williams hadn't told me that.

"You sure have turned into a lovely young woman. But then Malcolm had said you had grown into a beautiful intelligent woman. I just wasn't prepared to see it."

Malcolm was Pastor Williams's first name. I knew that, but I had never called him by it.

"Thank you," I replied, feeling the need to say something but not sure what I was supposed to say to this man.

He stepped back and waved for me to come into his office. "I see you've met Lincoln. He will be meeting with us. We have been without a secretary in the office for two weeks now, and Lincoln has been filling in, but I can assure you that we are all ready for him to go back to his other job. He's not very good at this one." There was a teasing tone in Pastor Keenan's tone.

I smiled and glanced over at Linc, who was leaning against a bookshelf, his arms crossed over his chest and a pleased smile on his face. He was ready to hand over the secretary position to me. I understood his excitement about me being there now.

"I would have started last week had I known you needed me. Pastor Williams said that I wasn't supposed to come in until today," I explained, feeling guilty for not coming in sooner.

"Malcolm wanted to make sure you had time to get settled and ready for your courses before you started work. I agreed with him. Besides, I think my son actually got better over the last week."

I glanced at Linc again. His grin was still in place, but he rolled his eyes as if he was amused with his dad.

"Okay, well, thank you. It didn't take me too long to get settled in though," I said, feeling the need to say something. I wasn't good with small talk.

"Good. I'm glad you're ready to dive in. Please, have a seat. Can Linc get you a water?"

I shook my head and sat down in the black leather high-backed chair that sat across from the pastor's desk. But instead of going to sit behind his desk, Pastor Keenan sat down in the chair beside me. Then he leaned back and smiled as he studied me.

"You will definitely be well received here. I imagine my daughter will be up here soon enough when she hears about you."

I didn't know how to respond to that. I wasn't sure I wanted to meet his daughter.

KRIT

I had been stood outside Blythe's apartment staring at her door for at least five full minutes. Since the night of the party, I had avoided her. Not sure why, because it wasn't like she was one of those females I had to avoid. She never knocked on my door or made any attempt at contact at all.

Secretly, I had been hoping she'd show up at my door all on her own if just to thank me for the iPod and earbuds I'd left her. Not that she had needed them this week. I had moved all parties to Matty's place. Blythe, however, never showed up. Not even in passing. So maybe I hadn't been avoiding her. Maybe she had been avoiding me.

And why the fuck did I give a shit?

"I'm not there." Blythe's voice filled the hallway, and I jerked my gaze from her door to find her standing at the top of the stairs.

Holy hell, she had on tight jeans with a pair of fucking pink heels. I let the image of her legs showcased in the jeans burn a spot in my memory as I trailed my gaze up them slowly. The clingy material of her shirt was cut in a modest enough style, but damn, it hinted at the body underneath.

"I haven't seen you all week." Her voice sounded nervous. "I wanted to thank you for the iPod. You didn't have to do that."

I mentally slapped myself and focused on her face and the words coming out of her mouth. She wasn't like normal girls. She was shy and unsure of herself. I had to remember that or I'd scare her away. Not that I could do anything with her. She would be too fragile for me.

"Uh, yeah, I did. Now I won't feel like an ass when we have a party," I replied with a smirk.

She grinned and reached up to tuck a strand of her long silky dark brown hair behind her ear. That hair was fascinating. As if she needed one more attractive feature on her already-perfect body. "I appreciate it. I really do. I started my classes today, so studying will soon be of extreme importance."

She moved toward her door and unlocked it before glancing back at me. I wasn't ready to let her disappear inside just yet. She was more comfortable talking to me today. I was suddenly curious. I wanted to hear more about her.

"Would you like some coffee?" she asked as she opened the door.

"Yeah, I'd love some," I replied, thankful for a reason not to leave.

She smiled at me, and I swear to God, the entire world around her lit up. How the fuck was this girl alone? Where was the man hovering over her and protecting her from every bad thing that came near her? She was too fucking unreal. Did her family think it was smart to just send her off like this? Were they idiots?

She slipped the backpack off her shoulder and dropped it onto her sofa. In a week she had made the place feel warm and inviting. There wasn't a lot of fussy shit around, and there were no pictures of her with friends or family, which was odd. Wasn't that, like, a girl thing?

"How did your classes go?" I asked, knowing if I didn't control the conversation, we would stand there in silence. Another thing I wasn't used to with girls. Normally, they talked my fucking ear off.

She filled the coffeepot with water then glanced up at me. "Good, but I wasn't worried about these two courses. Wednesday, I have to face Fundamentals of Public Speaking, and, well ..." She trailed off.

The pink color in her cheeks was enough. I knew what she meant. She didn't like attention on her. I had seen that myself at my party. But damn, how did she manage to get this far in life without being the center of attention wherever she went? "You baffle me," I said. "You don't want attention." I let my eyes trail back down to her legs in those jeans and heels, and my blood pumped harder just thinking about those legs and the things I could do with them. "Yet you have got to be used to drawing attention."

I lifted my gaze back up to see her face as she turned away from me and stared out the window instead.

"I'm working on blending in and hoping people will let me be," she replied

The pain in her voice didn't sit well with me. Had someone hurt her? And if someone had, who the fuck were they and how could they do anything to hurt someone so incredibly vulnerable and sweet?

There should be a dad or older brother or boyfriend making sure no one ever mistreated her. But I had seen no one with her or near her since she moved in. Why the hell was that? I didn't know her family, but I decided that I really didn't like them.

"Blythe," I said, liking just a little too much the way her name rolled across my tongue.

She turned her head to look at me. "Yes?"

I took a step toward her and then stopped. She would spook easily, and that wasn't what I wanted. I also didn't want her getting the wrong idea, because there was no way in hell I was taking on someone like her. I didn't do relationships. I had tried to have one, and I had fucked it up. Jess had been in love with someone else, so it hadn't mattered, but it had just about killed me.

I wasn't ever doing that again. I didn't do it well. But I could be her friend. I could be a damn good friend. I was good at that. "If you need anything, or anyone, you call me."

She studied me a moment then slowly nodded. She didn't ask me why or bat her eyelashes at me in a flirty way. Instead she just smiled. "Okay, thank you," was the only response I got.

"Give me your phone," I told her.

She walked over to her backpack, pulled out a smartphone, and handed it to me. I added my number then texted myself so I would have hers. "Here," I told her as I handed it back to her. "Promise me, if you ever need me, you'll call."

She nodded again. "I promise."

"Good." I grinned at her and walked over to sit down on her sofa. I propped my feet up on the table. "Now, come tell me all about your new classes."

She didn't move at first, and I wondered if I had pushed her too hard. I waited. Finally she moved and walked back to the coffeepot and poured two cups.

"How do you take yours?"

"Black," I replied.

She grinned as she brought the cups over and handed me one. "I didn't figure you for a cream-and-sugar guy," she said.

I was making her feel comfortable around me. Good. That was my plan. I wanted her to feel like she could trust me, because she needed someone to fucking trust. "What's your major?" I asked.

She frowned and stared down at her coffee for a moment. I thought maybe she was done opening up to me. Then she sighed. "I want to write books. But first I need a degree so I can have something to fall back on in case I'm a horrible writer and no one buys my books. So, I'm majoring in English."

Chapter Five

BLYTHE

For the next two weeks I found a rhythm. Classes, work, study, and occasional visits from Krit. My classes weren't bad, except for the public speaking one. I wasn't ready for that. I was trying to prepare myself for the day I had to actually stand in front of everyone and talk, but so far the professor hadn't called me out.

Work was great. Pastor Keenan had several counseling sessions in the afternoons, and I was left alone to handle the filing, answer the phones, and work on the different things he left on my desk to type up. A few times Linc had dropped by with doughnuts and a friendly smile. He even brought sandwiches one day from a deli in town and convinced me to take my break outside with him. He put me at ease, and for the first time in my life I wasn't constantly worried about what he might think of me. He just seemed accepting of my faults and he was nice.

I finally had a friend.

Then there was Krit. He also seemed to want to be my friend, and I was grateful that he was so nice. He always stopped by to check on me, and more than once he had brought Chinese food with him and said he needed my help eating it. He was curious about school, and he asked a lot of questions. Then he told me funny stories about his friends and things that had happened to them during performances. I always laughed so hard with Krit. But ... there was a difference. I was always on edge with him. I couldn't stop my head from escaping with images of Krit and playing out scenarios that I shouldn't think about with a friend.

I was attracted to Krit. I had been since the first time I met him, and while he was trying so hard to be a good friend, I was lying in my bed at night bringing myself pleasure with images of Krit in my head. That was the evil in me. It made me feel guilty every time I saw him. Especially on the mornings he stopped by and I was still dealing with the dream I'd had of him the night before.

Not one time had Krit flirted with me or given me any indication he was attracted to me. He was just a nice guy. A really sexy nice guy. I could stare at him for hours and never get bored. On nights that he did have his parties, there was a sick knot in my stomach. I knew he had a girl up there, and he was going to do to her the things I would never experience. Things that scared me, yet fascinated me. Things that I had only ever thought about since meeting Krit.

This infatuation I had with him was only getting worse. When he'd come down to my apartment and asked my opinion on two different shirts, he'd stripped off one to try on the other. I had lost my voice. The sight of his well-defined chest covered in colorful tattoos and the desire to touch them made my face heat up. I had felt flush and slightly off center. When he had left I felt so guilty. He saw me as his friend, not another girl that wanted something from him. Krit didn't make me uncomfortable by gawking at my body, so doing that to him was wrong and unfair. But then I didn't have a body like his. The kind that stops traffic.

This was where my head was when Linc showed up at work with a box of chocolate cupcakes. I pushed thoughts of Krit to the back of my mind and focused on Linc. If I could only look at Krit like I looked at Linc, my life would be so much easier.

"Break time? I have it on good authority from my sister that cupcakes don't get any better than these," he said with a serious expression and a sparkle in his eyes.

I glanced back at his dad's office door. He had just gone in there with a married couple, and if the phone rang and I wasn't there to answer it, then it would interrupt him. "Can we have the break in here so I can get the phone if it rings?" I asked him.

Linc nodded and pulled a chair up to my desk. "No problem," he replied. "Dad has a counseling session?"

"Yeah, and it just started," I explained.

"Then I have an hour of your time to waste." He winked at me and handed me a cupcake.

I was going to gain weight with all the sweets he brought me. But then I decided it didn't matter. I had gone most of my life without sweets, and I really liked them. The buttercream icing melted on my tongue, and I let out a small moan. So good. How I had lived my life without these kind of treats, I didn't know.

I opened my eyes to tell Linc thank you, but the intensity of his gaze stopped me. He wasn't eating his cupcake. His eyes were locked on my lips as he sat frozen. The only movements were the pupils in his eyes as they grew, and the vein pulsing in his neck.

"Blythe," he said in a deep voice that startled me.

"Yes?"

He didn't say anything for a moment. His eyes lifted only briefly to meet mine before they went back to my lips. I lifted my hand to touch my mouth to make sure there was no icing clinging to them that he didn't want to tell me about and risk embarrassing me.

He reached over and pulled my hand away from my mouth

gently, then moved in closer. His eyes never leaving my lips. My heart rate picked up and I nervously bit my bottom lip wondering if I should move or say something.

"I'm going to kiss you," he told me, and before I could let what he said register, his mouth was on mine.

It was my first kiss. His lips were warm and tasted like the mint of his chewing gum. I wasn't sure what I should do. I was curious about kissing, and I liked Linc—he was nice—but he was my boss's son. We were also in a church.

Mrs. Williams would hate that I was kissing a man in a church. She would call me filthy and dirty. But she was dead. I slipped a hand into Linc's hair and decided that I liked doing something that that woman would hate. When Linc's tongue ran across my bottom lip and pressed between my lips, I opened my mouth and let him inside.

"Told you those cupcakes were good," a female voice said, and then Linc's mouth was gone.

I dropped my hand back into my lap and turned around to see a female version of Linc standing in front of my desk, a knowing grin on her face. This was his sister. I had seen the pictures in the pastor's office. She hadn't stopped by in the two weeks I had been there, even though Pastor Keenan had said more than once that she would love me.

"You couldn't stand it, could you?" Linc said in an annoyed tone as he stared at his sister.

She cocked an eyebrow at him and shrugged. "You spend all your free time coming to visit here, and I knew it wasn't Dad you were bringing treats for. So I thought I would visit the new secretary and introduce myself."

Linc's hand moved to clamp down on my thigh.

His sister's eyes saw it, and she laughed and shook her head. "Seems you've got my brother all kinds of worked up," she said, then smiled at me. "I'm Lilah. Sorry I haven't been here to meet you yet. I've been busy getting things moved into my dorm, and I knew Linc was keeping you company every chance he got."

Lilah had the same dark hair as Linc, but it was longer and curled around her shoulders. She also had the same green eyes and long eyelashes. But she had a dimple in her right cheek that Linc didn't have. "It's nice to meet you," I replied. "And the cupcakes are amazing."

She beamed at me. "I know, right?" Then she shifted her attention to Linc. "You weren't exaggerating," she said to him.

I glanced at him, and he was covering up a grin with his hand and trying to make it look like he was casually rubbing it over his mouth. The laughter in his eyes told me differently.

I was missing something here.

"I have to go. I've got a lunch meeting in thirty minutes. I'll be back to visit when I'm in town next time. Be careful with him. He isn't as nice as he looks." Lilah winked, spun around, and then left the office.

"I would like to say she's not normally so annoyingly dramatic but I'd be lying," Linc said.

I was alone with Linc again, and this time we had a kiss between us. What did I say to him now?

His hand came up and cupped my face. "You okay? I ... Was the kiss okay? Or did I push things?"

Push things? I shook my head, unsure of what exactly he meant. "I don't think so," I replied, remembering the thrill of kissing someone. It had been fun. "I liked it," I told him honestly.

He let out a sigh of relief. "Good. I was trying not to cave in and kiss you, but you make it hard for a guy to concentrate on anything else."

I did?

Pastor Keenan's office door started to open, and Linc jumped up to move his chair away and walk toward the door to leave.

I could hear Pastor Keenan talking to the couple as the door stayed cracked.

"I'll see you tomorrow," Linc said, with a crooked grin. Then he left.

He didn't want his dad to see him here with me, but he had just kissed me. Something didn't make sense. But then I knew very little about guys. Maybe his dad would be able to tell we had just kissed and he would be upset that we did that in the church. I decided it was better that he left. I liked this job. I didn't want to lose it.

KRIT

I stood at my window watching the parking lot outside. There was nothing to see in the parking lot. I could lie to myself and say I was waiting on the pizza delivery. The truth was I was waiting on Blythe's car to pull in. Last night I had not gone to see her before my gig, and she'd been on my mind most of the night.

Several shots of tequila and two brunettes with nice size racks had been the only way to get Blythe out of my head. Heels clicked against the tile floor as one of those brunettes walked back into the living room. She'd excused herself to use the restroom. I glanced back to see all she was now wearing was the heels she had shown up in.

When I had opened my door fifteen minutes ago to see one of my one-night stands from last night standing there, I had cursed myself for bringing them back here. Now she knew where I lived. Getting rid of her would be harder.

Her breasts were real, which was nice considering they swayed heavily as she walked toward me. Last night this one had seemed more competitive than her friend. She'd wanted all my attention, and those were normally the ones that caused the trouble. I didn't have time for trouble. I had pizza coming and I intended to share that with Blythe before I went to Live Bay.

Blythe and her sweet smile and perfect body. That laugh that made me want to say or do anything to hear it again. And the way she sometimes forgot to guard herself and let her eyes wander down over my chest. The pink flush of her cheeks when I changed shirts in front of her. Which was entirely for my benefit. I didn't need anyone's opinion on what T-shirt to wear each night. I took them off when I was on stage anyway. I just liked giving Blythe a reason to look. She liked to look, and I liked that too much.

"I thought we might have more fun—just the two of us," the brunette purred as she stopped in front of me and ran her hands up my chest.

This one was wanting to make an impression. I could tell her that she wore too much makeup and her perfume was overpowering. If I was a nice guy I could explain that I just liked women. Sexy long legs and big tits. I loved touching them and fucking them. But I wasn't a nice guy.

I put my hands on her shoulders and pushed her down to her knees. She went willingly enough. "Take the edge off. That's all I got time for," I told her not sugarcoating this. If she wanted to walk out she was welcome to.

Her eyes lifted to mine and she smiled as if she'd won something. The girl was determined. Someone should have taught her that if a guy shoves you to her knees without kissing you then you should bite his damn dick off. No one told this girl that.

She quickly unzipped my jeans and tugged them down. I hadn't been wearing any underwear. It was way past laundry day, and I was without several items of clothing. I needed to wash some underwear.

My thoughts were on laundry when cool hands wrapped around my dick. Immediately my gears shifted and I pulled the stool up behind me and leaned back just as her lips slide over my still not fully erect cock. She needed to do a little work to get it on board with this.

Her tongue twirled around the tip before sliding it completely into her mouth and then bumping it against the back of her throat. The head slid deeper in than most girls allowed without gagging, and I realized I had a pro on my hands. My boy came out to play then.

Lifting my hips I shoved deeper into her mouth with a groan of pleasure. "That's it. You like it deep. Fuck," I muttered reaching down to grab a handful of her hair and hold her in place. She had started something I was about to finish. I rarely got my hands on someone who wasn't a gagger.

Her hands grabbed my thighs and she held on as I began moving in and out of her mouth with hard thrusts. Her eyes lifted to mine and a triumphant gleam was in them. That wasn't gonna help me, so I closed my eyes and pictured another pair of eyes. Those jewel-like eyes that were so big and innocent, yet curious.

Thinking about having her on her knees in front of me, taking me like this, made me reach back and grab the stool behind me as my body began to jerk its release. Shuddering I kept my eyes closed, and Blythe's face stayed there as my body relaxed. The sharp nails that had dug into my thighs brought me back to the real world, and I opened my eyes to see a smug smile on the girl whose mouth I'd actually just shot my load in. She wasn't Blythe.

Glancing out the window I saw Blythe stepping out of her car with her backpack slung over her arm. The skirt she wore had my complete and full attention. Those long legs of hers looked so damn smooth. Did she like to have them touched? Would she make sweet whimpers when I touched her?

"How long will it take until you can play again?" the female I had forgotten about asked.

I tore my gaze off Blythe as she walked toward the building. Our dinner would be here any minute and I only had an hour and a half to spend with her before I went to our gig tonight.

"I gotta run. That was great. Thanks," I said pulling my jeans up and zipping them before reaching for the T-shirt on the sofa.

Scanning the room I searched for my wallet, but noticed the girl still on her knees with a disbelieving expression on her face. What had she expected? I told them last night I just liked to fuck. Nothing more. She was the one who showed back up today. I didn't ask her to.

"You're just gonna leave?" she asked.

"Yeah, and so are you," I replied.

She didn't move. Shit. She was gonna be dramatic. I wasn't in the mood for dramatic. I shouldn't have let her give me head. Bad fucking idea, Krit. Make her think you owe her something.

"Listen, love. I told you last night I don't do girls more than once. You wanted to get naked and prance around in front of me and all I wanted was a release. You gave me that and we're done. Last night you got a helluva lot more orgasms than me. So we're even." The disbelief in her eyes turned to fury as she stood up. Those nice tits were appealing but I had better things to do. "Go get dressed. I gotta go," I reminded her as I pointed to the bathroom door.

"You're a bastard," she hissed.

"Yes I am. Now get your clothes on."

BLYTHE

After changing into a pair of cutoff sweatpants and a tank top, I dug my glasses out of my bag and put them on, then pulled my hair up into a messy bun to get it out of the way. Tonight I planned on writing, but first I had to find something to cook for dinner. I had bought several things at the store that I could easily make. I just wasn't sure what I was in the mood for.

On my way to the kitchen a knock sounded at my door and I stopped and stared at it. That had to be Krit. No one else ever came by. Glancing down at myself I debated on running back in the room and changing. At least jerking my hair back down and taking off these glasses.

No. I would not do that. Krit wasn't here to be impressed with how I looked. He probably just wanted advice on a shirt. I forced myself to walk over to the door just as I was and open it up.

Krit's slow grin lit up his face as he took in the way I was dressed. At least I could amuse him. "Aren't you too fucking adorable for words," he said.

I wasn't adorable but I wasn't going to argue with him. "Hey," I replied, then the smell of pizza hit my nose and I realized he wasn't empty handed. He was carrying a box from the pizza place down the street.

He held the box out so I could see it. "I need help eating this," he said with his entirely too sexy grin on his face.

Why he was here yet again with food to share with me I wasn't sure. Did he really like being around me? Was this what friendship was? I stepped back and let him walk inside. He stopped in front of me and lifted a finger and touched the tip of my nose. "Those glasses," he said and chuckled and shook his head. Then he walked toward the table with the pizza.

He hadn't looked like he was making fun of me and my glasses, but what had he meant by that? I closed the door and gave myself a moment to adjust to him being in here before turning to look at him. He was already walking into the kitchen to help himself to plates.

If he was teasing me about my glasses that was okay because friends teased each other. Right? I think they did. I could handle some friendly teasing. I knew I looked like a complete nerd in my glasses. It wasn't like I thought they were attractive. Krit was used to the women in his world being beautiful and perfect. Maybe that was why he liked me. He didn't get distracted by my looks.

That was a completely depressing thought.

"You gonna stand there frowning at this perfectly yummy pizza or come eat some?" Krit asked as he held out a plate to me.

I was being awkward again. He was here to be nice and friendly and I was making this weird. I shoved my thoughts about why Krit was here aside and forced a smile. He had brought me dinner. I wouldn't have to cook now. This was a good thing. I wasn't here to waste time with a guy anyway. I had a life to build. A book to write. I had goals.

"That's my girl," he said, as I took the plate from his hand.

I wasn't his girl. He didn't mean anything by that. Telling myself that didn't keep my silly heart from picking up its pace. But then all Krit had to do was grin at me or wink and my heart went into a frenzy. It was as if my body couldn't deal with the excitement that came along with Krit.

"How's the job?" Krit asked as he pulled out a chair and sat down.

I shrugged. Not much to tell him really. "Good. I enjoy it. I don't deal with a lot of people and the pastor is really nice." I didn't mention Linc. Especially after the kiss we had shared today. I wasn't ready to talk about Linc. I wasn't sure what I was feeling where he was concerned. And I didn't need Krit reading into anything I said.

"You ever gonna come listen to me play?" he asked, then took a bite of his pizza.

No. More than likely not. Going to a club where I knew no one other than a guy on the stage did not sound appealing at all. It sounded terrifying. However, I didn't want to hurt his feelings.

"I'm not sure. I don't do that scene, or I never have. I wouldn't even know anyone."

Krit studied me a moment. "You could bring a friend," he finally said.

A friend. I had two of those. At least I thought I did. I was still trying to figure out what constituted a friend.

"I'll see if I have one that wants to go with me," I told him, wanting to change the subject.

"You have that public speaking class yet?" he asked.

I nodded. I had suffered through it and somehow made it out on the other side alive. But that didn't mean I would always get out of being called on to go up front. "Not my favorite," I admitted.

"You really have a problem with attention don't you?" he asked as he finished off his first slice of pizza.

He had no idea how much of a problem I had with attention. He loved it. I hadn't seen him perform yet, but I could tell by the look on his face when he talked about it that he adored having all eyes on him. I had no doubt those eyes on him loved every minute of it too. Having a reason to look at Krit was always nice.

"I just don't have good experiences with it. ... I like to go unnoticed." I wasn't telling him any more. My past needed to stay in the past. This was my now and my future. I didn't want to bring all the ugliness and pain from my past into the life I had now.

"Problem with that, love, is that you're really fucking hard not to notice," Krit said with a small smile on his lips, but a sincerity in his gaze that made me think he didn't mean that in a bad way. Almost as if he was saying he liked what he saw.

"I try to blend in," I replied, not sure if I was misunderstanding him or not. I wanted to believe he meant that as a compliment, but how could he?

"That's a shame," he said, then reached for another piece of pizza.

I decided to change the subject and asked him about how he learned to play the guitar. Our conversation became easy then and relaxed. I loved hearing his voice and listening to him laugh.

What I didn't expect was that Krit would show up every evening like this and eat with me for the next two weeks. But he did. And I liked it. No, I didn't just like it ... I planned my day around it.

KRIT

It was becoming a habit. That was all. Nothing more. I was not addicted to her. I wasn't. Just a nice little distraction. Seeing Blythe in the evenings before I left for my gigs was a way to have a moment to just be me. Blythe didn't require me to be anything else.

Last night she had actually rolled her eyes at one of my jokes and thrown her napkin at me. It had taken every ounce of strength I had to stay in my seat and not grab her face and taste those full lips. She wasn't nervous with me anymore. She smiled at me and let me in when I knocked on her door.

Somehow she had become my level ground. The place I could go to find myself before I went out and entertained everyone. She didn't hang on me and beg me for anything. It was easy with Blythe.

Or at least I kept telling myself that.

If I acknowledged the truth, I would panic. So instead I was going to believe this was all I wanted from her. Just seeing her was enough. Hearing her laugh made my fucking day.

"Hey," she said, with that smile from heaven as she stepped back and let me inside her apartment.

"I got the pad Thai you like," I said, holding up the bag from the Thai place down the street. After watching her make those sweet little moaning noises as she ate it the last time I picked it up, I decided I needed to watch her eat it again.

Her eyes lit up, and she clapped her hands and bounced on her feet like a little girl. Women who looked like Blythe were not supposed to be so damn cute. Seeing her get excited over food made me want to feed her three meals a day.

"I made sweet tea just like you showed me. Come, taste it. I think I got it right," she said as she hurried to the kitchen.

Two nights ago she had said she loved sweet tea, but she didn't know how to make it, and buying it was too expensive. So I'd taught her how. You would have thought I was brilliant by the way she watched me and asked me questions. It was as if I was conducting a science experiment. Another thing about Blythe: she made me feel important. Needed. Like I was a part of her life that she relied on.

That felt fucking good. Too good.

But I was not addicted. I didn't care what Green said. Blythe was not an addiction. I hated that he had started accusing me of that.

I set the bag down on Blythe's kitchen table and followed her to the bar where she was filling up a glass of ice with tea from the gallon-size plastic pitcher I had brought her when I taught her how to make sweet tea.

"Taste it," she said with excitement dancing in her eyes.

If this tasted like shit, I wasn't going to be able to tell her. Not with her looking like that. Hurting Blythe was something I was incapable of. I would lie to make her smile. I had done just that last week when she had made me a grilled cheese and burned it. She had seemed so worried about what I thought, so I swallowed every last bite like it was the best thing I had ever put in my mouth.

Preparing myself for the worst, I picked up the glass and took a drink. The sweet taste was just right. She had nailed it. No bitterness in the tea—the perfect blend of ice and sugar. Grinning, I set the glass down and smacked my lips. "Perfect, love. That was fucking perfect."

"Really?" she asked, her eyes shining brightly.

It was times like this all I wanted to do was scoop her up and kiss her until we were both stripping off each other's clothes. Fuck. Shit. I was not going to think about that again. I had to stop thinking about her naked.

She was the kind of girl you had a relationship with. Not the kind you fucked because you couldn't stop lusting over her. She was also becoming important to me. To my sanity. I needed her. And fucking her would ruin that. This thing we had—I couldn't ruin it. I had never had this before, and it was too important to mess up.

"Really. Fill up my glass, and let's go eat," I told her as I turned away from those eyes and went to get plates out of the cabinet.

"You want a fork?" I asked her, already knowing the answer. She had attempted to eat the pad Thai with chopsticks last time, and it had been a disaster.

She laughed and nodded.

I grabbed us both a fork and headed to the table to fix our plates. This was what I wasn't willing to lose. I had never had a place where I felt like I belonged. This wasn't the kind of friendship I was used to, and I loved it. I woke up every morning thinking about what I would bring to dinner and what we would talk about. Things would happen during the day, and the first person who I wanted to tell was Blythe. In the short month since she had moved in, she had made herself the most important person in my life.

Fuck.

I turned around to see her grinning at me like I'd hung the moon, and my heart clenched. No. This was wrong. I wasn't that guy. She needed to see the real me. The me I was when I wasn't here eating dinner with her and talking about our days. She was looking at me with … oh, hell no. She was looking at me with something more.

I set the fork down and stared at the table. I had to remind her. She had to remember who I was. I was only worthy of her friendship. She had to remember we would always be just friends. This need I had for her company was confusing her. It was in her eyes. Those big beautiful eyes were so expressive and trusting.

Fuck. Fuck. *Shit!*

"I, uh, I'm running late. I gotta run. Didn't look at the time.

Sorry, but you have plenty of pad Thai you can eat. Uh, yeah, I'll see you ... later," I rambled. Panic was in my voice, but I couldn't help it. Backing up from the table, I forced myself to smile at her, but I didn't look in her eyes. I couldn't. I turned and got the hell out of there.

Protecting Blythe was my original intention. Someone needed to protect her, but damn it, I hadn't protected her from me. But there was still time to show her what she had forgotten during our cozy dinners. I was Krit Corbin. I was the lead singer in a band and I fucked women. Lots of them.

Chapter Six

BLYTHE

No one's sweet tea was that bad. But I couldn't figure out what else I had done. Krit had left my apartment like he couldn't get away fast enough. That was two weeks ago, and he hadn't been back since. That night, and every night since then, his parties had been going until late.

I used the iPod he left me and, luckily, it worked. I was able to sleep, and only occasionally did loud banging on the ceiling wake me; it made things rattle in my apartment. Other than that, I was okay.

I stood at my door for an hour last night trying to work up the nerve to open it and go upstairs to see Krit. Maybe I should apologize for something, but I didn't know what that would be. I had made sweet tea. He had liked it and gotten our plates.

Then … then he suddenly left. I had thought it was odd, but I believed him that he was running late and hadn't noticed the time.

But he didn't come back the next evening. And after a week had gone by, I knew it had to be me. I hadn't gone to his apartment to face him because I couldn't stand it if he was disgusted with me. I shouldn't have let him get too close. I shouldn't have gotten comfortable with him. I had been ridiculously excited about my sweet tea. He had shown me how to make it, and that batch had been my third attempt. I was so sure I had gotten it right.

So I let my guard down, and I was me. He had seen me. That was the only thing it could be. I let him see me, and what he saw sent him running. It was stupid. I should have known better, but Krit made me feel different. I wanted to trust him, and because I wanted it so much, I had.

Stupid girl.

"Frowning again? Third time this week I showed up to see your smiling face and it wasn't what greeted me."

I snapped my head up to see Linc standing in the doorway with a white bakery bag. He looked concerned. Why did he keep coming around? He hadn't kissed me again. But he brought me sweets and spent a good deal of time trying to make me laugh.

But I didn't let him in. I was careful with Linc. That was why he was still coming around. I should have been careful with Krit.

Linc lifted the bag in his hand. "Cream-filled doughnuts with the sprinkles on top, just like you like them."

I smiled at him. Seeing him helped me forget the sadness of Krit's absence. "You are awesome," I told him.

His smile got bigger, and he glanced back at the door. "Excuse me while I go buy some more doughnuts," he said with a teasing gleam in his eyes.

"Do not leave with that bag," I said, standing up.

Linc set the bag in front of me and put his hand on my waist before pressing a kiss to my cheek. He lingered there and inhaled deeply before pulling back. He had been greeting me this way since our kiss.

"I need to see you outside of this office. I was being patient with you because you seem so easily spooked and I didn't want to screw this up, but I really want to take you out. Please, go out with me. Tonight, anywhere you want. Your wish is my command."

I stood there staring at Linc as his words sunk in. He was asking me out on a date. I'd never been on a date. He seemed so hopeful. If I went and I let my guard down, would he run off and leave me too? This thing with him visiting me at work was safe. A date wasn't safe.

"I, uh …" What could I say? I didn't want to push him away. He was now my only friend, and I didn't want to mess this up too. Now that I knew what it was like to have friends, I liked it. I wanted friends.

"Please," he begged, tightening his hold on my waist. "I swear, I won't push you. You'll be in complete control. I just want to spend time with you."

Telling him no would be a mistake. I couldn't do that. I would just be careful not to be me with him. I would be what he wanted me to be. I could pretend. "Okay. But you need to plan the date. I've never been on one." Oh, crap. I was being me. Crappity crap.

Linc pulled back and frowned at me. I had done it. He was about to leave me too. He was going to see the real me. The ugly inside was going to shine through. I closed my eyes, unable to watch another friend run away from me. I just hoped he did it quickly.

"How?" was all he said.

How? What did he mean how? I opened my eyes and looked up at him while he searched my face. Was he looking for something? What did he see?

I couldn't do this again so soon. I was already sore from Krit's exit. I stepped back and sat down in my chair. "It's okay. Just go. I don't need excuses."

The doughnuts in the bag reminded me of the pad Thai that Krit had left me in his great escape. The sweet cream no longer appealed to me. I tried to focus on the papers in front of me.

Linc didn't move at first, but when he did, I held my breath and expected him to walk away. Instead he bent down. "What just happened?" he asked gently.

I turned to him, and my eyes collided with his. "You're not leaving?" I asked.

His frown deepened, and he shook his head slowly. "No, Blythe. I'm not going anywhere. I just can't figure out why you seem to think I would want to leave."

He didn't see it. I hadn't laid myself bare to him. He was still here. I let out a relieved sigh and smiled. "Sorry, I just thought that because I hadn't been on a date ..." *Shut up, Blythe.* I couldn't seem to stop saying that I hadn't ever been on a date.

"Was Malcolm very overprotective?" Linc asked me.

Pastor Williams, overprotective? Wait. He thought I hadn't dated because I hadn't been allowed to. He didn't think it was a bad thing.

"Yes," I lied.

Linc smiled then. "Good. He should have been."

If he only knew the truth. No. He couldn't know the truth. He'd run too.

"So, that kiss," he said, watching my face carefully.

I nodded. "First one," I admitted.

Linc's grin got even bigger. "Tonight, Blythe. I'll pick you up at seven."

We were actually going to go on a date. "I live at Sea Winds Apartments," I told him.

He stood up. "I know."

His dad's office door opened, and Linc took a step back and stuck his hands in his pockets.

"Linc, visiting again today. If I didn't know better, I would think you were trying to bribe my secretary with all the sweets you bring her."

Linc chuckled. "Yeah, well, maybe I am."

His father shot him a frown before turning to me and smiling. It was forced, but he was still smiling. "I have to leave early for a dentist appointment. Can you lock up when you leave?"

"Yes, sir," I replied.

Pastor Keenan turned his gaze back to Linc. "Walk me out, Son."

Linc looked frustrated but nodded. He followed his dad out and then turned back to me, holding up seven fingers before disappearing through the door.

KRIT

I was sitting in my favorite chair, a beer in hand, glaring at the wall, when the apartment door opened and Green strolled in with a smirk on his face. He closed it behind him and looked pointedly at me. "You're fucking stupid," he said, then turned to head to the kitchen.

He'd been telling me I was stupid since I had brought back two blondes two weeks ago and held our after-show party here. He was the only person who knew just how much time I was spending with Blythe and why I had moved our parties. I didn't tell him why. I just let him be pissed at me.

He stepped back into the living room with a bottle of beer in his hand and pointed toward the parking lot outside. "If you get up now, you can see Blythe dressed in a sexy little sundress and a pair of heels, getting into some preppy boy's Honda Accord."

What? I stared at him, letting his words sink in, then I jumped up and ran to the window. Sure enough, Blythe was walking across the parking lot. A guy about my height stood beside her, his hand settled on her lower back. Fuck that. Who was he? Blythe didn't get out enough to know people. She was too damn shy.

"You should have seen the guy drooling over her as she stood there with him and introduced us. She was completely unaware that the guy wasn't hearing a word she said. He didn't give a shit who I was. He just wanted to get her alone. She even asked about you. Wanted to know if you were okay. I told her she was welcome to come up anytime, but her eyes went wide like she was terrified and she shook her head. How the fuck you went from hanging out with her and making her laugh to the idea of her seeing you scaring the shit out of her I don't know."

Blythe climbed into the car and the douchebag holding her door leaned down and … Did he kiss her? He stood up, jogged around the back of the car, and climbed in. Then they were gone.

I walked back over to my chair and sat down. I wasn't talking about this with Green. He wouldn't understand. Fuck, right now *I* didn't understand. All I could think about was that guy kissing her. Touching her. My heart was pounding in my ears.

"Don't worry. I'm sure you'll have one or more hot babes to have a cheap fuck with tonight. Just like last night. No need to worry about the one girl you wanted to actually talk to and wasn't a used groupie. You made sure to shut her out."

Closing my eyes, I refused to listen to him. "She is just a nice girl I spent some time with. I made her feel welcome—that was it. Don't give a shit who she dates," I replied in a bored tone, then took another drink of my beer and picked up the remote control.

And that lasted about five minutes.

Throwing the remote down, I reached for my phone and sent a text to Blythe.

ME: WHO'S THE GUY?

I deleted it before I could send it. That wasn't the right thing to send to her. It would give her the wrong idea. I wasn't jealous. I just wanted to protect her, if no one else was going to fucking do it.

ME: THE BAND WILL BE PLAYING AT LIVE BAY TONIGHT. ABOUT TIME YOU CAME AND LISTENED.

I sent that one. And I waited. A minute later my phone lit up.

BLYTHE: I'M OUT WITH A FRIEND TONIGHT.

No shit.

ME: BRING YOUR FRIEND, TOO.

A minute later there wasn't a response. I stared at my phone for five more minutes, then decided I was acting like a damn chick. Tossing my phone on the sofa, I stood up and headed back to the bathroom to take a shower. Blythe wasn't mine to protect.

Chapter Seven

BLYTHE

KRIT: BRING YOUR FRIEND, TOO.

I had read that last text from Krit at least ten times over the past two hours. I didn't respond to him. I wasn't sure how. He had ignored me completely for two weeks, and now this.

I glanced over at Linc. Dinner had been nice. He had talked a lot about his family and soccer. He was a big fan of soccer. The problem was, nothing he said made my heart flutter the way it did when I looked down at Krit's text message.

Linc hadn't asked much about me during dinner. He had told me a lot about himself, and I had listened. Krit always asked me about myself. I had to find ways to gloss over the truth about my past, but at least he asked me.

"Where to now? Any suggestions? Mini golf maybe?" Linc asked, breaking into my thoughts. I felt guilty even comparing him to Krit. That wasn't fair. Linc was a nice guy, and he liked me. Krit was … I didn't know what Krit was.

Glancing back down at my text, I let the words fall out of my mouth before I could stop them. "There's a band playing at Live Bay tonight. You met the bass player when you came to pick me up. I haven't gone to listen to them yet."

What was I doing? Linc had mentioned playing mini golf, and I'm asking him to take me to a club. Did pastor's sons even go to clubs? Shaking my head, I looked up at him. "Never mind. That's not an appropriate place to go. I'm sorry I mentioned it."

Linc grinned as he turned the car around. "I've been to Live Bay before, Blythe. Jackdown is a great band. I've heard them play several times. They headline the place and bring in the biggest crowds. If you want to hear them play, then I'll gladly take you there."

"Oh. Okay. If you're sure it's okay with your dad. I don't want to upset him."

Linc's face got serious for a second. I would have missed it had I not been looking at him. A forced smile quickly formed on his lips. "Not worried about my dad. I think I made that clear to him once this week already," he said.

I wanted to ask him what he was talking about, but I didn't. We were pulling into the parking lot of Live Bay, and all my excitement about seeing Krit perform took center stage in my head.

"Parking is fierce tonight. I'll let you out at the door, and you can wait for me inside while I go park around back. I don't want to make you walk that far in the gravel with those heels."

Linc stopped in front of the entrance. I didn't want to walk in there alone, but I didn't want to sound like a baby, either. He was trying to be nice. "Thank you," I said before opening the door and stepping out.

The muffled sound of the music inside filled the night air as I walked toward the door. A guy with a tight black T-shirt on and the largest arms I had ever seen in my life stood there. Both of his arms were wrapped with chainlike tattoos. I lifted my eyes to meet his and realized he was watching me. An amused smirk was on his face.

He opened the door and nodded for me to go inside. "I'll let your man pay your cover. You go on in, sweetheart."

My cover? Did you have to pay to go inside? Maybe I should pay. This was my idea. I reached for my purse. "No, I'll pay for both of us," I told the large man.

"Baby, if you pay, I'm gonna personally kick his ass for letting you. So you need to walk your sweet tail inside."

Oh my. Okay.

I managed a nod and hurried quickly inside. A low chuckle from behind caused me to blush. I wasn't sure how I felt about some stranger calling me sweetheart and baby. I wanted to wait for Linc, but I didn't want to wait close to the door and to that guy.

Inside the club, Krit's voice filled the place, and I spun around to see him standing on the stage, grinning down at the girls screaming his name. "Damn, y'all look sweet tonight. Got me all kinds of worked up," he said. He was shirtless, and that in itself was something to scream about. I understood their excitement. He reminded me of a god, standing up there. His beautiful body showcased by a pair of jeans that hung perfectly on his hips gave the crowd a view of his lower stomach and the promise of what was underneath.

I moved closer, wanting to see more. He was laughing at something Green had said, and the dimples that fascinated me flashed out at the crowd. The blue of his eyes was electric tonight. More intense than they normally were. There was an unreal quality to them.

He slid his hand down his lower stomach and just inside the top of his jeans and winked at some girl up close to the stage. The screaming started up again, and he threw his head back and laughed. The muscles in his neck stood out, and my gaze soaked him in. Every inch.

When he looked back out at the crowd, his eyes shined with amusement—until they locked on me. Then he went completely still. I had moved closer to the stage than I thought had. Slowly, a real smile touched his lips, and it was as if no one else was in the room. I stood there, unable to move away. He had me spellbound.

His tongue touched his bottom lip, and then he puckered his lips in a kiss before reaching for the guitar behind him and slipping it over his shoulder. "Let's do this," he said, breaking our connection and looking back at Green.

Green was watching me too. I lifted my hand and gave him a little wave. He grinned and gave me a nod.

"There you are. I couldn't find you in this place. It's crawling with people," Linc's voice was in my ear, and I jumped, startled. I had forgotten about Linc. One look at Krit, and all other thoughts had left me. I was a horrible date. I started to apologize for walking so far away from the door when I heard it: Krit singing for the first time. His voice was already one of my favorite sounds. But hearing him sing ... It was something more. The thick warmth of his voice curling around the words sent a thrill through my body.

I couldn't talk to Linc right now. I had to listen to this. Krit had commanded the attention of the entire place with just a few words.

Just another night, baby, and you're just another girl.
I don't do mornings and I never will.
You wanted a taste and I wanted a distraction.

Don't go begging for more because I like the chase, not the
kill.

It wasn't all-consuming, girl—you gave it too easily.
You know what you got into, but you still begged me.
Don't leave your phone number—I'm not gonna call.
Say it, baby. Scream it all you want. I've heard it all.

Krit wasn't playing the guitar anymore. Both of his hands were on the microphone in front of him as he sang the words with a smirk on his face. It was as if he were singing to all the girls. They called out his name and reached up toward him as he stood there, almost making love to them with his words.

They all want to save me. They all want to own me.
But I've been owned before. That ship has sailed.
She took my soul a long time ago when she walked out that
door.
So don't think you're gonna win me.
I'm not a prize and you won't score.
Nothing left inside to gain. I'm empty there, and she's to
blame.

I've broken hearts and left them in a trail behind me. But
they only had me one night.

She owned my heart for years, then took it with her in her
   flight.
I liked the escape you give me, and I'll take it without
   remorse.
I don't even care if you fake it. I'm using you more, no reason
   for force.

Krit's eyes met mine, and I froze. Seeing him like this, in his element, made it difficult to do anything but stare at him. He owned the place. The real smile that I knew wasn't part of his act tugged at his lips before he leaned back into the mic.

It wasn't all-consuming, girl—you gave it too easily.
You know what you got into, but you still begged me.
Walking away is my favorite part because I know I didn't lose
   my heart.
You want more than I can give. Someday you might see.

They all want to save me. They all want to own me.
But I've been owned before. That ship has sailed.
She took my soul a long time ago when she walked out that
   door.
So don't think you're gonna win me.
I'm not a prize and you won't score.
Nothing left inside to gain. I'm empty there, and she's to blame.

Walk away now if you want to keep your innocence.
Run like hell girl if you're not ready for me.
Everybody is the same and no matter how sweet you
look ...
There will always be only one face I see.
You've been warned and that's all I can do.
Let's forget the talking and the wasting of my time.
This is all about me, babe. I'm not worried about you.
Just another night, babe and you're just another girl.

They all want to save me. They all want to own me.
But I've been owned before. That ship has sailed.
She took my soul a long time ago when she walked out that
door.
So don't think you're gonna win me.
I'm not a prize and you won't score.
Nothing left inside to gain. I'm empty there, and she's to
blame.

"You want to find a seat and get something to drink?" Linc asked close to my ear. I didn't want to stop looking at Krit or miss a word that came out of his mouth. But I was here with Linc, and I couldn't stand here completely soaking up Krit. That was rude.

"Um, yeah," I replied.

Linc's hand wrapped around mine, and he pulled me back through the crowd and toward a tall table over in the corner that didn't have people around it. A group of people at the table beside it looked like they needed more than one table. Linc must have been thinking the same thing. "Excuse me, but is this table free or are y'all using it?" he asked a guy with long blond hair and a face that belonged on television, it was so perfect. He didn't even glance in my direction when he answered. "It's all yours, dude. We're good with just this table."

"Thanks," Linc replied.

"You're Lilah Keenan's brother, aren't you?" asked the girl beside the beautiful blond guy. Her smile was friendly, and she was as perfect as the guy whose arm was possessively wrapped around her shoulders.

"Yeah, Amanda Hardy, right?" Linc replied.

The girl grinned. "Yep. Thought that was you. How's Lilah?" the girl asked.

"She's good. She leaves again for Tuscaloosa this week."

Amanda Hardy turned her pretty eyes to me. She wasn't even wearing makeup. All that beauty was natural. "We haven't met, I don't think. You didn't go to Sea Breeze High, did you?"

I shook my head. "No. I'm not from here," I replied, then realized I hadn't told her my name. I felt like an idiot. She seemed so nice. Nothing like the girls back home who looked like her.

"Amanda, this is Blythe Denton. Blythe, this is Amanda Hardy. Blythe is working at the church for my dad," Linc informed them for me.

"Blythe?" another female voice asked. I hadn't looked at anyone else at the table because from the one glance I had taken, the group looked intimidating. Forcing myself to look away from the safe connection I had made with Amanda Hardy, I found what looked like a Victoria's Secret model smiling at me. Where Amanda was very natural, this woman was all fixed up, but she was still gorgeous. The kind who stopped traffic.

"Yes," I managed to reply, and returned her smile.

"I believe you live in the apartment beneath my brother," the blonde said. I didn't need her to say more. I saw it then. The blue of her eyes was identical to Krit's, and her hair was the same white blond—except hers was long and full of curls.

"Are you … Krit's sister?" I asked.

Her smile went from pleased to brilliant. "Yes, I am," she replied.

"Krit?" Linc asked, reminding me that he was there beside me.

"Krit and Green are roommates," I explained to him. I turned back to Krit's sister. "Linc has only met Green."

The blonde flicked her gaze to Linc then back at me. "I'm Trisha. It's nice to meet you, Blythe."

"This is about to get fucking interesting. I need another beer first." A deep drawl from the guy at the back of the table caused Trisha to roll her eyes as she shot an annoyed glare in the guy's direction. I took a quick glance and saw a well-built guy with dark eyes and thick lashes. He had dreadlocks pulled back in a ponytail that hung down the back of his neck. *Intimidating* wasn't even a strong enough word for him. His face was striking, but the rest of him was terrifying.

"Shut up, Dewayne. Don't start shit," Trisha snapped.

"I was gonna leave, but I think we might need to stick around for a few minutes," the beautiful blond guy said.

Amanda gave me an apologetic smile and then elbowed the guy still holding her close. He only chuckled and then bent his head to whisper in her ear. The pink blush on her cheeks had me turning away from them to look at Linc.

He took that as his cue. "Well, it was nice to see you, Amanda," He looked at the blond guy. "And Preston. We need to get a drink and grab this table before it's snatched up," Linc said politely.

I smiled at Amanda and then at Trisha before giving them a small wave and following Linc to the table beside them. I didn't want to talk about Krit just yet, and I had a feeling Linc was going to ask me about him. I had seen the look in his eyes when Trisha had recognized my name. Which gave me a secret thrill. Had he told his sister about me?

"Did you go to school with all of them?" I asked, curious to know more about Trisha and her friends. I hadn't seen any of them at his parties.

"Yeah. But we didn't run in the same crowds. Amanda and my sister were friends. Her older brother, Marcus, is a part of that group. I hadn't heard that Amanda was dating Preston Drake." He lowered his voice. "I'm surprised her brother allows that. Preston isn't known to be a one-woman guy. And Marcus, being his best friend, knows that better than anyone."

I felt like I was watching an episode of *Dawson's Creek*, listening to this. "He seemed like he was unaware of any other female in the world," I said honestly. That good-looking blond guy had spent the majority of his time staring at Amanda while holding her close to his side.

"I noticed that. Little Hardy must have managed to tame the beast," he said with a chuckle. "I'm gonna get a Coke. You want anything?"

I wanted a sweet tea, but I wasn't sure they had that here. "Um, sure. A Coke will do," I replied.

He nodded and stood up. "Be right back."

Linc hadn't gotten far when someone moved back his chair. It was Trisha. She sat down on it. "Hello again," she said.

"Hi." I wasn't sure why she was at my table. Then I took a quick glance back at the stage and noticed Green announcing that they were taking a break and would be back in fifteen minutes.

"I don't have much time before he gets down here," she mumbled.

Who? Krit? Would he be mad that she was talking to me?

"Anyway, Green told me you were new in town, and I wanted to invite you to lunch one day."

Green told Trisha about me. Not Krit. My stomach knotted up. I managed to nod. "That sounds nice."

She beamed at me, and I felt even more insecure. Why would someone like her want to spend anytime with me? And did I want to take the chance that she would see the true awkward me the way Krit had? Trisha would drop me just like Krit did. Green was still friendly, but he wasn't asking me to hang out with him either.

"Perfect. What day is best for you?"

"Tuesday. I get out of my last class at eleven, and I don't have to be at work until one thirty."

Trisha grinned then glanced up and scrunched her nose. Even that looked good on her. "Here he comes," she said.

I turned to see Krit walking our way. His eyes were locked on me, and he was smiling that dimpled smile that meant he really was happy. Good. He had meant what he'd said in the text message.

"You came," he said to me while ignoring the table beside me, the one full of his sister's friends.

"You asked," I replied, unable to keep the silly smile off my face at seeing him again after two weeks without his visits. I had missed him.

"I thought you had a date."

I had told him I was out with a friend. I hadn't said *date*. I started to reply, when I was cut off.

"She does," Linc said as he set my Coke on the table and slid it over in front of me. "I'm Linc, her date," he said to Krit in his ever-polite tone of voice. "You must be Krit, the neighbor."

Krit's happy smile was gone. In its place was an annoyed frown I had seen before. "Her *friend*," he corrected Linc.

Linc seemed unaffected by Krit's clipped tone. "I'm sorry. I didn't know. She hadn't mentioned you before tonight," Linc responded.

What? Did he really just say that? I swung my eyes to Linc and noticed the sudden change in his demeanor. He wasn't calm, cool, and collected. He was tense, and the smile on his face was fake.

Krit's hand moved from the back of my chair to rest on my back. "How did you like the set?" he asked me as if Linc hadn't just been rude.

"I loved it. You sounded amazing. I had no idea you could sing so well." I was gushing. I knew it, but I couldn't seem to help it. There was a reason why women threw themselves at Krit. He was like a magnet, and it was hard to pull away from him. When he got close, you just wanted to get closer.

Krit lowered his head until his mouth was at my ear. "I've missed you," he said softly.

I hadn't gone anywhere. I wanted to point that out, but then Trisha was watching us with undisguised interest, and Linc had given up the nice-guy smile. I was here with Linc, and I had to remember that.

I picked up my Coke and smiled at Linc. His frown eased some. "We're glad we came. It's a great way to end the evening."

Trisha ducked her head and covered her mouth, but her eyes were dancing with laughter. She then composed herself. "Come on, Krit, you're ignoring everyone else. Let these two enjoy their date. You can talk to Blythe later," Trisha said, standing up. To me, she said, "Tuesday at eleven fifteen, meet me at the Pickle Shack. It's less than a mile from the college, so you should find it easily." She reached for her brother's arm, tugging him away from me. "Come on," she said in a stern whisper, and led Krit to her table.

Krit didn't say goodbye to me, but then, Trisha might have caused a scene if he had. I tried to block out the laughter behind me and not listen to what they were all saying. I could hear the dreadlocks guy saying something about being shot down, and I winced, wondering if he was talking to Krit. They misunderstood the situation. I didn't want to hear Krit correct them. That would just have been embarrassing.

Couldn't they look at me and tell I wasn't Krit's type? He was completely out of my league. Glancing over at Linc, I realized he was too. Yet there he sat.

"I didn't realize you were so tight with the lead singer of Jackdown," Linc said, then took a slow sip of his soda while studying me.

I shrugged. "He lives above me and when I first moved in, we did talk a lot and stuff, but then he just kind of stopped coming by. I haven't even seen him in a couple of weeks." I wasn't going to tell him about our dinners together, the ones that had stopped with no explanation.

"He's bad news, Blythe. I don't know him, but everyone has heard of him. Jackdown is pretty big around the southeast. Krit is … well, for lack of a better word, he's a male whore," he said quietly, so the table beside us wouldn't hear him.

I nodded. I already knew Krit slept with a lot of girls. "I know what Krit is like. We were just friendly. Nothing more. I'm not his type anyway."

Linc nodded in agreement. "No, you're not. I'm glad you realize that."

The ache in my chest couldn't be helped. Hearing Linc confirm that I wasn't tall and beautiful like the girls Krit brought back to his place was painful. Knowing it and hearing it from someone else were two different things.

I wasn't in the mood to stay. I wanted my apartment and my

pajamas. I wanted my silence. Taking one more drink of my soda I stood up. "I think I'm ready to go home now," I told Linc.

He looked relieved, which only made me feel worse. Our date had started out nice, but it hadn't ended well. I wasn't the only one ready to escape it.

"Of course," he said standing up. "Let's go."

KRIT

"I like her," Trisha announced as I watched Blythe walk away with that guy. "She's gorgeous and really sweet."

"Linc's a really nice guy. He was always friends with everyone in high school. I can't think of one person who didn't like him," Amanda added to the conversation.

A pair of tits pressed against my arm. I wasn't in the mood. My head was somewhere else. Shrugging off the unwanted female, I turned to look at Amanda Hardy. "You know that guy?" I asked. I didn't want to let this bunch know I gave a shit that Blythe was on a date. They would all misunderstand and harass me about it endlessly.

Amanda nodded and bit her bottom lip nervously.

"She's right. Guy's nice," Preston said. "He always did that Christian teens group thingy in the mornings. But he wasn't like the other religious kids. He even stopped one night when Marcus and I had a flat tire. I didn't have a spare or some shit like that, and Marcus wouldn't call his dad because I was so hammered. So Linc gave us a ride."

This wasn't something I wanted to hear. Preston Drake liking someone so completely different from him meant this Linc guy probably was fucking perfect for Blythe.

Shit.

"Do you like her?" Trisha asked me. My sister wasn't one to beat around the bush. She was a straight talker. I just wish she'd chosen to ask me this without all her nosey-ass friends watching me.

I shrugged. "She's not my type. But, yeah, she's a friend. Glad to know the guy she's with is worthy of her." I took a swig of my beer. "I need to get back. Fifteen minutes are almost up." I never made it backstage on time. They were all thinking just that as I walked to the door leading to the stage.

I ignored the girls trying to get my attention. I just needed to get the hell away from everyone and hit something. I didn't want to fucking care that Blythe was on a date. She wasn't someone I could mess with. She was fragile. The more time I had spent with her, the more I realized just how fragile she was. I wasn't good with fragile. I broke shit. I'd never forgive myself if I broke her. That would likely destroy me.

But could I just cut her out of my life? I'd missed her like crazy the past week. She made me laugh. Really laugh. And damn, I smiled all the time when she was around. I loved watching her find herself and her independence. It made the darkness that seemed to live in my chest ease up.

Blythe made me feel whole inside. I'd never felt whole. There was always this emptiness. I had tried everything to fill that dark ache inside, but nothing had ever worked. Until Blythe smiled at me.

"Break's up," Green said, as he came through the door and slapped me on the back. "Cheer up. You're thinking too much about this. Just be her friend. Be her *motherfucking friend*. That's it. Try it. You might find you like it."

I watched as my best friend grinned at me and nodded before turning to go back onstage. Green had been the only person in my life to really know me. He knew my dark places and he knew why they were there. Not even my sister knew everything. I couldn't tell her; she'd blame herself for not protecting me. For leaving me. But Green knew. He'd seen it.

Should have known I couldn't hide my battle with Blythe from him. He saw it all over my face. Was he right? Could she be my friend? Jess had been my friend. Sure, I'd wanted in her pants most of the time, but in reality she had been my friend. She'd accepted the dark side of me and she'd understood it. She also had been one of the toughest people I knew. Hurting her was impossible. At least for me. I knew I'd never break her.

Blythe wasn't Jess. She was so innocent and … hell, she was precious. I closed my eyes and let out a string of curses. I was so losing badass points for that thought. Who the hell thought a girl was precious? Not fucking Krit Corbin.

"Think about it later, dipshit! We got a crowd to please," Green yelled at me from the stage.

He was right. I shoved thoughts of Blythe to the back of my mind and put on my game face. Trisha would be watching me, and I needed to get her off the scent. If she thought I wanted Blythe, she'd bust her ass to get into my business. I loved my sister, but she was hell to shake when she got something in her head.

Chapter Eight

BLYTHE

There was no party that night. I had expected one, but the noise never came. I did hear feet walking around upstairs around midnight, but that was it. Nothing else. Linc had tried to be casual with his questions, but I could tell he had been curious about Krit. My answers were appeasing him.

When he had walked me to my door, he had kissed me. Like before, it had felt good, and the closeness had been nice. His taste was warm, and the gentle touches of his tongue against mine had been exciting. I had been happy to stand outside and kiss him for hours. But Linc had ended the kiss and then let out a deep breath before kissing me on the forehead and saying good night.

It had been my very first date, and it had been everything I had expected it to be. Linc had met all my expectations. I enjoyed his company, and I really enjoyed his kisses. Linc was nothing at all like Krit. Yet I still felt like I was waiting for him to realize I wasn't worth his time—like Krit had.

Worrying about losing something I didn't really have was pointless. Today I didn't have to go into the office. On Saturdays it was closed because Pastor Keenan prepared for his Sunday sermon. I had spent my last few Saturdays studying, but today I wanted to do something else.

Yesterday had been payday, and it was time I splurged on a few more items of clothing. Pastor Keenan hadn't complained about my jeans, but on the days I wore my sundress or one of the skirts I had worn to church back home, he made a point to mention that he liked how I was dressed. He never said that about my jeans.

I was lacing up my tennis shoes when a knock at the door startled me. It was ten in the morning on a Saturday. I had no friends. I couldn't think of one person who would be at my door at this time. Tightening my laces, I stood up and went to open the door.

Krit standing there in a pair of jeans, looking too incredibly tempting for any female to deal with this early. The shirt he was wearing fit tightly enough that each of his six-pack abs muscles was outlined. I hated that shirt. It made me think things. Things I had to stop thinking where Krit was concerned.

"Morning," he said, with a slow grin.

He'd caught me ogling his abs. Crap.

"Morning," I replied, and forced my eyes to stay on his face. Not his body. If only his eyes weren't so pretty.

"You had breakfast yet?" he asked.

I shook my head as I stared at him, confused. Krit didn't get up at ten ever. He partied all night and slept most of the day.

"Good. There's this place I know that has incredible pancakes, and I want some pancakes," he said, then nodded toward the stairs leading down to the parking lot. "Come on. Eat breakfast with me."

I should ask him why he was there. Why he wanted to have breakfast with me after he made it clear these past two weeks that he was done with this friends thing we had. I should ask him if this was because I had been on a date last night. But I didn't do any of those things. Instead I reached for my purse and slipped it over my arm. Then turned back to him. "Okay," I replied.

The dimpled grin on his face that never ceased to surprise me made my stupidity worth it. He stepped back and let me close and lock my door. Maybe he planned on explaining his exit from my life. Maybe there was a reason he had run from me like I had a disease.

"I'll drive," he said.

Frowning, I paused. "Do you have a car?" All I had seen him drive was a motorcycle.

He smirked. "Not anymore. I sold it," he replied. Then he brushed his thumb over my cheek. "You scared of my bike?" he asked.

He was touching me. I let my eyes fall to his lips. They were fuller than Linc's. They always looked so soft. His mouth was also wider than Linc's. Would he kiss differently? Would it taste as good? The flash of metal in his mouth I had seen before would be there in his tongue. Could I feel it when his tongue touched mine?

"Blythe." His voice sounded deeper than before.

I jerked my eyes off his mouth and looked back up at him. "Yes?"

He let out a shaky-sounding laugh and muttered something I didn't understand. "You gonna ride my bike?"

His bike? He meant his big scary motorcycle. Was I? I wanted to. It would let me wrap my arms around him and feel his abs. Okay, maybe death was worth getting to feel Krit's abs. I managed a nod. "You have an extra helmet?"

Krit slid his arm around my shoulders and started walking us toward the parking lot. "Sweetheart, I wouldn't put you on my bike without something to protect this pretty head."

He smelled good. I took a deep breath and inhaled his clean scent. I wasn't sure what soap he used, but it reminded me of the sea.

"Did you enjoy your date last night?"

I nodded, afraid that if I said the wrong thing, he would remove his arm from around my shoulders and then I wouldn't get to smell him.

"Amanda said Linc's a nice guy."

I nodded again and decided I probably should join this conversation instead of just answering with head gestures. "Yeah, he is."

"Good," was his reply.

Good. That simple word felt funny in my chest. It wasn't a pleasant feeling. Why? Did I want him not to like Linc? That would be silly.

He didn't say anything else, but he didn't move away from me either. When we reached his motorcycle, he pulled out a smaller helmet. It was silver and very feminine-looking. I hadn't expected that. He must have had this for the females he gave rides to.

I put the helmet on my head and started to fasten it, when Krit moved my hands away and did it for me. Then he tightened the straps. I watched his face as he seemed focused on making sure my helmet was nice and secure. My heart did a little fluttery thing that I couldn't help.

"Nice," he said when he was done. Then he winked and threw a long leg over the bike. It reminded me of every movie I had ever seen of the sexy bad boy climbing onto his motorcycle. Krit held his hand out to me. "Come on, love."

I slipped my hand in his and managed to climb on the back without making a fool of myself. I had never ridden on a motorcycle.

"You're gonna need to slid up close to me. Wrap your arms around my waist and hold on tight," he said over his shoulder.

I had a few inches between us. The thought of sitting with my legs open like this and Krit fitting snugly between them was as terrifying as it was exciting. I reminded myself that this was just a ride. He had girls on his bike like this all the time. It was no big deal. I placed both of my hands on his waist. He reached down and grabbed them, tugging me up against him until my chest was pressed against his back. Then he took my hands and placed them on his stomach. I had to take a steady breath when I felt the ripples under my hands. It was almost enough to make me forget the fact I was plastered against Krit's backside.

"That's better," he said with a pleased sound to his voice. Then he started the engine. The vibration ran through my body, causing me to cling tighter to him.

A chuckle came from him before we started to move. I closed my eyes at first and tried to think of something else. I was sure that if I saw cars moving around us, I would panic. We hit a bump in the road, and my chest and crotch bounced up against his hard back, snapping me out of my fear and slinging me right into something else, something entirely different.

Sucking in a quick breath, I let the heat from Krit's body seep into me. He felt very, very good. Better than anything else I could ever remember. The rock-hard abs under my hands were so tempting. I wanted to tug his shirt up just enough so that I could slip a hand underneath. The colorful skin that had the snake tattoo on it had been burned into my memory.

I gripped his T-shirt tightly in my fist to keep from doing just that. I couldn't feel him up. He'd think I was crazy. If I wanted to send him running away from me again, all I had to do was something like that. He wasn't flirting with me. I knew the difference now. Linc flirted with me. His eyes always had a playful gleam that told me he was interested in me. That he wanted to spend time with me, and he like being around me.

Krit's eyes didn't have that twinkle. He was just friendly. Maybe that was it. Maybe I had stepped over some sort of invisible friend line that I didn't know about before, and then he had run off. Was he giving me another chance to prove I could be a friend and not treat him like every other girl out there?

Was that what he wanted from me? For me to be an escape from his reality? I let go of the tight hold I had on his shirt and smoothed the fabric out without rubbing his stomach. I didn't press my hands as tightly to him, and I eased away from him so that my breasts weren't touching his back. Krit needed a friend. Someone not in his world, someone who didn't expect him to drink, party, and entertain them.

And I wanted to be that for him. I wouldn't think about his

muscular body or his pierced tongue. Those would be off-limits. I would think of him as a friend. Someone who I didn't have to impress and who didn't have any expectations of me or me of him. We would just accept each other.

Krit pulled into the parking lot of a cute little diner. The coastal blue color of the wood-framed building had white trim and a large front porch. If it didn't have the big sign out front that read, SUNNY-SIDE UP, I would have thought this was someone's beach house. The parking lot still had several cars outside even though it was kind of late for breakfast and too early for lunch.

Once Krit had parked, he took one of my hands and helped me off the bike. My legs felt a little funny, but the feeling went away quickly. I started to take off the helmet, when Krit turned around and finished the task for me.

"Thanks," I said, smiling at him with what I hoped told him I wanted to be his friend. I would be willing to be whatever it was he needed. No one had ever needed anything from me before. The idea that he might need me for something made me feel special.

"Did you enjoy it?" he asked, hanging the helmet on the handlebars before glancing back at me.

"Yes. Once I realized I wasn't about to die," I answered honestly.

Krit laughed then reached for my hand. "Come one, love. Let's go eat. You're gonna love the food here."

KRIT

I should have fucked someone last night. It was screwing with my head. Getting up at the ass-crack of dawn just so I could take Blythe to breakfast was insane. I could have gotten some sleep and taken her to dinner. And having her on the back of my bike was a terrible idea. We should've taken her car.

This was going to be my attempt at salvaging the friendship we had started. Thinking about how good her tits looked in that tank top and how much better they had felt on my back was not what this was supposed to be about. I was gonna have to call Brit when I got finished. She would take the edge off.

"You're really talented. I enjoyed hearing you sing last night," Blythe said in that sweet musical voice of hers.

I hoped the fact that I was imagining her naked and wrapped around my body wasn't all over my face. "I'm glad you came. My sister enjoyed meeting you. Green had mentioned our new neighbor, and she is always curious." More like Green told Trisha I was making up reasons to go visit our new neighbor all the damn time.

"She was really nice. I'm having lunch with her this week," Blythe said, smiling, but I could see the nervous look in her eyes. "I mean … I hope that's okay. I don't mean anything by it. Just she asked me to go to lunch. She seems really nice and all, and I haven't made any friends, exactly."

That stung. I deserved it, but it still stung.

Her eyes flew open more, and she shook her head with a hor-rified expression on her face. Damn, she was adorable. "I mean. You, of course. I mean, I think we're, I mean, you're, I mean, uh. I know you're a … friend … kind of …" She stopped trying to make sense of her ramblings. Then she pressed her lips together and dropped her eyes toward the table.

I had fucked with her head, running off like I had. Most girls would have shown up at my door demanding attention. Blythe had just accepted my absence and gone on with her life. She didn't demand anything of anyone. Girls who looked like her usually used their beauty as weapons. She didn't make any sense. She acted like she deserved to be treated poorly.

"About that," I said, knowing I needed to apologize. She didn't lift her eyes to meet mine. "I'm sorry I ran out on you that night and that I haven't been by to see you since. I had some shit going on in my head, and I was worried. … I just didn't know. … Fuck." I needed to just say it. Get it out there. "I didn't want you to get the wrong idea about what we were doing. About why I was showing up with dinner and coming around so much. You're not the …" I wasn't going to say she wasn't the kind of girl I fucked because it sounded wrong. "I like being around you. You make me smile and I like that. I missed you these past two weeks and I would still like to be your friend. If you would consider me as a friend, that is," I finished.

She lifted her eyes to meet mine, and the relieved look in

them told me all I needed to know. She didn't want more than a friendship with me anyway. I wasn't going to hurt her. She knew she was too good for me. Even if she seemed completely in the dark about her beauty, she knew I wasn't the kind of guy she deserved.

"I'd like that. I have fun with you too. And I missed you. I don't expect anything other than friendship."

The plate of pancakes I ordered was set down in front of me, and the same exact order was set down in front of Blythe. There was no way she could eat all that, but I figured what she didn't finish I would.

"This looks really good," she said, grinning, and then a giggle escaped her lips. "I can't believe they have whipped cream on them. And peanut butter."

I winked at her before picking up my fork and knife. "Sweetheart, if pancakes don't have whipped cream and peanut butter on them, then they aren't worth eating."

She licked her lips, causing me to almost drop the damn forkful of gooey goodness into my lap. The fantasies I'd had about her tongue. Shit! I had to get a grip.

"I've never actually had pancakes," she admitted.

This time I did drop my fork.

Chapter Nine

BLYTHE

Pastor Williams hadn't called me in the month that I had been gone. It wasn't that I expected him to, really, because we had never talked much, but then again he had been my guardian for my entire life. Did he not care if things were working out for me? Or was he just glad that I was gone? More than likely, it was the latter.

I only had one photo from my childhood, and it was one a teacher had taken of me with my classmates in the fourth grade. She gave each student a copy in a heart-shaped frame for Valentine's Day. I was never given a phone with a camera, and things like Facebook were off-limits to me. If Mrs. Williams had ever seen me doing anything like that, I would have paid for it.

Looking around my apartment, I realized there was a

coldness to it. I had nothing to show for my life. Nothing to remember it by. I wanted memories that I could cherish. There was no reason to be sad because of my past. What I needed to do was focus on my life now. I had friends now. I also had a phone with a camera, and a laptop.

When I walked in the door, I wanted there to be photos of people in my life that made me smile. I wanted to see moments I would always remember. If I didn't want to be different, then I needed to learn how to live like a normal person. I had thought coming here, that hiding out in my apartment and writing, was all I wanted to do.

I knew now I had been wrong. I hadn't known about the things in life: like how good a kiss felt or how nice it felt to be held by someone. I had never had someone tell me about themselves and listen to me talk in return. Having had a taste of both, I wasn't willing to go back to being that girl who closed herself off from the world and everyone who might hurt her.

I was also pretty sure that Mrs. Williams had been wrong about me. People liked me here. No one cringed or whispered about me when they saw me coming. Oftentimes people would turn to look at me and smile. They didn't see the ugly evil that Mrs. Williams had always claimed was inside me. I was almost convinced she had been lying. She hated me because of my mother, but I wasn't a bad person. Good people liked me. No one treated me like I was a walking sin.

Just maybe I was worthy of love.

Krit had taken me to breakfast yesterday, and we had then gone for a longer ride on his motorcycle along the beach road. When we had gotten back, he had come inside and we had talked about my classes. He had read me the lyrics of a song he was writing and asked me what I thought. It was late afternoon before he left to get a nap before his performance that night.

Linc had called later that evening to ask if I wanted to see a movie. The idea of getting to be close to someone again and feeling connected had sounded wonderful, so I had of course told him yes. Both Linc and Krit had been around me enough to know if there was evil in me. They would have seen it by now and been disgusted by it. Both of them seemed to genuinely like me.

A knock on the door brought me out of my thoughts, and I looked up from my computer screen, where I had intended to write some of my book. The door opened, and Krit stuck his head in. His eyes scanned the room until they found me, and then he smiled. The smile that always made me feel like warm honey was running through me.

"You really should lock this door," he said as he stepped inside.

"Why? To keep out the riffraff?" I asked teasingly, then cocked an eyebrow at him.

He shrugged. "Well, you left it unlocked and look what happened."

I nodded and gave him a serious frown. "I can see what you mean. Maybe I should get an extra bolt," I replied.

Krit grabbed his heart. "Ouch," he said, then fell back into the chair, facing me. "That was deep, love. Fucking sharp."

I rolled my eyes and leaned back in my chair. "You'll survive. I'm positive of it."

Krit propped up both of his feet on the coffee table in front of him and studied me for a moment. "Come tonight and listen to the band. We're at Live Bay again because of a scheduling change this week. You can sit with Trisha. You didn't get to hear much the other night."

This was where us being friends was going to be difficult. Telling him I had a date with Linc to see a movie shouldn't be a big deal. But for some reason it was hard to say so out loud. I didn't want him to think Linc was more important, though I had a feeling Linc wasn't asking me out again because he wanted just to be my friend.

"You have plans already, don't you?" he said before I could come up with something to say that wasn't awkward.

"Linc asked me to go to the movies with him tonight," I admitted. I had no reason to feel bad about this. No reason at all ... but I did. Dang it.

Krit let out a sigh. "Fine. He asked first. It's all good. But

Thursday night I'll be playing at Live Bay, and I want you to come."

Okay. We could do this. He was making it easy, and I was making it harder than it had to be. "Deal," I agreed.

Krit nodded, but he didn't seem happy. "You eating on this date?" he asked.

Linc hadn't said anything about dinner. He'd just invited me to a movie. I shook my head.

Krit pulled his phone out of his pocket. "Good. I'm starving. What time is he going to be here?"

"Six," I replied.

"That leaves us with two hours," he said, and a smile had replaced his frown. "Thai or Italian? Or do you want to get those fajitas from that Mexican place again?"

He was ordering us takeout. I didn't want to feel that squishy feeling in my chest that made me feel tingly. At least not where Krit was concerned. But oddly enough, he was the only person who managed to trigger that feeling.

"Not that hard of a question, love," he said, reminding me that I needed to answer him.

I had bad memories of Thai food. "The fajitas sound good."

"That's my girl," he said as he dialed the number to the Mexican place. I knew he didn't mean anything by it, but I had never been referred to as belonging to someone before. The simple *my girl* meant more to me than he realized. In fact, if he

knew how deep that struck with me, he would run off again—
and this time he'd possibly never come back.

I studied my screen like I was actually thinking about what
to write next, but I listened to Krit order food. He acted like he
belonged there in my place. Maybe that was supposed to freak
me out, but it didn't. It did the exact opposite.

When he hung up, I had gathered enough courage so I could
turn to him and blurt it out before I realized how stupid I
sounded.

"Can I take a picture of us on my phone? I don't have a picture of us … and I'd like one."

Krit glanced around the room, as if noticing for the first
time that I didn't have a picture of me with anyone, and then his
eyes came back to me. "Only if you text it to me so I'll have it
too."

Smiling in relief at him not laughing at me or running off
again, I stood up and walked over to him. Before I could figure
out how to take the photo exactly, Krit grabbed my hand and
tugged me down onto his lap. "I'll take it and send it to you," he
said, then pressed a kiss to my cheek and snapped a photo with
his phone. Laughing, I pulled away to tell him I wanted one
where I could see his face, but he grabbed my head and pressed
my face to his cheek like I was kissing him and took another
photo.

When he let go of my head, I saw the wicked gleam in his

eyes and laughed harder. "Look at the camera, love," he said before sticking his tongue out and licking the side of my face.

Shoving him off me and wiping my face with the palm of my hand, I couldn't even pretend to be grossed out. It was the first up-close view I had had of his tongue piercing, and I was a little more than fascinated.

"Most women beg me to lick them, and I give it to you for free and you push me away," he said with a fake pout on his face.

"You're crazy." I giggled.

"I'm the good kind of crazy, though."

I wasn't going to argue with him about that. He was definitely the good kind of a lot of things.

"There, I sent you all three of them. And I'm posting one on Jackdown's Instagram because I'm so fucking photogenic."

I wouldn't disagree with that. "Hmmm" was the best I could do in response. Telling him he was anything less than beautiful was a lie. I needed to get up and off of him. I started to move, when his hand clamped down on my leg. "Hey. I didn't say you could get up yet," he said as he messed with his phone. One hand stayed on me as if that was all it took to keep me here.

When he was finished posting the picture, he looked up at me. "What's your Instagram?"

"I don't have one."

His pierced eyebrow shot up. "Everyone has Instagram. Why the hell don't you? Face like yours needs to be shared daily."

How was it that he could say the sweetest things one minute and the dirtiest things the next? I shrugged and hoped I wasn't blushing. "Don't really do social media. Never have."

Krit didn't push me to say more, although I could see he wanted to. It was like he knew my boundaries and didn't cross them. One day, if I was ready to talk about my past, he was the only person I could imagine talking about it to. But not right now. I wasn't there yet.

"Want to see a picture of me with long hair?" he asked, changing the topic and moving his attention back to his phone. The amused look on his face when he found it made me want to take a picture of him. I loved how expressive he was.

"Look at this," he said, tugging me closer so he could show me his phone instead of handing it to me. I tried not to think about being all cuddled up to him, and I focused on the picture.

His hair was the same color, but it brushed his shoulders. He looked like a surfer gone alternative. His face was younger too. "How long ago was this?"

"About three years, I guess. I hated it long, but the girls liked it," he explained as if that was the answer for everything. The girls would like him without hair. Surely he knew that.

"I like it better now," I told him, and moved back again. Being so close to him that his breath tickled my skin was too much.

A knock sounded on the door, and Krit pinched the inside of

my thigh. "Food's here," he said before taking me by the waist and standing me up.

"Already?"

Krit shot me a crooked grin and shrugged. "The owner's daughter and I know each other."

Not surprising. I wouldn't be requesting Mexican again. No! Wait. That was not the correct response. I shouldn't have cared about what females Krit knew. He and I were friends. I wasn't going to ruin our friendship for him or me.

"I'll go get the plates," I told him.

"You got sweet tea?" he called out after me.

I stopped and thought about lying to him. Telling him I ran out of stuff to make it. But I didn't want to lie, and there was also a chance he might see the tea bags if he went through my cabinets.

"No, I don't have any made," I replied, then hurried into the kitchen.

KRIT

If she had just said no then I wouldn't have noticed. But she'd stopped and frozen up on me for a minute. That was what gave her away. And I felt like a piece of shit. I was a piece of shit. Damn it. She loved sweet tea, and she'd been so proud of herself for making it right. And I had screwed that up for her by being an ass.

Well, she was gonna make some more sweet tea, damn it. I was gonna stand right there with her while she did it. If I had to stand over her daily, she was gonna keep sweet tea in her fridge because she liked it. I didn't want her associating it with a bad memory. Not when teaching her how to make it was one of my favorite memories.

I placed the food on the table and headed into the kitchen. She was getting two plates, and the frown on her face told me she was worrying over the sweet tea thing. I didn't deserve her time. I wasn't good enough to get her sweet smiles, but she gave them to me anyway.

"Where're the tea bags at, love?" I asked, walking over to stand behind her.

She tensed up.

I placed my hands on her shoulders and gently squeezed. "I was an asshole. You scare me, and I didn't know how to handle it at first, but I'm good now. I won't run off on you again. I don't think I can even if I want to. The idea makes me fucking sick to my stomach." I stopped because I had opened my mouth and was saying all kinds of shit I had no business saying. Regrouping, I finished. "We're gonna make some sweet tea. And every time I come over here, you better have your sweet tea in the fridge. Not for me, but because you like it. I want you to have the things that make you happy."

She relaxed under my hands and then she nodded. "It was

silly. I should have kept making it," she said, then turned to slay me with the most sincere, honest, fucking precious smile on the face of the Earth.

There was a tight painful feeling in my chest that was completely unfamiliar, but it hurt like a motherfucker and breathing was difficult.

"I'll get the tea bags and sugar. You boil the water," she told me, completely unaware something was happening in my body that was freaking me the hell out.

I managed to nod and move over to the stove. Fumbling, I filled the pot with water. No reason for the clamp on my chest to be there. What was wrong? She had smiled at me. That was it. Sweetest smile I'd ever seen, but still, it was just a smile.

"The other night, that was my first date. Not just with Linc, but my first date ever. I'm not good with guys. I don't understand them, and sometimes I do things that I shouldn't and react ways that are ridiculous, and I don't realize it. So, if I do something dumb or say the wrong thing, just tell me. I promise, I'll get better."

I couldn't turn around and look at her just yet. I knew I needed to because that was the most she had shared with me about her past, but fuck, how could I look at her while I processed this? Fury, confusion, bafflement, and pure icy cold jealousy swamped me at one time.

Her first date? How in the hell was that possible? She was

almost twenty years old. Did they keep her locked away in an attic?

I tried hard not to let the fact Linc had been her first at something eat me alive. I wasn't going to date her. I didn't date, for starters. I tried that once, and I sucked at it. But I didn't like sharing her either. She was mine. No, she wasn't. She was my friend. Boundaries. I needed some boundaries in my head. Blythe was my friend. She made me happy. She was not mine. She never would be because I didn't want someone to be mine.

"You're not moving." Blythe's voice sounded worried. I was worrying her.

I let out a breath and relaxed my face into what I hoped was a casual expression. Glancing back over my shoulder, I gave her a reassuring smile. "From what I've seen, you're pretty damn near perfect. Don't apologize. Anything that happened with us before is because I'm fucked up. Not you, love. Never you."

I turned back to the pot of water and lit the gas on the stove top. I couldn't stand there and watch the water boil, so once I was finished, I turned back around to face her. She was wringing her hands and watching me.

Reaching over, I grabbed one of her hands to make her stop. "I meant what I said. When I act like an ass, it's because I'm all kinds of fucked up. You are perfect, Blythe. I swear. Stop worrying, and let's go fix our plates. Those fajitas smell incredible."

The tension in her shoulders eased. "Okay," she replied, and started to walk toward the table. The she stopped and glanced back at me. "For what it's worth, I don't think you're fucked up. I think you're perfect too."

So not what I needed to hear her say. She was going to kill me slowly, and I was going to let her because I wasn't going to be able to stay away from her.

It was time I faced the facts.

I was addicted to Blythe Denton. More addicted than I'd been to anything in my life.

Chapter Ten

BLYTHE

Linc didn't show up at work on Monday, but he did text me several times. He had to go to Mississippi for his dad for the next few days. He didn't give me details, and I didn't ask for any. Something about his text seemed like he was trying to avoid an explanation. Two dates and some doughnuts didn't make me his girlfriend. I had no reason to expect an explanation.

Krit, however, did show up for dinner that evening with cheeseburgers and fries. We ate at the table like we always did, and he asked about my job and made me laugh with stories about his bandmates. I was always sad when it was time for him to leave, but I didn't let him know.

*

Tuesday at eleven fifteen I pulled up to the Pickle Shack. I was incredibly nervous about eating with Krit's sister. I had spoken to her for maybe ten minutes at Live Bay. If she started asking questions about Krit and me, I could answer truthfully, but I was afraid my pink cheeks would tell her something else.

The hope that she could be a friend and maybe my first real female friend outweighed all my other fears. I wanted to do this. I just needed to prepare myself for questions about my friendship with Krit.

Walking into the restaurant, I immediately spotted Trisha. Her blond hair and gorgeous face were hard to miss. She waved at me, and I explained to the hostess that I was meeting a friend before walking over there.

"You came," she said, smiling brightly at me as if she thought I wouldn't have shown up. I found it hard to believe people ever turned her down. Male or female.

"Yeah, sorry, I'm a bit late. Traffic getting out of the parking lot after class was backed up."

She shrugged as if it was no big deal. "No worries. I just got here myself. I had to take some cupcakes to Daisy's class. It's her birthday today. Daisy's my daughter," she explained.

Trisha didn't look older than twenty-four at the most. I couldn't imagine how she had a child in school already.

Her smile grew, and she leaned on the table toward me. "I

know what you're thinking. Daisy is actually my youngest child," she said with a twinkle in her eye. "Brent is ten and Jimmy is thirteen. My Daisy May turned nine today." She paused as I let the fact she had a thirteen-year-old sink in.

"Rock and I adopted them two years ago," she said with a happy sigh. "You met Preston Drake at Live Bay the other night. The beautiful guy with the surfer hair. Remember him?"

I nodded. That had been the guy with his arm around Amanda. He was hard to miss.

"Jimmy, Brent, and Daisy are all his younger siblings. His mother was … She wasn't mentally healthy. She had some addictions, and the only reason they lasted with her as long as they did was because Preston sacrificed everything to take care of them. When his mother passed away, he was going to take them all in, but Rock and I had been trying to get pregnant, and the doctor had just recently told us it was impossible. I wanted those kids," she said as tears welled up in her eyes. "Daisy May hadn't even been able to talk plain back then. She had been neglected by her mother, and she clung to any attention she got from females. Now, don't get me wrong, in her eyes Preston Drake walks on water. She loves Rock and even calls him Daddy, but he knows that Preston is her number one." Trisha wiped at her eyes and laughed then shook her head. "Sorry. I get emotional sometimes talking about it. Especially when I realize how blessed I am to have them."

I watched as the beautiful woman talked about these kids who had needed a mother, and I was amazed at how much she loved them. They weren't her kids, but she loved them as if they were. I hadn't known that was possible. I often told myself that Mrs. Williams hated me because I wasn't hers. Because she hadn't given birth to me. But seeing Trisha tear up talking about these kids who she obviously adored made my heart squeeze but also made me feel empty inside.

"Wow," I managed to say. I knew I needed to say something. She had just told me a lot in the ten minutes I'd been sitting here. "That's a really great story. Those kids are very lucky to have someone like you and your husband in their lives. Many kids don't get that." I stopped talking when I realized how much I was about to give away.

"Can I get y'all something to drink?" a waitress asked, interrupting my slipup. I had never been so thankful to be asked what I wanted to drink in my life. I knew that whatever I told Trisha was going to get back to Krit. As much as I wanted a female friendship, we didn't have that yet. I wasn't ready to trust her with my story.

"Diet Coke," Trisha told her. "And some pickles, please. Extra ranch."

"Sweet tea," I replied.

The waitress turned and left, and Trisha looked back at me. "The fried pickles are amazing. You'll love them. Anyway, enough about me. Tell me about you. All I know is you moved here for school, and my brother has taken a keen interest in you. Which never happens by the way, so you have me completely fascinated."

I didn't have much I could tell her about me. And I needed to clarify my relationship with her brother before she got it any more confused in her head, keeping in mind she'd repeat this conversation to Krit. I tucked some hair behind my ear as I gathered my thoughts.

"Well, I grew up in a small town in South Carolina. Extremely small. We had two traffic lights in town, if that tells you just how small. My mother died during childbirth. There were complications. She didn't have any parents or other living family. She was an orphan and was raised in the system since she was ten. The church she attended was the largest church in town." I paused, because honestly I didn't know why Pastor Williams and Mrs. Williams had taken me in. They hadn't wanted me. That much was obvious. They never said anything even remotely as touching as what Trisha had said about her kids. And they also never had kids of their own. I wasn't sure if that was because they couldn't or because Mrs. Williams wasn't the motherly type.

"Um, and well, I don't know why exactly, but the pastor at the church my mother attended and his wife took me home with them. I wasn't adopted or anything, but they kept me and raised me." I wasn't going to give her any more details about that part of my life. The truth hurt, and hiding it was impossible. I was too expressive. "I wanted to go somewhere different for college and be close to the water. I hadn't grown up near water. Pastor Williams is friends with Pastor Keenan, so he lined up a job for me here with him, and I enrolled at the local college. So that's it," I said, happy with my explanation and hoping she didn't dig into it any more.

The waitress set drinks and small round deep-fried slices of pickles down in front of us. I had never had deep-fried pickles before, and I wasn't sure if I liked the idea of them. It seemed wrong.

"Do y'all know what you wanna eat?" the waitress asked.

I glanced down at the menu and realized I hadn't even looked at it. "What's good?" I asked Trisha.

"Do you eat tuna?" she asked.

I nodded. I had eaten a lot of canned tuna growing up, and I wasn't a fan, exactly, but I didn't want to tell her that. I liked it well enough. I'd just had too much. She gave me a reassuring smile and turned back to the waitress. "Two seared tuna paninis please. With the chips," she said, then turned back to me. "Trust me." She winked.

I had no idea what seared tuna was because they didn't have that in a can. I nodded and returned Trisha's smile. She was hard not to smile at. "Okay," I replied.

Once the waitress walked away, Trisha turned her eyes back on me. "There are a few things that seem odd about your story, but I have the feeling you're telling me what you feel safe telling me right now. I respect that, so I'm not going to dig. Now, tell me about you and Krit."

She was seriously blunt. It was as scary as it was refreshing. You didn't have to wonder what she was thinking, that was for sure. She would just tell you.

"Krit is my friend …," I began. "He has been very kind and thoughtful from day one. He makes me laugh, and he always seems to know when I need to laugh. He's special. I don't imagine there are many guys like him out there. I don't have much—well, any experience really—with guys, but from what I can see, Krit isn't like most of them. He has a really big heart, and he doesn't seem to realize how special he is. Which makes him even more special." I was rambling, and from the wide-eyed look on Trisha's face, I was not doing a good job of hiding my feelings for her brother.

"Special," she repeated slowly, as if she needed to let that word sink in. My face grew hot, and I knew my cheeks were flaming. Dang it, I sucked at this.

"I don't think I can remember a time in my life when anyone ever called my brother special and meant it the way you just did." The pleased look on her face made me calm down a little. Maybe she did get what I had been trying to say. He was a good friend.

"I needed a friend when I moved here, and he noticed that and filled the void. I don't imagine most guys, especially ones who look like him, would do something like that for someone like me. He has beautiful girls on his arm all the time. They throw themselves at him. Yet he took the time to be my friend." Much better. I felt like patting myself on the back.

Trisha stared at me as if she were trying mentally to dissect me. I decided I would take one of those pickles now, because I needed something else to think about other than Krit's sister reading too much into my words. The last thing I needed was for her to go tell him I thought he was special.

"Can I ask you something?" she finally said, breaking the awkward silence.

I nodded, and chewed the fried pickle, which was surprisingly tasty.

"Do you really mean what you said?"

I swallowed and stared at her. Did I look like I was making it up? "Uh, yeah, I meant it. He's—" I could not say special again. I sounded like an idiot. I needed more adjectives in my vocabulary. Well, I had more where Krit was concerned, but they weren't safe to use around his very perceptive sister. "Krit's wonderful. But then, you're his sister. You know that."

A slow smile stretched across her face. "Yeah I do," she replied.

Before things could get any more intense and I could make an even bigger idiot of myself, the food arrived.

"Tonight we're having a party for Daisy May at Amanda Hardy's mother's house. She has a pool, and Amanda wanted Daisy to have a pool party. It will be friends and family. I'd love it if you could come. Krit has a thing tonight, so he will only be stopping by to give Daisy a gift and, knowing him, grab a piece of cake. But I want you to meet everyone. My friends. Amanda will love you, and since you're new, I know meeting people who are a part of this town would be nice."

I didn't like crowds and parties, but lately I was getting better. A child's birthday party wasn't like the wild parties Krit had, and Trisha was right. I'd like to meet more people. I wasn't doing well getting to know my classmates. I got to my classes on time and hurried out as soon as they ended. This kind of setting seemed safe.

"Thanks. I'd love to come."

KRIT

Britt collapsed on top of me as she fought to catch her breath. I wasn't one to cuddle after sex, but I'd give her a minute before moving her off me so I could take a shower. I hadn't planned on having sex with Britt today, but she'd shown up around four, had basically stripped, and then had gone on her knees right there in my living room.

I was pent up, and since she was so very willing and determined, I let her help me unwind. Turning my head, I glanced at the clock. It was almost five. *Shit!* I needed to get something for dinner and go down to Blythe's.

"Off you go," I told Britt as I moved her and climbed out of the bed.

"Wait. I want a round two," she said in a voice I knew was meant to be sexy, but right now I had more important things on my mind.

"Got plans, babe. But thanks." I paused and waved at the bed. "For that."

Reaching for my phone, I headed for the shower. I needed to text Blythe and let her know I'd be a few minutes late. More like thirty. Fuck, I wouldn't even have time to talk to her today.

My phone lit up, and I glanced down to see my sister's name. I opened the text message.

TRISHA: DON'T FORGET THAT DAISY MAY'S BIRTHDAY PARTY IS AT SIX THIRTY AT MARCUS'S MOTHERS HOUSE.

Shit! I threw the phone down on the counter and turned on the shower. I hadn't bought Daisy a present yet, and she had told me she wanted a sparkly pink purse and lip gloss when I'd asked her last week. I didn't know where the hell to buy a sparkly pink purse.

I took the fastest shower in history and wrapped a towel around me. Then I grabbed my phone to text Blythe. I wasn't going to be able to make it to dinner tonight. Not that I had told her I would be there, but now it was just kind of an understood thing with us again. I didn't want her to expect me and then I didn't show up.

ME: NOT GONNA BE ABLE TO DO DINNER
TONIGHT.

I hated sending her a text. She was my friend and just a friend, and it was normal for me to tell her I couldn't show up in a text. I waited for a response, but one didn't come right away, so I went to grab some clothes and get dressed.

Britt was pulling on the short skirt and hooker heels she had worn over here. How she walked in those without breaking her ankle, I didn't know. "Where you hurrying off to? You got hours before you gotta be at the club," she said as she tugged her bra back on.

My phone vibrated, and I jerked it out of my jeans pocket where I had just tucked it in.

BLYTHE: THAT'S FINE. I'LL SEE YOU LATER.

That was it. She didn't ask why or act upset. She was just okay with it. Why did it bug the hell out of me that she didn't expect more from me? Women always expected more. It was what kept me from getting too close to one. I didn't want to give them more. But Blythe ... She expected nothing. Fuck, that drove me crazy.

It was now ten minutes after five, and I still had to find a pink sparkly purse and lip gloss. Where the hell was I supposed to even look for those?

Britt walked over to me with a pleased smile on her face. Why was she still here? We were finished, and I had shit to do. "Where you off to in such a hurry?" she asked again as she slid her hand up my arm and into my hair.

Shrugging her off, I grabbed my wallet and stuck it into my back pocket. "My niece has a birthday party," I explained. See, this was normal. Britt wanted to know why I was leaving her. Where I was going. She was demanding answers by not getting the fuck out of my house. This was what women did.

Not Blythe.

But then I hadn't ... Hell, I couldn't even think it. If I let myself think about being with Blythe the way I was just with Britt, I would get the hard-on from hell. Shaking my head, I walked away from Britt and into the living room.

"You seem angry. Normally, you're much more laid-back and happy after you fuck," she said as she followed me.

"Normally, you get your shit on and leave," I shot back at her.

Britt rolled her eyes and put her hands on her hips. "Are you grumpy because you have to go to a kid's birthday party?"

I opened the door. "I have to go find a sparkly pink purse, Britt. I don't have time for twenty fucking questions," I growled in hopes she'd get the hint and leave.

She laughed and walked to the door. "You will never find a sparkly pink purse on your own. For once in your life, you need me, Krit Corbin. Come on, I'll show you where to find that purse."

Of course Britt would know where to look for the purse. Why hadn't I thought of that? Slightly relieved, I started down the stairs after her. The moment Blythe's door came into view, though, my bad mood was back. I liked my evenings with Blythe. Seeing her smile and listening to her talk—they were what I looked forward to all day. If Britt hadn't shown up and started sucking my cock, I wouldn't have run out of time. Disgusted with myself, I headed down to the parking lot.

"Are we taking your bike?" she asked.

No. The last girl who had been on my bike had ruined it for me with anyone else. I didn't like the idea of anyone other than Blythe being wrapped around me when I rode. "Let's take your car," I said, and walked toward her silver Camaro.

Chapter Eleven

BLYTHE

I had almost backed out of going to the party. Hearing Krit and some girl going at it when I went to his apartment earlier had made me ill. I wasn't ready to face him just yet. Knowing the sounds he made during sex made me feel funny. I admitted to myself that I was insanely jealous of whoever that was screaming his name.

His text that he wouldn't be able to have dinner with me was thoughtful. He hadn't had to say anything. It wasn't like he had said he would be there. I hadn't wanted to respond to him, because I was aware that he was texting me after his wild sex. Ignoring him was rude, though. He was being nice, so I couldn't be rude. I had typed my reply three times and erased all three, finally settling on something simple. Friendlike.

I was sure that Trisha had told him I would be at the party, and so he would expect to see me there. Backing out now would also be rude. Trisha had been so nice today and had even refused to let me buy my meal. She insisted that she had invited me to lunch and she was paying. I reached over and picked up the gift I had wrapped in glitter paper. It had taken me an hour this afternoon at the toy store to decide on something for this little girl I had never met. I didn't want to arrive empty-handed to her birthday party.

After much debate, I had settled on a jewelry-making kit. It even had supplies so she could paint the stones with designs of her own. I would have loved something like this as a kid. I hoped I had bought the right thing for a nine-year-old girl.

A tap on my window startled me, and I turned to see the porcelain perfect face of Amanda Hardy. Her friendly smile eased my anxiety some, and I opened my door and stepped out.

"I'm so glad you came. Trisha said she'd invited you. She really enjoyed lunch today. I'm so coming to the next lunch," Amanda said as I closed the car door behind me.

"It was fun. Trisha is really a great person." I glanced back at the large house. "It was really nice of her to invite me."

"You're Krit's friend. He doesn't have many of those ... of the female kind, that is. In all honesty, we were curious, but now that Trisha has spent time with you, she sees why her brother has grown attached to you."

141

I had to clear this up before we walked into that house and Krit showed up. "Oh, he's not attached to me. That's not it at all. He's just being nice. I'm new in town, and he's a nice guy," I explained. If Krit walked into this party and everyone acted like I was anything other than his friend, he might take off on me again. I didn't want that.

Amanda nodded, but a smile stayed on her lips. She wasn't getting it.

"No, I mean it. Really, I swear, he is just a friend."

Amanda started to say something, when a silver Camaro pulled into the driveway going a little too fast and doing a perfect U-turn to fit into the last parking space. I glanced back at Amanda, who was looking at the car, frowning. Apparently, she agreed that they had been driving a little too fast in a driveway.

The driver's door opened, and two long legs exited before the rest of a tall model-thin body came with them.

I heard Amanda mutter something, but I couldn't focus because the sight of Krit getting out of the passenger door wearing a pair of sunglasses and looking like the sex god he obviously was took my breath away. Not just because he wore his jeans better than any man on Earth or that he reminded me of every childhood fantasy of a bad boy with his aviator sunglasses on, but because he was getting out of a car with her. I never saw him with the same girl twice, but I'd seen him with her before. The first time I'd been in his apartment, she'd been in his lap.

Was she who he was doing in his apartment earlier? I tore my gaze off him and looked back at her. The smug smile she wore on her face said that yes, she was in fact who I had heard screaming his name and begging him to do it harder. My face heated, and I turned to look at the house. I had to deal with this. It was life as Krit's friend.

"Blythe?" Krit's voice called my name, and I tensed up. Crappity, crap, crap. I didn't want to talk to him just yet. My stomach still felt sick and knotted up. I was sure my face was red too. Why was my face red? It wasn't like I had anything to be embarrassed about. I hated the fact that I acted like an idiot in situations I wasn't familiar with.

Amanda's hand touched my arm, and I knew that if I was going to salvage this friendship with Krit, I had to turn around and act like nothing was wrong. Like seeing him with this girl I had heard him with earlier wasn't hard on me. Forcing a smile onto my face, I turned back to look at him.

"Hey," I replied as I watched him walk toward me in big purposeful strides, like he was afraid I was about to bolt and he was getting to me before I could. The pink-and-white-striped gift bag in his hand caught my attention. It looked so girly and out of place with him. That made me really smile.

"What are you doing here?" he asked, and that snapped me out of my moment. He sounded angry. Oh no. Was coming here stepping too far? I should have asked him if this was okay. I assumed he wouldn't mind, but he hadn't asked me to come with him. He had asked the tall goddess with him instead.

"Uh, Trisha invited me. We had lunch today. I, uh ..." He still looked upset. This was bad. I had messed up again. And this time I knew what I had done wrong. "I'm sorry. I should have asked you if you were okay with me coming. I thought your sister would have told you. I didn't think."

Krit ran his hand through his hair as the frustrated look on his face only intensified. I needed to leave.

I turned to Amanda and handed my gift to her. "Take this in, will you? Tell Trisha I said thanks so much for inviting me, but I have something I forgot that I can't miss. A study thing for one of my classes," I blurted out, and shot Krit an apologetic smile. "I really am sorry," I said, hoping the tears suddenly clogging my throat weren't obvious.

"Who are you?" the girl who was now clinging to Krit's arm asked in a bored tone.

Yet another situation for Krit he hadn't been prepared for. He kept me neatly in a certain part of his life. He didn't invite me into other parts of it. I should have thought about him and asked him. "I just ... I'm his neighbor. Uh, okay. I'm gonna go," I replied, unable to look at her.

"No, you're not," Amanda said as her hand clamped around my arm firmly, surprisingly firmly for someone as small as she was. "This is my friend Blythe. She is also Trisha's friend, and she's here for the birthday party because we want her here. Now, if you'll excuse us." She turned and headed for the house, pulling me with her. I wasn't sure I could get my arm free of her tight grip even if I tried. "Don't look back. Just come on," she whispered.

What? I needed to leave. She did not understand. "Really, Amanda. I need to go. He doesn't want me here, and this is his family. I should have asked him." I was pleading now. If she didn't let me go, I was going to start begging.

"Krit is an ass. He has always been an ass. And Brittany has a thing for singers. She's been after Krit for years. Why she is with him, I have no idea, other than to tell you he is an ass."

This was wrong. Krit was not an ass. I had blindsided him by showing up here. He reacted the way anyone would. "He's not an ass. I am. I should have asked him if this was okay. I don't think sometimes."

Amanda opened the front door and pulled me inside. Then she turned to look at me. She stared at me for a minute, then a sad smile touched her lips. "You are so not an ass. And I love Trisha, but you're too good for Krit," she said, then nodded toward the sound of people. "Come on in. This is my mom's house, but make yourself welcome. Let's go see the birthday girl and give her this sparkly present she's gonna love," she said, handing the gift back to me. "Then we will get you—and me—a drink. I need one after that."

We rounded a corner and came into a large kitchen that looked like something out of a magazine. Balloons were everywhere, as was the color pink. A tall three-tiered cake sat on the bar with pink and white stripes on one layer, and pink and white polka dots on another layer. Then the top layer was white and had the number nine and the name Daisy in pink. A pink sparkly crown sat on the top. It was the birthday cake of little girls' dreams.

"That is one fabulous cake," Amanda said as we entered the room. Trisha spun around, and her smile brightened when she saw us.

"Isn't it? Can you believe Rock ordered this? He went to the bakery and everything two weeks ago. I told him to get her a princess cake. He sure is an overachiever," she said with a laugh. "I'm glad Amanda found you and helped you find your way in here. I was going to call Krit and see if you could just ride with him, but then I forgot."

Oh no. Not a good thing to say when Krit would be coming in behind us at any moment.

"Probably good you didn't. He came with someone. I'm pretty sure Blythe wouldn't have wanted to ride with them." The distaste in Amanda's tone didn't go unnoticed by Trisha. She stopped and looked at Amanda. The questions were there in her eyes, but she wasn't going to ask them with me standing there.

"If I had known she needed a ride, I would have driven

myself," Krit said as he entered the room. There was a hard edge to his tone as he shot a glare at Amanda.

I couldn't look at him. I jerked my head back around to stare at anything but Trisha or Krit. I didn't belong there. I didn't belong anywhere. I knew that. I had always known that. Being there was wrong.

"Didn't know you were bringing a guest," Trisha said in a tight voice. Just what I needed. For her to get upset with him too. They were all jumping on him like he had done something wrong. It wasn't fair. I ruined everything. Mrs. Williams had told me that more than once. I had wanted to believe she was lying to me, but I could see that she had been right.

"Didn't know you had invited Blythe," he repeated in a clipped tone.

I winced. He was angry about that. Why hadn't I asked him about it first?

Trisha took a step toward him, her eyes slanted, and she looked ready to slap him. "This is Daisy May's birthday party. Not a place you bring an uninvited guest. One I should have been told about." Trisha had raised her voice. This wasn't good. They were about to fight. I could see the look on Krit's face, and he wasn't going to back down from this. Trisha's husband was huge, and I didn't imagine he would be okay with Krit raising his voice to Trisha.

This mess was my fault. I had to fix it.

"Don't. Please. I think that y'all have the wrong impression here, and Krit is being treated unfairly." I looked at Trisha. "What I told you today was the truth. I wasn't trying to keep a secret. I was being honest. Krit and I are friends. That's it. He also wasn't expecting me to be here. I didn't ask him if he was okay if I came. I should have." I waved a hand over to where he stood with his date. "As you can see, he brought someone. Someone of his choosing. And that's okay, because he is just a friend. He isn't doing anything wrong. I'm the outsider here. I'm the one who doesn't belong. And if you invited me because you thought that Krit would want me here, then I am so sorry I gave you that impression." I took a deep breath, then looked at Krit. "I really am sorry. I didn't think. I told you I would mess up, because I don't always know the right thing to do." I set the gift on the counter. "Thanks for inviting me. I really enjoyed spending time with you today. But this is a party for friends and family. I'm making it tense and awkward with my presence," I said as I looked at Trisha, willing her to understand.

Then I walked to the door, making sure I didn't get too close to Krit or his date. I just wanted to go back to the safety of my apartment. I heard whispering, and I walked faster. They were talking about me, and that was something I was used to.

Luckily, I got outside and to my car before Amanda could decide to keep me from leaving again. I had left the door unlocked, which I never did. The shock of seeing Krit with that girl had made me forget all about it. I climbed inside, thankful for the security of my car so that the tears burning my eyes could fall now in peace. Reaching into my pocket, I pulled out my keys and fumbled with them through the tears now freely flowing and hindering my sight. Once I had the key to the car, I managed to shove it in the ignition. The car cranked.

Then the passenger door opened, and Krit was sitting down beside me.

KRIT

She was crying.

Holy hell, something in my chest exploded. I had made her cry. Sweet precious perfect Blythe. What sick worthless motherfucker makes someone like her cry? Me and my worthless ass. God! I should have stayed away from her. I'd been selfish and had wanted to be near her because of how she made me feel, how being near her filled me and made me have a complete feeling. But I would sacrifice my soul never to have to see her cry. To know I did this was worse. A thousand times worse.

"Blythe," I managed to get out through the thickness in my throat. "I am so sorry, sweetheart. Please, god, love, please don't cry," I begged, and reached over to wipe the tears streaming down her face. I didn't want to do this there. I wanted to hold her. Fix this. God, do anything to make her smile and forget this ever happened.

I opened the car door and got out and walked around to her side. Reaching in, I took her hand and pulled her out and into my arms. I needed to hold her just for a minute. I was taking us home, but first I had to feel her close to me. She was stiff in my arms, and that sliced through me like a hot blade. I deserved it. I'd handled this completely wrong. I knew her insecurities, and I didn't take them into consideration when I reacted the way I did. She had misunderstood me.

"Krit!" Britt's voice reminded me that she was still there. Shit. Blythe moved to get away from me, but I held her tightly to my chest. She was very confused about Britt, and I intended to clarify that. But first I had to get her to stop crying.

"Come on, I'm driving," I told Blythe as I wrapped my arm around her and tucked her to my side to keep her from running off from me. She went, but she was like a robot. She didn't mold into my side or cling to me in any way. She was so damn tense, it hurt.

After I got Blythe in the passenger seat of her car and buckled her up, I headed for the driver's side. Britt stood with her hands on her hips and a scowl on her face. I didn't have time for her drama. Blythe was likely to bolt on me if I didn't get this car moving.

"Thanks for helping me find the purse. I have something important I have to deal with. I gotta go," I said, not looking at her as I climbed into the driver's seat.

"Important! Really! You fucked me like a wild man in *your bed* just two hours ago, and now you're running off because she's crying?"

Closing my eyes, I gripped the steering wheel tightly to keep from reaching out the window and strangling her. That was not what I wanted Blythe to hear. I got the hell away from Britt and her loud mouth. She used to be easy. Now she was a pain in my ass. Today was the last time I'd take her to my bed. It was a massive mistake to begin with.

"I'm sorry about her," I said, hating that I even had to bring her up around Blythe.

"Don't. It's okay." She sniffed, and I glanced over at her to see her wiping her face with both her palms. "You shouldn't be leaving, Krit. It's your niece's birthday party," she said softly. "I just ruin everything." The pain in her words were my doing.

"Do not ever, ever, say that again. Do you understand me? Don't ever." I swallowed hard and took a deep breath. I had to gain control of my emotions. "You make everything better. Why can't you see that? Who fucked your head up so bad that you can't see how amazing you are? And God damn it, Blythe, you're unbelievably gorgeous, and you don't know that, either. How is that even possible, love? You have a mirror. You can see that your outside package is just as beautiful as your inside. It shouldn't be possible for you to be so damn blind when it comes to yourself."

She didn't say anything. I glanced over at her, and she was

staring at me like I had lost my mind. Her eyes were wide and confused. The red-rimmed swollen puffiness even looked adorable on her. Did she even have to be a pretty crier? Damn it, I needed her to have a fault. Anything. Something to put me on a more even playing field with her.

"Fuck, you're even perfect when you're eyes are swollen. Ain't fair, love. How do I deal with that? Hmmm?" I turned back to the road and focused on getting us to the apartment. I needed to get a washcloth and clean her tear-streaked face. Then I needed to hold her. I wanted to hear her laugh. Right now I would settle for a smile. Anything other than that hurt look in her eyes.

When I had stepped out of Britt's Camaro, and Blythe had been there staring at me with a panicked look on her face, I hadn't been prepared for that. I was frustrated that I hadn't had time for Britt to take me back to the apartment so I could get my bike. She'd had to come with me, and that frustration multiplied when I saw Blythe looking at Britt.

I didn't want her near Britt. Britt was a part of my life I didn't like Blythe to see. Blythe was the good part of my life, and Britt was part of the darkness I didn't want touching Blythe. That all hit me at once, and I hadn't handled Blythe correctly. She assumed she was completely to blame. For what? Coming to a party my sister had invited her to? How did Blythe get into her head that she was wrong for that? I was the jackass, and Amanda and my sister were in complete agreement.

Blythe had picked up on their anger toward me and rode in like my avenging angel to make sure no one blamed me. She wasn't going to let them attack me in any way. Even though I deserved it. I had gone to the party intent on getting Blythe and fixing the mess outside. But then she had gone from her typical shy nature to standing up in a roomful of people she didn't know that well. Blythe defended me with a look on her face that blatantly dared anyone to argue the fact that I was innocent.

No one in my life had ever done that. Not even my sister. I was positive at that moment, when my sweet quiet Blythe was loudly telling a room of people who knew better that I was a nice guy who was treated unfairly, that I would follow her off the edge of a cliff if she asked me to.

I pulled into her parking spot under the apartments and quickly got out of the car and went around to get her. She had already started to get out, but I grabbed her hand and pulled her close to me. Then I locked the car before tucking her keys into my pocket.

"Come on," I said gently, and threaded my hand through hers. She wasn't as stiff as before, but she wasn't warming up to me either. She let me hold her hand, but she kept her distance.

When we got to her door, I pulled out her keys and unlocked it, then I went inside, taking her with me. I went directly to the sofa and sat down while bringing her with me and tucking her into my lap. I wrapped both of my arms around her. I bent my head and rested it in the curve of her neck and throat, and inhaled her sweet scent.

I was completely obsessed with her. *Addicted* wasn't a strong enough word. She had surpassed my addictive tendencies, and I was full-blown obsessed. There was nothing I wouldn't do for her. All she had to do was ask. I would give anything up just to get to hold her like this again.

"Krit," she said in a quiet voice.

"Yeah?" I wasn't ready to stop smelling her yet. My lips were pressed against her soft skin, and I liked having them there.

"You have to go. You have to sing tonight," she reminded me.

I had forgotten. I had never forgotten about a gig before, but tonight it was the last thing on my mind. There wasn't any room for anything other than Blythe. Sighing, I leaned back, and with one hand dug my phone out of my pocket. With the other hand, I held on to her for fear she'd get up and leave me.

I pressed Green's number.

"Tell Daisy May I said happy birthday," Green said into the phone. "And now get your ass here."

"I'm not coming tonight," I told him, lifting my eyes to lock on Blythe's.

"What? What do you mean you can't come tonight?"

"I have something more important. Someone more important that I need right now," I told him.

He didn't respond, and I knew at that moment, he realized what and who I was talking about.

"Well, shit," he grumbled. "Okay. I'll see if they are good with me covering tonight. You go deal with—" He paused a moment. "You know what you're doing, right? Don't break her."

Her big confused eyes were watching me closely. "It's me that you should be worried about. I'd jump off a cliff, you know?"

He let out a low whistle. "Damn. Okay. I'll talk to you later."

I ended the call and dropped the phone. Then I slipped my hand up to cup Blythe's face. "I need you to understand something," I told her. "From the moment you walked into my life, you have never ruined anything. You light up the things you touch. You're gonna trust me enough to tell me why you seem to have this completely warped view of yourself. But I'll earn that trust first."

She leaned into my hand, and for the first time some of the tension in her body eased. "I think you're very confused about me. I don't know why you don't see me correctly," she said softly.

I hated that. I hated that she thought I saw something no one else did. My sister fell in love with her today. It was all over Trisha's face when I walked into that kitchen. She was ready to take a side, and it wasn't gonna be mine. And Trisha always took my side. Today she'd found someone else she was willing to turn on me for. And instead of making me mad, it made me want to laugh. It wasn't just me Blythe charmed—it was everyone. But she didn't fucking see it. Amanda Hardy had come close to taking a bat to me. She'd won her over in even less time.

"I'm gonna spend my life convincing you of how wrong you are," I told her.

Blythe bit her lip and ducked her head. Dark locks fell over her face, blocking me from her eyes, and I couldn't have that. I tucked the hair back behind her ear. I wasn't worthy of her, but I needed her. I couldn't keep this up. I wanted to be around her all the time. I didn't want to have to make up excuses to see her.

"This thing with you and Linc …?" I started to ask, then stopped myself. What would I do if she said they were serious? Respect that? Hell no. Linc might be right for her, but did he need her to breathe?

She shrugged. "He's a friend. We went on two dates," she replied.

That was enough. I didn't want her thinking about it too much. She might realize Linc was the better option. I slid my hands into her hair and pulled her head to me. Then I cupped her face in my hands again. My heart started slamming against my ribs as her breath drifted over my skin. She was so close. So damn precious.

Tilting my head, I pressed my lips to hers, and the sharp intake of breath then immediate response from her body as her hands flew up to grab my shoulders and squeeze made me light-headed.

She tasted like warm summer sunshine and crisp apples. All the goodness I'd seen from a distance but never experienced was there with the gentle flick of her tongue against mine. I wanted to soak in this moment and devour her all at one time. I wrapped my arms around her and pulled her tightly to me until her chest pressed against mine and her erratic heartbeat matched my own.

I couldn't get enough of her. I tore my mouth from hers, and a groan of protest escaped her lips as I trailed kisses down her neck. I tasted her with my tongue and ran my hands down her sides and back up again, trying so hard to keep them safe. She was innocent. If I let myself go, I would scare her, and that was the last thing I wanted. Winning her trust was everything. I wanted to be worthy of something. If I could be worthy of her trust, maybe that would make this okay.

Chapter Twelve

BLYTHE

My body was on fire. There was no other explanation. Everything was sensitive. And I mean everything. Parts of me were throbbing that I hadn't had throb before. My breasts felt so full and achy, I wanted to scream for Krit to help me. Each time his hands slid up my sides and his thumb came so close to brushing the side of my boobs, I stopped breathing.

That mixed with the feeling of his tongue flicking out and running over parts of my neck and collarbone was enough to cause heart failure. He was experienced. He would know if this was dangerous, right? Because I wasn't sure I could handle much more. I needed something, but I didn't know what or if it was normal. As good as it felt, it scared me.

The metal bar that pierced his tongue touched just under my chin as he made his way back up to my mouth. A whimper filled the room, and it took me a moment to realize that it was coming from me. I didn't know I could make noises like those. If I wasn't battling so hard to keep oxygen flowing in and out of my lungs, I might have been embarrassed by my reaction to his kisses. I wanted him to stop and let me breathe but then I was terrified he wouldn't do this again.

"Sweetheart," he said in a hoarse whisper as he nuzzled my neck and licked me again. He was being tender and gentle. I trusted him. My mind was screaming at me that I shouldn't trust him but my heart wanted to. It wanted to so badly.

I tried to form words to tell him to slow down and give me a moment, but I just pressed closer to him. His heat was the only thing my body seemed to want right now. His hand slid back up my side and this time his thumb was so close to the side of my boobs. I was wearing a bra but it wasn't thick. I already dealt with big enough boobs, I didn't want to make them look any bigger with padded bras. So the thin fabric of my sundress and the satin of my bra wasn't much barrier from the gentle touch of his thumb. He was almost there.

"What do you want, Blythe," he said as he pulled my earlobe into his mouth and sucked on it causing me to tremble.

I could tell him now to stop and slow down. I could use this moment to remember why this was a bad idea. I had never done anything like this. But I didn't. Because more than anything else I wanted his thumb to stop teasing me. I wanted his hands on my breasts. My nipples were aching so bad and if he didn't grab them I was going to have to.

He ran his nose along the line from my ear to my chin, then pressed a kiss to my lips. "Tell me, sweetheart. What do you need?"

"Touch me," I begged, too incredibly past the point of need to be humiliated.

His hands moved, and his thumb was gone, causing me to cry out in frustration. Then the zipper at the back of my dress slowly slid down, and I stopped breathing, unsure if this was what I wanted. Having his hands on me was one thing, but seeing me was another. What if he didn't like how I looked?

I couldn't stand the idea of him walking away and leaving me there after I had been given a taste of this. Of him. The straps of my dress fell away and slid down my arms. I kept my eyes closed tightly and tried to inhale and exhale.

"Jesus," he said in a reverent tone that didn't sound like he was praying at all.

I opened my eyes to see his hands cover each of my breasts. I let out a strangled sound, and he inhaled sharply as his eyes swung up to meet mine. I needed more than that. The heat from his palm was teasing me. The achiness grew, and I felt as if my boobs had swollen under his touch.

"Always so perfect," he muttered as he lowered his head, his eyes still locked on mine. He pressed a kiss to the top of each mound. Then finally his hands moved, gently squeezing, and then his thumbs pressed against each nipple. I let out a scream and arched into him again.

Krit's eyes flashed brightly as if something inside of him had suddenly lit on fire. "Fuck, love," he said, right before he touched me again.

"Please," I begged this time, then I cried out. I wasn't sure what I was begging for, but I was desperate for it.

His hands left me, and I was ready to snatch them and put them right back, when my bra fell open and Krit was pushing it down my arms. Then it was gone.

I was bare. For the first time in my life, someone was seeing me naked. The terror that should be there wasn't. Not with Krit. It felt right. His hands came up to cup each breast. He squeezed and inhaled sharply again as he fondled them. I began to squirm and plead. This wasn't me at all. I couldn't believe how I was acting.

Instead of freaking him out, my actions seemed to excite him. He began to get more aggressive as he pinched each nipple and tugged on them. He sent me into a frenzy of panting, and I had to grab his arms to keep from falling. A strange haze was coming over me, and I was scared of it and clambering closer to it all at one time. *More* was all I could think about.

When a wet heat pulled a nipple in, my eyes snapped open and I cried out Krit's name. His lips were wrapped around my nipple while his eyes were locked on my face. Then he began to suck, and I lost any train of thought I had been pitifully holding on to. With each tug of his mouth, I could feel the bar in his tongue rub against my sensitive flesh. I grabbed at him as everything began to spiral out of control around me. I was going under, but the pleasure coursing through me made me not care where it was I was falling. Grabbing handfuls of Krit's hair, I began crying out his name and holding him to me. I couldn't bare the idea that he might stop this. Nothing had ever been this amazing.

The flame that was consuming me burst wide open and swallowed me as I trembled and lost all conscious thought other than the blissful wonder that had taken over my body.

Slowly, the wonderment began to fade as I sank back to Earth. My head was tucked against Krit's chest, and one of his hands was wrapped tightly around me while the other one caressed my back in lazy strokes. I didn't move. I liked the way it felt being held like this.

I would have to face him soon enough. Right now I wanted everything he was willing to give before he got up and walked out of there. I knew without a doubt this was not a "friend" thing. It wasn't okay for friends to do what we had done. Yet I had begged him to touch me. I had pushed him to do what he'd done.

He turned his head and pressed a kiss to the side of my head. "You back with me?" he asked in a tender voice that was too much for me at the moment. What had I done?

"Yeah," I said, not looking at him or moving from the comfort of his hard chest.

He continued to run his fingertips down my bare back. "Are you okay?" he asked.

I nodded.

"That was your first orgasm, wasn't it?" he said. But it wasn't a question.

I nodded a second time. It was my first everything. And I didn't want it to be a mistake. It would kill me if it was.

He kissed my head again then tangled his hands in my hair and let the strands fall from his grasp before returning to stroking my back.

"Thank you," he said in a husky whisper.

Why was he thanking me? I was the one who had just been shown what heaven was like. Not him. I pulled back just enough so that I could look up at him. He didn't ease his hold on me. He tugged me close to him again.

"Easy, love. I'm being a good boy, but you just fell apart in my arms and looked like every fucking fantasy that I've ever had. And if you show me those perfect titties again, I can't promise I'll be able to keep being a good boy."

A smile tugged at my lips just before a giggle broke free.

How was he able to do that? I was nervous and worried, and with one sentence he eased my nerves and made me laugh.

"They're jiggling, sweetheart. Please have some mercy on me and be still," he said as he hissed through his teeth and pulled me back up against his chest tightly. "There, that keeps them out of sight and still."

I couldn't even remember what it was I had been going to say to him, so I cuddled back into his chest and lay there. I didn't want him to leave. Ever. This was perfect. I didn't even care that I was topless.

We sat there quietly as he continued to run his fingertips down my back, and then he moved to my arms and shoulders. I sank deeper into him and then wrapped an arm up around his neck.

His breathing changed, and I realized he had stopped rubbing me. I moved to look up at him. He snapped his eyes closed and took a deep breath.

"Go put a bra on and one of those big-ass sweatshirts of yours. Please," he said as he continued to sit there with his eyes tightly closed.

"I took those to the Goodwill," I explained.

He let out a frustrated growl. "Fuck."

He liked the way I looked. He was trying to be good and not touch me again. The silly smile on my face only got bigger. If he liked touching me, I wanted to do that again too. I loved the way he had made me feel.

"Krit," I said, reaching out and touching his face.

He flinched then leaned into my hand. "Yes, love?" He didn't open his eyes. This was becoming amusing.

"Can we do that again? I mean, if you're trying to be good because you don't think I want you to do that again, then you're wrong. I liked that very much."

Krit let out a shaky laugh and covered his face with both of his hands and rubbed it hard while groaning. "God, sweetheart. If that was all I wanted to do, then I would take you up on it, but that's not all I want." His voice lowered as he let his hands fall to his lap and his eyes lock on my chest. He stared at me hungrily before lifting his eyes to look at my face. "I want you flat on your back underneath me while I fill you over and over. I want to hear you scream my name while you fly off into that happy place with me inside of you, being squeezed by your tight little pussy as it convulses with an orgasm around me. I want you to claw at my back and beg me while I kiss every last inch of this body. But I'm not going to do that tonight. Because I don't deserve it. I'm not sure anyone on this Earth is worthy of that. Of you. So, I need you to go get covered up and then come back in here and cuddle up with me on this sofa while we'll watch a movie."

I wasn't sure how to respond to that. What he described I wanted very much. But I wasn't sure I was ready for it. That kind of connection and vulnerability. Then there was the girl:

Britt. It had been just a few hours ago that I had heard her screaming his name. No. I wasn't ready. As wonderful as that sounded, he had been with someone else today. I couldn't be that girl for him. One that was okay with sharing him. I wasn't sure I could handle seeing him with other girls now that he had touched my boobs.

I moved off of him, covered my chest with my arms, and headed to my bedroom. My sundress hung forgotten on my hips.

KRIT

She was asleep. Her breathing had changed over the past few minutes, and while she watched the movie, I had watched her. I'd known the moment she recalled Britt's words about me fucking her. It had been all over her face. When she retreated to her room, I had sat here with the fear she might not come back out. All I needed was to hold her.

Like with everything else, Blythe hadn't acted like any other girl. I would have been made to pay for it had Blythe been like the others. But she'd changed into a pair of little pink boxers that really didn't do much to cover her, and a large T-shirt that almost covered the shorts up. The idea that the shirt could have belonged to a guy was driving me nuts.

Without a word she had walked over to the sofa and curled up beside me. Then she handed me the remote and told me to find something to watch. It was impossible not to touch her. Luckily, she was okay with me constantly feeling her skin and playing with her hair. We hadn't talked much, but her body had told me all I needed to know. She trusted me, and she forgave me.

That was enough for now.

I sat there with her asleep in my lap for an hour and watched her as she turned and wrapped her arm around my waist and buried her face into my stomach. It was a good thing she was sleeping because other parts of me were not dealing well with the fact that her head was in my lap. My cock, for example, had other ideas.

Finally, when I knew I needed a very cold shower or things were going to get painful, I picked her up and carried her back to her room. The bed was a mess, which made me grin. Blythe didn't seem like the type who left her bed unmade, but she had, and it looked like she did this a lot.

Laying her down, I straightened the covers and then tucked her in. Placing a kiss to her nose and forehead, I forced myself to turn and leave. I didn't have the willpower to crawl into bed and just hold her. The image of her coming in my lap was burned into my brain and on repeat. She'd been beautiful.

I took her keys and locked her in as I left. I would have to set my alarm to get back down there early enough in the morning to give her the keys so she could go to school. I wanted to see her again anyway. I really wanted to wake up in bed with her, but that wasn't safe. I couldn't take more.

Going up to my apartment, I knew Green had come in an hour ago. I had heard him and the silence that had followed. He hadn't brought the party home, and I owed him one. For covering for me tonight and understanding that I didn't want everyone there messing things up.

The door was unlocked when I walked inside, and Green was sitting in the recliner with a beer, watching late-night television. His gaze swung to meet mine as I closed the door behind me. I owed him more of an explanation. He had taken that one small explanation on the phone and handled things.

"Thanks," I said as I sank down onto the sofa.

"Yeah. That ain't gonna do it. I need more than that," he said, and cocked an eyebrow at me.

I nodded. He was right. He deserved more.

"Trisha invited Blythe to Daisy May's birthday party. Trisha had lunch with her today and, well, you know what Blythe's like. You spend five minutes with her, and you're sucked in. You want to get closer," I let out a chuckle and shook my head. Damn, I was sunk. "Anyway, then I showed up with Britt, which was a stupid move. I was surprised to see Blythe, and I handled it wrong. She assumed I didn't want her there because for some goddamn reason she thinks the worst of herself. And Amanda and Trisha were about ready to murder me from the looks on their faces." I turned and looked at Green as the emotion in my throat started clogging me up again. Fuck, if this didn't get to me every time I thought about it. "She stood in a kitchen full of people she didn't know and informed them all they were being unfair to me. That I was innocent and that she didn't want anyone upset with me." I stopped and swallowed hard. "She fucking said it was her fault."

"She defended you," he said, and I could see he understood. I didn't have to get mushy and act any more like a pussy than I was already. He got it.

"Yeah, she did."

Green took a long drink of his beer, then leaned forward and sat it down on the table before looking over at me again. "She sees you. Not the guy the others see. She sees *you*. The guy I've known all my life. The one you don't share. That guy. She saw him when she first looked at you." He leaned forward, resting his elbows on his knees as he looked directly at me. "Thing is, I know for a fact people can only see what you allow them to see. You let her see you. I watched you let her see you. Before you even knew her, you'd let your guard, and all those fucking walls you have built around you, down." He stood up and stretched. I let his words sink in, and I realized he was right. "She's seen the asshole the rest of the world sees. Problem is, you let her see the real you first." He shrugged. "Maybe that isn't a problem. But I guess you'll determine that. Just don't fuck this up. Because, dude, almost every man alive would kill to be in your shoes."

I watched as my best friend walked down the hall to his room. His door clicked closed behind him.

Chapter Thirteen

BLYTHE

The smell of coffee woke me up. Confused, I stared at the ceiling and tried to figure out when I went to bed last night. A cabinet closed in the kitchen, and I shot up out of bed. Just before I went into full-blown panic, last night came back to me as my sleepy mind began to catch up with the rest of me.

Krit. He had been there. I'd fallen asleep in his arms. Spinning around, I looked down at my bed, but the other side didn't look like it had been slept on. The covers were much neater than they normally were, but the other pillow was still unused.

I slipped into the bathroom to brush my teeth and my hair before walking out to the kitchen to face him. Not that it mattered much. He had been quiet last night when I had come back into the living room after changing. I didn't have to ask him to know he had been rethinking things.

I had to reassure him that this changed nothing and that we could still be friends. I wouldn't act weird and get upset over him dating his slew of women. But for my sanity, I could not allow what we did last night to happen again. It had been … It had been the most … There were no words for what that had been.

Quietly, I made my way into the kitchen and stopped and watched him as he poured a cup and started fixing it the way I liked it. At least he didn't look like a man who was about to stop being my friend. Had he stayed there all night? On the sofa maybe?

"Good morning," I said, hating the sleepy sound still clinging to my voice.

Krit jerked his head around then slowly let his gaze drift down my body and back up again. He had seen me in my oversize T-shirt and boxers last night. He picked up the cup in front of him and brought it to me.

"Morning," he said, a grin tugging at his lips.

At least he didn't look like scared runaway Krit.

"Made you coffee," he said as I took the cup from him.

"Thank you."

He stood there close to me even after I took the cup and we stared at each other. He was the pro at this kind of thing. I had no idea what I was supposed to say. So I waited.

"Was it too much to ask for you not to look so damn good in the morning?" he asked as he reached out and wrapped a strand of my hair around his finger.

"I brushed it," I admitted.

He chuckled softly. "Next time I want to see it pre-brushed."

Next time? There would be a next time? I didn't want to get too excited. He could mean the next time he stays over and watches a movie and puts me to bed.

"I have a gig tonight about an hour away. What time do you get off work?" he asked as we stood there, my coffee forgotten in my hand. Krit's blue eyes could make you forget your name when they were focused on you.

"Uh, four," I replied in a little bit of a daze from his intensity. He was never this close and intense before yesterday.

"I'll pick you up at six. I want you to go with me."

As if any female with a beating heart could tell him no. I simply nodded.

He grinned, and his dimples came out. I reached up and touched one before I could stop myself.

His grin slowly faded as his eyes flickered with the heat I remembered from last night. "What you doing, love?"

"I like your dimples," I replied honestly.

He reached for the coffee he had given me and I let him have it. He set it down on the counter beside him then picked me up and set me on the other counter, leaving him standing snuggly between my legs.

I wasn't sure what he had planned on doing until he cupped my face with both of his hands and held it as if I were breakable. His eyes locked on mine then dropped to my lips. "I was gonna be good and not kiss you this morning. But I don't think I can do that."

I didn't want him to be good. "Okay," I said, almost afraid to talk. I didn't want him to change his mind.

He moved in closer, and then his mouth was on mine and his tongue was teasing my bottom lip. I opened for him and moaned in pleasure as he slid inside. Just like before, I had to grab ahold of him for fear of losing myself somewhere. My head felt light and my heart pounded so hard, I knew he had to hear it.

My body started tingling again, and I needed to squeeze my legs together, but he was standing between them. His hands drifted to my waist, and I wanted to beg him to touch me again. Moving my body closer to him, I hoped to get a brush of his chest.

But before I could feel him, he was gone.

I opened my eyes and he was standing back just a little bit, taking quick short breaths. His eyes were still on me, and I had to bit my tongue to keep from begging him to come back.

"That," he said, and tilted his head back and stared at the ceiling. "I have to get control of that."

I disagreed. I thought he needed to have less control of that. I had thought kissing Linc had been fun and had felt warm and nice. Well, kissing Krit made my body go into a wild frenzy of feelings that made me lose my mind. It was explosive.

I sat there and watched as he got his breathing evened out. Then he finally looked at me again. The smirk on his face made a giggle bubble up, and I covered my mouth to keep him from hearing it. But he heard it anyway.

"You think this is funny?" he asked, taking a step toward me. The sexy look on his face excited me.

I nodded and watched him as he battled with himself about getting closer to me.

"What if I yank that T-shirt off your body and put my hands back on those pretty titties? Hmmm? Would that be funny?" The playful look in his eyes was meant to tease me, but the way he described it made my body feel flush all over.

"No, it wouldn't be funny at all," I replied a little breathlessly.

"It wouldn't?" he asked, stopping just before he was between my legs again.

I shook my head.

"Then what would it be, little dancer?"

"Wonderful," I replied honestly, and his eyes went wide before he cursed and backed up.

"Shit, love," he said, walking over to grip the counter where my coffee had been left. "You're gonna drive me mad."

I didn't want to drive him mad. I just wanted him to touch me again. I had woken up thinking I could never let it happen again, yet here I was ready to throw myself at him. Facing the truth was hard. I could say things in my head all day long. But if Krit wanted to touch me, I wasn't sure I could say no to that.

I felt like someone had doused me with cold water. What did that make me? I was willing to let him touch me and kiss me, and then what? Go touch and kiss someone else? Or … or … sleep with them? I pushed myself off the counter and decided to leave my coffee in the kitchen. It was too close to him, and suddenly I needed some distance.

Krit thought I was gonna drive him mad. Well, he was making me crazy.

He looked worried when his eyes met mine again. "Where you going?" he asked.

"I need to get ready. I have class in forty-five minutes," I explained.

He nodded and picked up my coffee. "Take this," he said.

I took it from him.

"I'll see you at six," he said before making his way to the door.

When he reached it, I couldn't keep my mouth from blurting out the question that was burning a hole through me.

"What are we doing, Krit?" Because this didn't feel like friends. At least not to me.

He paused and gripped the door handle tightly. Then he

glanced back at me. "Let's not label it. Let's just go with it," he said, then jerked the door open and left.

I took a drink of my coffee, then set it back down. My stomach felt sick, and I wasn't sure I could handle that now. I wouldn't push him for anything. That would only push him away. I would go tonight and see how things worked with us while he had all those females throwing themselves at him. If he acts like I'm just a friend and does things with them backstage or flirts, I'll know. I will have my answer.

Krit will just be my friend. Nothing more. No matter how much I wanted more with him, I couldn't allow myself to feel too much. He already had so much of me. And if I let my emotions get in the way and hope for more, then I could ruin what we have now, which is friendship.

KRIT

My plan for going back to bed had failed. Blythe's question was hammering away over and over in my head. She'd asked for something. It hadn't been the way most women did it, but she'd done it nonetheless. She had wanted me to make promises.

Terrified of saying something I would regret, I had gotten out of there as fast as I could. If it had been any other female, I would have laughed and told her nothing. We're doing nothing. But Blythe—I couldn't be flip with her. She'd been honestly asking me for an answer. I hadn't given her shit.

Which made me feel like shit. She deserved more than this.

"You get any sleep?" Green asked as he walked into the living room in a pair of boxers and his hair sticking up all over the place.

"Yeah, some."

Green squinted against the sun coming in through the blinds I had opened. "You must not have come up with an answer you like," he said, then yawned. "'Cause you look like you've been punched in the stomach. Ain't no man who has had sexy little Blythe in their arms should look like that."

Green was an even better choice for Blythe. I hated to admit it, but it was true. He was going to be a lawyer. He wasn't terrified of commitment, and he didn't screw around as much as me. He'd actually done a relationship before. One that worked. Not one he'd fucked up.

Banging on the door jerked me out of my thoughts.

"What the hell?" Green growled as he stalked to the door.

His angry snarl immediately evaporated as my sister pushed him aside. "Go put on clothes," Trisha ordered him, then swung her gaze to me. Shit. She was pissed.

"*You*," she said, pointing a finger at me like I was five fucking years old, "had better tell me you fixed that mess from last night."

"Not your business, Sis," I replied. She didn't have her scary-as-hell husband there to stare me down and dare me to be a smart-mouth.

"Maybe it's not. But I'm making it my business because I love you," she snapped.

"How do you figure that you barging into my place and yelling at me means you love me?"

She glared at me and shook her head. "Sometimes I want to slap your face and knock some sense into you."

I would threaten her in return, but we both knew I wouldn't lay a hand on her. I loved her bossy ass too much. "What do you want? To know I took Blythe home and apologized? Well, I did. I brought her home. We talked, and I told her I was sorry even if her stubborn ass thinks it was her fault, which I can't for the fucking life of me figure out why she is convinced of that. She stood up for me, Trisha. She fucking stood up for me. Who the hell does that? What is wrong with her?" I could see by the look in my sister's eyes that she saw too much. So I shut up. I was talking more than I should.

Trisha let out a deep sigh and then laughed. "It happened," she said as tears started filling her eyes. "I didn't think it would. I knew it wasn't Jess. I love that girl, but I knew it wasn't Jess. I even told Jess that one day the right girl would come along and you'd know. She'd rock your world. That she would heal you. Fix what they did to us." A tear slid down her face, and she sniffed.

"We deserve to be loved, Krit. I got that a lot younger than you did when Rock came into my life. He showed me unconditional love, and he healed me before I was jaded and hard. But you—"

she covered her mouth as a sob escaped"—you didn't. I left with Rock to get away from it all, and there was no one to save you. No one to show you that you were worthy of love. I was too young to know what you needed. I failed you, and you got jaded. You built walls. You learned to use all those good looks to charm girls out of their panties and good sense, but it meant nothing to you. They weren't filling your void." She stopped and wiped her face.

I didn't say anything because I didn't want to accept this. She was wrong. This was wrong. My past and what I was were too twisted for anyone to fix. I didn't want to be fixed.

"She fills your void," Trisha said when I didn't say anything. "Don't lose this. Fight for it."

"I'll only hurt her," I said, because it was true. "And I'd rather die than hurt her."

"Oh, Krit. She sees it. Why can't you?"

I didn't want to hear this anymore. My head was already a mess.

"She sees what?" I asked.

"She sees where she belongs."

I shook my head. Only my sister would think that I was worthy of Blythe. Anyone else who knew me knew that wasn't true. "I can't."

Trisha looked like I had kicked her puppy. We stood there in silence for several minutes. I expected her to fight me more, but she had given up already.

Green cleared his throat, and I turned to see him standing there with clothes on and his arms crossed over his chest. "Well, I sure hope that preacher's son is worthy of her then, because if you don't snatch her up, he's waiting in line. If it's up to her, you're the winner, but if you bow out, then Linc has an easy in."

Once I had thought I understood jealousy. I had seen the girl I was sure I loved in the arms of another man. One she wanted. One who she deserved. But that hadn't been jealousy. It had been loss. Jess had been a lot like me. Hell, Jess may have been just like me. When life had felt lonely, I knew Jess was there.

This burning possessive fury that was pumping in my veins at the thought of Linc touching Blythe or seeing her orgasm or kissing her lips was all consuming. I'd never felt this before.

"Krit, meet jealousy. It's a bitter bitch," Green said with an amused grin.

Chapter Fourteen

BLYTHE

Pastor Keenan had just stepped out to go to lunch with his wife, when a white paper bag was placed in front of me. I had been so focused on typing up the letters that Pastor Keenan had left for me that I didn't hear Linc come in.

"You're back," I said as the smell of fresh doughnuts hit my nose. "And you brought treats."

Linc's smile seemed off, but I didn't mention it or ask him if he was okay. We weren't that close yet. "I figured if I was going to abandon you for a few days without warning, I should come with a peace offering."

It was hard to believe so much had happened in just a few short days. Why did I feel guilty when I looked at him? I had no reason to feel guilty. We had been on two dates, and he had brought me some sweets to the office. Nothing more.

But what if he asked me out again? Did I say yes? Did I want to say yes? No. I didn't want to say yes. I wanted Krit. Problem was, Krit didn't want just me. He wanted to see how it went. There was no request that I not see Linc anymore. If this ended badly with Krit, I didn't want to have lost a friendship with Linc because of my feelings for Krit. There had to be a way to juggle both.

"Okay, those thoughts are way to deep for a doughnut," he said as he sat down on the edge of my desk.

I looked up at him and his handsome face. He didn't scare me. He was very safe. I wasn't in danger of getting hurt by him. That all sounded like the better choice.

But it was the easy choice.

Krit had the power to hurt me because I cared about him. I wanted him. I craved being close to him and hearing his laugh. I didn't feel all that when I was with Linc. Did that mean Linc was the friend and Krit was the one I could love?

"Deep thoughts again," Linc said, leaning down to cup my face in his hand. "Why the deep thoughts? Are you okay?"

He was so sweet.

"I'm sorry. I was lost in work when you came in and—" I stopped. I was lying. I didn't like lying, but that was exactly what I was doing. I shook my head and let out a sigh. "No. That's not true," I admitted.

Linc's concerned frown deepened. "What is it?"

I had to lay it out there for him. He deserved to know.

Keeping him on the side for when Krit dumped me was wrong. I wasn't going to be evil. I refused to believe I was evil, and I wasn't about to start doing bad things now. "You met Krit," I said, and when he nodded slowly, I decided not to give him time to say anything. I had to talk, and if he said anything bad about Krit, I would immediately go on the defensive mode. He would judge Krit without knowing him.

"Well, he's a friend. A good friend. We eat dinner together most nights. He brings takeout over before he goes to sing at whatever club he's at that night. Anyway, I like him. I like him more than he likes me. I like him as more than a friend, and he isn't that kind of guy. He likes to stay free and doesn't do relationships. I knew and I still know this, but I still can't help the way I feel about him. So, I'm dealing with how to keep my friendship with him from being harmed because I let myself care about him in a way he wasn't asking for."

Linc didn't say anything. He turned his gaze to stare at the wall across from him, and the muscles in his jaw tightened. I had needed to talk to someone about this, but Linc wasn't the person I should have unloaded on. But at least he knew the truth now. I wasn't lying to him.

"Has he kissed you?" Linc asked in a deep even voice. One would never guess he was upset in any way unless they knew he didn't normally talk in a voice that deep.

"Uh." Again I didn't want to lie, but I was pretty sure you

weren't supposed to kiss and tell. Should Linc have even asked me that question? I didn't ask him who he had kissed. This wasn't a fair thing to ask me. "I don't think that is the point of this conversation. You asked me if I was okay, and I didn't want to lie to you."

"So he has," Linc said, and stood up from the desk.

"I didn't say that."

"You didn't have to," he replied almost too calmly.

I wasn't sure what to say then. I didn't expect this reaction.

"I need to go. I'll see you later," he said without looking at me, then left the office with long fast strides.

Well, that was great. Now I had to work with his dad and deal with that awkwardness. Guess that friendship was over, but at least I had been honest. I wasn't going to lie and hurt someone to benefit myself. That would never be me.

Standing in front of the mirror, I stared at myself. I wasn't sure how I was supposed to dress to even go to this club. I didn't have the kind of clothes I had seen Krit's normal dates wear. This was the closest thing I had to sexy. Maybe. The dark blue sundress was strapless, so that was something at least. The flowers on it, however, had made me feel pretty in the store but didn't really seem like something you would see at a club. It was short, and the girls at Live Bay the other night had been wearing short skirts. So, that might make up for the fact that it was a floral print. Looking down at my feet, I had on a pair of blue ankle boots. They seemed to give more of an edge to my dress. This was the best I could do. I just hoped Krit wouldn't be embarrassed by me.

I glanced back at my closet and looked at the jeans hanging there. It was still eighty degrees most nights. The idea of being in a packed club in this heat wearing jeans seemed miserable. But maybe they would be sexier.

A knock on the door told me my time was up.

"Where you at?" Krit's voice filled the apartment. "And why isn't this door locked?"

Smiling, I stepped out of the bedroom. "I like the riffraff who finds their way in here."

Krit turned to look at me with a grin that froze on his face. He let his eyes trail down my body slowly and back up again. Then he let out a low whistle. "Damn, love. You make innocent and sweet sexy as fucking hell."

I let out the breath I was holding. I passed inspection. He wasn't embarrassed. "Oh, good. I wasn't sure what to wear to this," I admitted.

He walked toward me, and the tight black jeans he was wearing with black combat boots made my mouth water. "Truth is, little dancer, you could wear a granny gown and turn heads." He reached for my waist and pulled me close to him. "You ready to do this?"

If he meant kiss, then, yes, I was very ready.

He kissed the tip of my nose and stepped back, a playful grin on his face. "Let's go. The guys are waiting on us downstairs, and Matty, like the dickhead he is, will start blaring the horn in a minute."

I grabbed my purse and followed him to the door. He stepped back and let me go first, then he held out his hand for my keys. I gave them to him and watched as he locked the door up tight and then handed the keys back to me. "Time to party," he said with a sexy wink.

KRIT

Green was standing outside the black Escalade that we had bought from Matty's dad. It was our traveling vehicle. It was roomy enough and had the power needed to pull our trailer with the instruments.

"Whose car is that?" Blythe asked when she saw Green standing there, arms crossed and looking annoyed.

"The band's. It's what we travel in," I explained.

"Nice," she said, smiling.

"Glad y'all could join us," Green drawled when we got to the door.

"Shut up," I snarled, and held Blythe's hand as she climbed inside. They had left the back for us. Normally, I rode up front, but being tucked in the back with Blythe and everyone else in the front sounded pretty damn good.

The short little dress she was wearing rode up as she bent over to climb in the back, and the blue satin of her panties peeked out. I heard Green's sharp intake of breath and shoved him back so he couldn't see her ass. Then I climbed in behind her to make sure no one else saw her either.

Green was laughing as he climbed in after me and sat down in the middle. Legend was sitting up front in the passenger seat, and Matty was driving. Legend glanced back. "What'd I miss?" he asked as Green continued to be entirely too amused.

"Nothing," I snarled.

Legend's eyebrows went up, and he nodded before turning back around. "Got that," he mumbled.

"You always make him this testy?" Matty called back, looking at Blythe through the rearview mirror.

Blythe tensed up beside me, and I was ready to get out and smash all their faces in. Leaning back, I slid my arm around the back of the seat and pulled her closer to me. "Ignore them. They get like this before we perform," I told her.

She relaxed into me. "Do they not like for you to bring women?" she asked.

Unfortunately, she asked just loud enough for Green to hear her. He let out another laugh and turned to look back at her. "He takes 'em home, Blythe. He don't bring 'em with him. You're a first."

Her head snapped back up to look at me. I didn't meet her

curious gaze. I knew what she wanted to know, and I had no idea what the answer was. This morning I had been ready to put her at a distance when I left her apartment. I had been mentally preparing myself to keep the friend thing going, and nothing more. Then Green said the one word that sent my monster inside into a frenzy—*Linc*. I didn't like the idea of anyone else spending time with Blythe. No one else needed her laugh like I did. No one else knew how to make her laugh, and no one else made sure she had everything she needed for her sweet tea. That was all me.

The word *mine* kept rearing its head too, and I kept pushing that away. No one was mine. I didn't claim women. Not my thing. If I was going to claim anyone, it would be Blythe, but then the idea of hurting her was too much.

One argument with Jess, and I had gone off and fucked two girls backstage. Jess hadn't given a shit. She'd been fine. She was tough, and she had her own walls. I couldn't penetrate them. But Blythe, hell. What if I did something like that to her? What if I snapped and hurt her that way? I couldn't think about it. Hurting her would destroy me. I wouldn't be able to pull out of that.

But then the name Linc taunted me. I couldn't lose her to him, either. I couldn't share her. She was ... *Fuck!* That stupid word again. She wasn't mine. She was her own person. She was her own beautiful perfect person. She didn't belong to anyone.

"Krit?" Her soft voice broke into my internal battle and I gazed down at her.

"Yeah, love?" I asked, wanting to kiss the frown off her lips. I didn't like making her frown.

"Where will I sit while you sing? I won't know anyone there, will I?"

I pulled her tighter against me. "You'll stay backstage. You can watch from there, and when I take my breaks, we can hang out together."

She let out a sigh of relief. Had she actually thought I was going to send her out into that crowd alone? Probably. The girl didn't have a clue.

"I'm excited about hearing you again. This time without the interruption of having to talk to my date," she said.

I was pretty damn excited about that, too. I wouldn't have to pretend I didn't care that some other man was near her. Making her smile. Buying her drinks. "Good. I'm gonna sing that song I've been working on. I got it right one night last week. I know the way it ends now." I knew because I admitted to myself who the song was about. Who I was singing it to. Once I admitted that the song was for Blythe, I was able to finish it. My screwed-up issues all came pouring out, and the song was pretty badass. I was happy with it.

"Can't wait to hear it," she said, snuggling closer to me.

If she kept that up, I was going to forget we weren't alone.

Blythe shifted and crossed her legs. My eyes were instantly drawn to the movement. The short little sundress rode up, leaving all the soft silky skin of her thighs bare for me to see. I wasn't able to stop my hand before it decided to move on its own accord.

I ran a finger up her leg from her knee to the top of her leg. It was like cool silk. "You cold?" I asked, unable to look away from my hand on her thigh.

"No," she said softly.

"You feel cold," I told her, and opened my hand to cover her thigh. I moved it back down to her knee and back up to the top, where I paused and left it. Then moved down to her knee again. It was an attempt to heat her skin, but in reality I just wanted to touch her.

I felt her tremble, and my need kicked in. Leaning down, I whispered in her ear. "Open 'em for me."

She lifted her gaze to meet mine, and I watched her take shallow breaths as she uncrossed her legs. She didn't open them at first. I held my breath as I waited to see if she'd do it. I wanted to grab her knees and push them open, but I knew she had to make this decision.

When her legs began to ease open, my head went a little foggy and all I understood was need. I needed her. Laying my hand on her thigh, I slowly eased it up, letting my fingers trail the inside of her legs. Each tremble that went through her thighs sent my blood pressure up another notch. She was as fucking excited about me touching her as I was about her letting me.

The damp satin that met my fingertips woke the caveman in me who wanted to beat on his chest and roar. She was wet and so incredibly hot. Leaning down more, I pressed my mouth as close to her ear as I could and whispered, "You're wet. Do you get this wet for me all the time?"

She closed her eyes and nodded. I kissed her cheek and slipped a finger inside the lacey edge of her panties.

"Oh, God," she choked out, way too loud for the horny and nosey fuckers in the car with me. I moved in front of her so they couldn't see her face, and shot them all warning glares. They didn't see her. No one got to see her like this. I shouldn't have touched her in the car.

"Shhh," I said as I pressed a kiss to her mouth to muffle her sounds, and then moved my hand away from the hot wetness that had teased me. I wanted that. I wanted that so fucking bad, my body felt like it was on fire. This time I was the one trembling when she moaned her disapproval. I moved my mouth over hers and slipped my tongue inside the sunshine I craved. How the hell I'd thought I could taste this and go back to not being able to had been crazy. My addictive personality was full-blown out of control with this woman. She kept her legs open, and the temptation to slide my hand back up there was too much. I took her knee and closed her legs as I kissed her.

A small whimper escaped her as I held her legs together. She was so willing to let me touch her, and that was only escalating this thing I had for her. She had no idea what she had walked into with me. Lifting the finger I had touched her with, I inhaled her arousal and my cock throbbed in my jeans. I was past being surprised at her having no flaws. She even smelled incredible. I broke the kiss and sucked my finger before her essence was gone. Just a taste.

I lifted my eyes to see her staring at me with her mouth gently open in surprise. I pulled my finger free and smiled at her. "You'd have to *taste* like nirvana too, wouldn't you, love?"

Her cheeks turned a bright red, and she ducked her head.

"Dude, you're gonna have us all so fucking worked up when we get there, we're gonna have to find someone to get the edge off before we warm up. Could you tone it down?" Matty called back.

Shit.

"Ignore them. They can't see shit. I'm blocking their view," I assured her when her cheeks blazed brighter.

"Don't have to see her, man. Those whimpers ..." Green said, trailing off.

Fuck!

I had gotten so lost in it that I hadn't realized she was making loud enough noises for them to hear her. I didn't want them to hear her noises. I didn't want anyone to hear her noises. Those were my motherfucking noises. *Mine*. Pulling her into my lap, I pressed her head against my chest as I glared at all of them.

I hated them all. Every fucking one of them. That wasn't theirs to hear. They didn't get to hear her. She was making those noises for me. *Me*. Stupid nosey assholes.

"Krit." Blythe's sweet voice broke through the red haze that had started to blind me.

"Yeah, love?"

"I'm sorry," she said, laying her hand on my chest, almost as if she expected me to move it off me.

"What are you sorry for?" I asked, racking my brain for something she should be apologizing for.

She glanced toward the rest of the guys then back at me. "I didn't mean to make any noises," she said quietly.

Damn. Fucking sweet. I was bad for her. I wasn't what she deserved, but I'd be damned if I let anyone take her away from me now. No one had ever needed me. And no one had ever defended me. Blythe had managed to be both. Someone who needed me to take care of her, someone who was as alone as I felt and who would defend me even when I didn't deserve it.

I ran the back of my hand over her cheek. "Don't apologize for that ever again. It was my fault. I lost it for a minute there. I should have been more careful."

She pressed her lips together, but the smile trying to break free was curling up the corners of her mouth.

I leaned down to press my mouth to her ear and asked, "Is that a naughty thought that has that grin tugging on your lips?"

She nodded, and I reminded myself why sliding my hand up her thighs was a bad idea.

"We're here! Thank *fuck*! I gotta get away from these two," Green said as he opened the door and jumped down out of the car.

Legend laughed and got out, but Matty looked back at me. "You need me to leave the car going for a little bit? We can get set up first."

I started to say no, when Blythe shivered in my arms. I changed my mind. "Yeah, lock us in," I told him.

He shot me a thumbs-up and got out.

"Is that what you wanted, love?" I asked her as I slid my hand between her thighs.

She leaned up and pressed a kiss to my mouth. When I opened mine so I could taste her, she pulled my tongue into her mouth and began to suck on it. Fuck me, that was hot. My hand was on the wet crotch of her panties again, cupping her instantly. She was even more damp than she had been earlier.

A moan escaped her as I pressed my palm against her heat. "That feel good?" I asked.

"Yes, please." She panted as she moved herself over my hand and started kissing my mouth again, greedily this time. She was obviously fascinated with my tongue ring. This was the first time she had spent any time exploring it.

I let her play a little before I slipped two fingers under her panties. The moment I made contact, she threw her head back and bucked against my hand. Never had I had a woman come apart on me from something so simple. Watching Blythe's innocent expression flare up with desire was something I'd never get enough of. No one had touched her like this. No one had seen her the way I had.

As terrified as I was about hurting her, I was beginning to think I might need to worry about me. Blythe had managed to wrap me up so tightly that I couldn't imagine life without her now. I needed her to live.

"Please," she begged, panting as her heavily lidded eyes gazed up at me.

I slid a finger inside her tight entrance, and she gasped and stilled in my arms. I moved my hand and pressed exactly where I knew she'd feel it most. Her eyes flew open wide, and she grabbed my arm and tugged on it weakly. Then she cried my name.

"Easy," I whispered against her temple as I pressed a kiss there. "I've got you. Just let it come, sweetheart."

Blythe wrapped her hand around my forearm and squeezed. I took that as my cue to continue. With more tenderness than I'd every shown anyone in my life, I began to slide my finger in and out of the tight greedy hole squeezing me with a promise of how fucking mind-blowing it would be when I was buried inside her.

I didn't have much time. One of the guys would be banging on the damn door any minute. I wanted to see this. I was craving it just as much as her body was. Using the pad of my thumb, I brushed her swollen clit and felt it throb under my touch.

Blythe trembled and whimpered at the contact. My body was screaming at me to take her. Rip her panties off and bury myself inside the tight heat that I knew would change my world. But my head knew I had to be careful. She was fragile, and I needed to cherish her. I would make myself worthy of this.

I began making circles with my thumb as her point of pleasure pulsed with each touch.

"Krit, I'm gonna … I need to … please." Blythe was gasping for breath and holding on to me as if her life depended on it. "Make me come."

Another thing I'd realized. If Blythe asked me for anything, I'd give it to her. With one final pump of my finger, I pinched her clit and watched as Blythe bucked wildly and cried out my name.

I was obsessed with Blythe Denton.

Chapter Fifteen

BLYTHE

I wrapped my arms around my knees as I sat on a bench to the right of the stage behind the wall. I had a perfect view of Krit. I could see Matty, too, but Green was too far over, and Legend was behind Green. They were amazing.

It was their fourth song of the night, and so far I had seen a bra and two pairs of panties thrown at Krit's feet. There were also several notes and pieces of paper up on the edge of the stage. I wasn't sure what that was about. Maybe there were something like fan letters.

This was a part of Krit's life, and I knew he loved it. The attention from women was something I couldn't change. I didn't want to change him. He wasn't mine to change, though the way he had acted after we got out of the Escalade had been different.

Remarkably different. His hand was on me at all times. Even when he walked out onstage to check his equipment, he had kept my hand in his.

Girls had been screaming his name then, and he'd turned back to them and waved. One had even told him she loved him, and he'd winked at her. But all along his fingers had been threaded with mine, and his hold on me was tight, as if he was afraid someone was about to come snatch me away from him.

As if he could hear my thoughts, he turned to look back at me while he was singing. The grin on his face made my heart skip a beat and my stomach feel funny. I lifted my hand and waved at him, and his grin just got bigger.

It wasn't the first time he had done that tonight. He was doing it a lot. I had worried that he would realize I was in the way and regret bringing me, but he wasn't acting that way at all. He really hadn't acted that way when we'd been in the car. My panties were uncomfortably damp now, but wow, it had been worth it.

I was worried about it though. That hadn't been a friend thing to do. It had been intimate and something I never imagined I would do with someone I wasn't in a relationship with. But with Krit, I forgot about all that and took whatever I could get.

Not having a mother to talk to growing up and not having a father who made me feel secure had warped me somehow. That was all that made sense. This intense feeling I had for Krit. This need to be touched by him. To belong to him. I had always wanted to belong to someone.

When I was fourteen, a girl in our church had been tragically killed in a car accident. I had sat at her funeral watching as her mother had bent at the waist as sobs had racked her body. The girl's father hadn't been much better. He had fallen on his knees and rested his head against the girl's casket as his shoulders shook. It had been heartbreaking to watch. But the entire time I'd sat there, I'd wondered what that girl's life must have been like. She had known a love like I had only dreamed about.

Then it had hit me. No one would cry if I died. No one would care. I wouldn't have parents who were so overcome from their grief that they couldn't stand up. I wouldn't even have friends who had tissues wadded up in their fists as they stood and silently sobbed in their seats. That day had marked me.

Krit didn't know any of this. He didn't know what he was getting himself into with me. I wasn't like the girls who threw their panties at him hoping for one night of pleasure in his arms. I couldn't get up the next day and walk away like he meant nothing to me. I wasn't wired that way. All my life I had been alone and isolated. Would I love naturally? Or would my love be a twisted, broken love? Would I love in a way that smothered and made people run away?

Was I even lovable? There was a reason Pastor Williams and Mrs. Williams didn't love me. There was a reason no one ever got close to me or showed me love. Had I tried to love when I was younger and had it been wrong?

I glanced up from the spot on the floor I had been staring at while I was lost I my thoughts to see Krit walking toward me. Had they finished the set? He had said they did three tonight with twenty minute breaks in between.

Glancing behind Krit, I saw Green scowling as he followed Krit offstage. Was something wrong? I hadn't been watching them. Did I miss a fight?

Krit was in front of me, immediately taking my hands and pulling me up. "What's wrong?" he asked, a concerned frown etching his beautiful face.

"What's … I don't know? I—" I stopped talking when Green grabbed Krit's shoulder and jerked him around.

"What the hell was that? We had five more minutes. We could have done another song. We were scheduled to do another song. Did you not look over the fucking lineup?"

Krit took a step and got in Green's face. "Don't. Fucking. Interrupt. Her." He snarled then shoved him back, causing Green to stumble.

The instant fury that lit up Green's eyes sent me into motion. He was going to hit Krit. I wasn't going to let him hurt Krit. I jumped up as Green got in Krit's face.

"We are working! She was fine. You could see her. What the fuck is wrong with you? This is our job, asshole. You can't go doing shit like that when we have a packed house!"

Krit shoved him again. "Don't tell me what the fuck to do."

I had to stop them. This was about me. I wasn't sure why Krit had come offstage, but I knew it was about me. I had to fix this. I didn't want Krit fighting with his best friend.

"Stop fucking shoving me, you pansy-ass motherfucker!" Green roared, and lunged for Krit.

I moved fast, putting up two hands and jumping in front of Krit to stop him. The force of impact when Green didn't stop hit me directly in the chest. It was as if someone had put a vacuum in my lungs and sucked all the oxygen from the room. Nothing was getting in, and panic gripped me when I realized I couldn't breathe.

"*Fuck!*" Krit yelled, and his arms were around me. He was doing something to my chest as he begged me to breathe. I was trying to breathe. It wouldn't work.

"Baby, please breathe," he was pleading, and I wanted nothing more than to do that, but I couldn't. It hurt, and the terror that I was about to die settled over me.

"She got the air knocked out of her. She's gonna be okay," Matty said in an calmer voice.

And then the vacuum left, and the air I had been fighting for filled my chest as I gasped loudly and bent over. Krit was holding me against him as me muttered sweet things over and over while he rocked me back and forth.

"Take him out of here," Matty said.

I couldn't look up to see who he was talking to, but I grabbed Krit's arms to hold on to him in case they were talking about him.

"Not me, baby. I'm not leaving you," he said as his hand began running down my hair as if he were petting me. "Not going anywhere."

"I was going for him. I didn't mean to hit her," Green said, sounding panicked.

"When Krit is sure she's okay, he is going to beat the motherfucking hell out of you. Go with Legend and let him calm down first." Matty's words were more of an order this time.

"I'm so sorry. God, baby. What were you doing? You … God." He took a shaky breath. "You couldn't breathe. He hit you so hard and you went down and fuck, sweetheart. I've never been that scared in my life."

I was able to breathe again without pain, and I had to fix this. This wasn't Green's fault. I didn't know he wasn't going to be able to stop. I thought he would stop from hitting Krit if I was in front of him. "He was gonna hit you," I said, wincing from the pain in my throat.

Krit went still a minute, then his hold on me tightened.

KRIT

"Fuck," Matty whispered.

He'd heard her.

It was me who couldn't breathe now. I had thought it was an accident. But she'd fucking done it on purpose. To protect me. Holy hell.

"I'm gonna go …," Matty trailed off. I listened to his footsteps until he was gone before pulling back and looking down at Blythe.

"You got in front of six-foot-three, one hundred and eighty pounds of muscle because he was going to hit me?"

She nodded. "It was my fault he was going to hit you. I was just going to stop him."

She was going to stop him. This girl. Never in all my life did I imagine there was anyone like her. Never.

"Sweetheart, how did you intend to stop him? I could handle him. I've kicked his ass many, many times." I cupped her chin in my hand. "I had rather had him kick my ass than to have anything happen to you. That was fucking unbearable. You can't do that to me. If you get hurt, I won't be able to handle it."

She sighed, and her eyes looked back toward the stage. "I made this worse. I'm sorry. Can you go fix things with the two of you so you can get back onstage?"

The distressed look on her face meant I wasn't going to be able to leave. I wanted nothing more than to take her back home and hold her all night. But she was really upset about this. I had overreacted. She had been sitting over here staring at the floor with the saddest lost expression, and I couldn't think straight. I had to get to her.

"I'll get Green, and we'll go back onstage. But you have to promise me that you won't try and save me again. I take care of you. Not the other way around," I told her.

She reached up and touched my face. "Then who will take care of you?"

No one had ever cared about that before. That wasn't something I was going to tell her, though. "You safe in my arms is all I need. Okay?"

She frowned and glanced away from me. "I'm not agreeing to that," she said.

God, she was adorable. I pressed a kiss to her head. "Come with me to get the guys," I told her as I stood up and brought her with me.

"You won't do anything to Green then?" she said, sounding hopeful.

"No." Until you're asleep tonight. And then I'm beating his ass.

The look on their faces when Blythe apologized to Green and explained she was just trying to keep him from hitting me was priceless. Green looked like he might be sick, he was so upset over hurting her. If I hadn't held her in my arms as she fought to breathe that could have possibly been enough punishment for him. I wasn't going to feel better until I busted up something on his body. Preferably something that Blythe couldn't see. I'd have to be careful with his face. She wouldn't understand.

When we walked back onto the stage, Green whispered. "I would've never hurt her on purpose."

I nodded, but I wasn't responding.

"This ain't over, is it?" he asked.

He knew me better than that.

"You hurt her. She was fucking protecting me. What do you think?"

Green hung his head, and the pained look on his face made me feel a little better. But he still had no idea what seeing her like that had put me through. Then the fact that she had defended me again and been hurt for it. I was going to hurt someone, and Green was number one in line.

Matty took over the mic, knowing Green and I needed time to adjust to what had just gone down before we were ready to entertain the crowd.

The girls chanting my name and throwing panties and papers with their phone numbers on them normally made me get that rush in my system. Tonight I had to keep from cringing, knowing that Blythe saw all this. She heard it. When I had looked back at her and she'd been so lost in her thoughts, I had been worried that she'd heard or seen something that upset her.

Getting to her and reassuring her had been all I could think about. I glanced back at her, and she smiled at me. The excited gleam in her eyes was all I needed. I wanted to entertain her. I wanted her to enjoy watching me. I turned off the anger simmering inside and focused on that sweet smile.

When we finished the song and Matty had taken over to give me time to calm down, I turned back to the band and nodded. They knew that meant it was time for the new song. The one I'd written since Blythe had come into my life. It was hard and real. Fans would love it, and every time I sang it, Blythe's face would be the only thing I saw. She had inspired it, even if I intended to change the bitter facts in the lyrics. She was changing everything for me.

I've always had an addictive personality—
Take a little then want a little more.
Being told no isn't okay with me.
They call it obsession, but I know it's more.

I know they tell you to stay away from the devil,
But, baby, come a little closer, open my door.

I turned and held her gaze. Her eyes were sparkling with something I didn't understand, but damn, it felt like it was all mine.

They say I'm bad for you.
They say I'm wrong for the innocent, I'll only burn you up.
But I'm addicted now, and there's no changing that.
I just may be bad for you, but this lesson you're gonna learn.

Accuse me of insanity or desire to possess.
I've heard it before but never like this.
I'd tell you not to fear this, but then I'd be a liar.
You lost your free will right after our first kiss.

I know they tell you to stay away from the devil.
But, baby, come a little closer. Open my door.

They say I'm bad for you.
They say I'm wrong for an angel, I'll only burn you up.
But I'm addicted now, and there's no changing that.
I just may be bad for you, but this lesson you're gonna learn.

Good girls should stay away from the dark corners.
Temptation will always lurk within the turn.
Keeping you pure may be the only thing that redeems me.
But I never asked not to burn.

Chapter Sixteen

BLYTHE

There were a lot of them. All of them had tiny tops and tinier bottoms. I stepped back from the women being let backstage by a large guy dressed in black. I could feel several of them looking at me.

"Who is she?" one of them asked in an annoyed tone.

I turned to the large guy who had the muscles of a body-builder and a T-shirt on that was so tight, it was in danger of ripping. He frowned at me. "How did you get back here? I don't let the girls in until last song."

Nervously, I glanced back at the stage, but I had moved so that I couldn't see Krit anymore. Swinging my gaze back to the man, I told him, "I came in with the band."

His frown turned into a disbelieving smirk. "Yeah, right.

Heard that before." He stepped toward me and held out his hand. "Come on, sugar. I bring back the girls the guys pick out, and you weren't one of them. I didn't even see you around the stage all night."

Uh-oh. Glancing back at the stage, I knew Krit would be done soon, and he would inform the guy I was really with the band. Problem was it didn't look like I was going to be able to keep this guy from sending me away.

"Come on," he said, motioning me to take his hand. "This isn't something you want in on. I have no doubt they'd have picked you out of a crowd, but you look terrified. This isn't where you need to be. These boys like to play."

"I really did come with the band. I'm a friend of Krit's," I explained.

One of the girls burst out laughing, and several others joined her. My face felt like it was on fire.

"You are so not Krit's type," one of the girl's said in an amused tone.

"Nice try," another one piped up.

The guy gave me a pity smile. "Come on now. Let's get you out of here."

I didn't want to stay back there with those women anyway.

"Fine," I replied, but I wasn't giving him my hand. I didn't know him.

I stepped around him and shoved my way through at least

fifteen girls. What the heck did four guys need with fifteen girls? Was that even possible? I ignored the sick knot in my stomach. It was likely that Krit would get a couple of these girls pawing all over him, and he'd forget about me until he was done. I would be stuck out there in the crowd, alone.

"Blythe." Krit called out my name, and relief swamped me. I wasn't going to have to go out there and face all those people. "Get the fuck away from her," he ordered as he jumped down the steps and shoved the guy much bigger than him as well as a couple of the girls until he had his hand wrapped around my arm.

"Where are you going?" he asked, looking panicked.

I turned to look up at the guy in black. "He was sending me away," I explained.

"She's really with you?" the man asked incredulously.

"Did she fucking say she was with me?" Krit roared as he pulled me beside him and wrapped his arm around my shoulders.

"Yeah, but they all say that," he said defensively.

"Does she look like the rest of them?" he asked in a hard voice. He was angry. Again.

"No. I'm sorry, dude. You never bring a girl with you."

"I will from now on. You'll see her again. Make sure the others know this one is mine," he ordered. Then he looked down at me. "Let's get out of here."

"Okay," I replied, but the women behind us drowned my voice out. They were trying to get Krit's attention.

"He's taken, beauties, but I'm so fucking not," Green called out over the women. Then Matty and Legend joined him.

Krit walked us to the back door that we'd arrived at earlier.

"Are we leaving them?" I asked, glancing back at the crowd.

"Yeah, they'll be a while. I have a car picking us up. I was prepared for this," he replied, then pressed a kiss to my head. "Next time someone tries that shit again, you call my name real fucking loud. Got it?"

Next time? My heart fluttered. There would be a next time.

"Okay," I replied.

"I'll make sure they know who you are at the next place. I should've thought of that tonight."

The possessive way he sounded made me want things I couldn't have. I knew in my head that Krit didn't mean what I wanted him to mean. But with him touching me and holding me all the time, it was hard to remind myself that he was just affectionate. I just wasn't positive this was safe for my heart. I had never loved anyone. A month ago I would have said I had no idea what love felt like. However, I was beginning to think that this might be it. And I knew that was not what Krit wanted from me.

A black Lincoln Town Car was waiting outside. Krit walked over to it and opened the door. "Get in," he said with a grin.

When we were both inside and headed back to Sea Breeze, I relaxed against Krit. My eyelids were feeling heavy, and I enjoyed his warmth as I slipped into my dreams.

I woke up tucked into my bed, but I wasn't alone. I lifted my head to look down at the hard drool-worthy chest I had been sleeping on. It wasn't as soft as my pillow, but it was so much better. I took in the sexy musical note tattooed on his pec—it was perfect for him. I wanted to trace all the ink on his chest and arms, but he was still blissfully asleep. With his bad boy smirk gone and his long eyelashes brushing his cheekbones, he really did look like a fallen angel.

I remembered waking up with him carrying me last night, and then again when he pulled my boots off. Then his warm body had climbed into bed with me, and I had been drawn to him.

Glancing at the clock, I realized I had only thirty minutes to get to class. Krit was a late sleeper. I didn't want to disturb him, so the kisses I wanted to cover his chest with would have to wait. With extreme care, I eased out of his arms. When my feet hit the floor, I peeked back at him to make sure he was still sleeping. Seeing him lying there in my bed made me ache for things I'd never have.

I had lived within my walls for a long time. Why couldn't I keep them up around Krit, and protect my heart? Shaking my head, I realized no woman would be able to turn away from that.

If you were lucky enough to have Krit Corbin in your life, you didn't push him away. You soaked up every minute and made as many memories as you could.

I got ready and took a shower as quietly as I could, and decided against using the hair dryer because it would wake him. Slipping on my jeans and a new blouse I had bought for work, I picked up my heels and tiptoed out of the room.

Taking the notebook out of my backpack, I quickly wrote Krit a note and taped it to the door before I headed to school. I was going to be late for class, but I just didn't care. I had woken up in Krit's arms this morning. It was a perfect day.

KRIT

Waking up without Blythe in bed had sucked. But waking up in her bed with her smell enveloping me was pretty damn nice. If I couldn't wake up to her, then waking up in her bed with her pillow under my head was a close second. I had hoped I would wake up when she got up to get ready. I wanted to see her. Starting the day and not seeing her sucked.

I was in so deep. Funny thing was, I didn't give a shit. I would gladly drown in her if she'd let me. For the first time in my life the hole that was always empty was full. I wasn't trying to find something to curb a desire I couldn't name. The unsatisfied feeling that had chased me and sent me from one addiction to another was gone. I was …

Satisfied.

I wanted to see my girl. *My girl.* I liked the way the words sounded. Letting her go was impossible. Hell, staying away from her for a few hours sounded like torture. I wasn't going to make until this afternoon. Rolling over, I inhaled her scent in the sheets before getting out of bed. I went to grab my shirt and decided I was going to leave that here. I wanted her sleeping in my shirts. The other one was going to have to go.

Getting a shower was important, then I was going to find her. I knew when her classes were today, and if I missed her at the college, I would head over to the church. The piece of notebook paper taped to the door caught my attention.

Krit,

Good morning. You were sleeping so soundly I didn't want to wake you. Thanks for staying with me last night. You're surprisingly very comfortable. Do you still want me to come to Live Bay tonight? If not, it's okay. I know I caused a lot of problems last night. I did enjoy it though. Thanks for taking me. Hope you slept well.

Blythe

Did I still want her to come? Chuckling, I shook my head. It was time I cleared some things up. It was my fault that she was so confused. I hadn't been clear with her, and I hadn't been sure this was what was best for her. I knew now it didn't matter anymore. She was what fixed me. With her I wasn't broken.

A redhead wearing Green's T-shirt was standing in the kitchen drinking a glass of orange juice when I opened the door. I glanced around, and Green wasn't anywhere. Fantastic. He hadn't gotten rid of his one-nighter.

Her eyes lit up when she saw me, and then her gaze fell to my chest. I wasn't in the mood for this. I wanted to go find Blythe.

I didn't say anything as I headed for Green's room and banged on the door. Then I opened it. A blonde was still wrapped up in the sheets and curled around his back. "Get up. Get 'em out. There's one drinking my juice," I barked.

Green lifted his head with one eye open and scowled. "What time is it?"

"After ten. Get them out before she eats my shit," I said, then flipped on his light.

A string of curses came from Green and the girl in there with him as I headed back to my bathroom.

"Turn off my light, you fucker!" he called out.

"Don't push me. I still plan on beating your ass," I replied back before slamming the door behind me.

The girls were gone by the time I'd showered and dressed. Green glared at me as he sat on the sofa with a cup of coffee in his hand. His hair was sticking up all over the place, and he had only managed to pull on a pair of sweatpants.

"You came home in a bad mood," Green grumbled.

"No. I came home to get ready and go see my girl. I didn't like seeing some strange chick drinking my damn juice."

"Your girl? Something happen last night?" he asked.

"Not what you're thinking, and that's not your fucking business," I snapped. I didn't like him thinking about Blythe and sex in the same sentence. It was some insane caveman shit that had taken over me, but I couldn't control it or tap it down.

"What am *I* thinking?" Green asked, a confused expression on his face.

I headed for the door. He was being a dick on purpose, and I didn't have time to beat his ass. I didn't want to miss Blythe before she left school and went to work.

"Krit," Green called out. The way he'd said my name made me pause.

"Yeah?" I asked, glancing back at him.

His eyes were big, and he had sat up straight. The disbelief on his face had left his jaw hanging slightly open. "You," he said, and shook his head as his eyes studied me like I was some strange creature from outer space. "You haven't ... Y'all haven't ... had sex?"

I dropped my hand from the doorknob and took one step toward him and stopped myself. Controlling my possessiveness was going to be a challenge. "Don't," I warned. "Don't even *think* about Blythe and sex in the same sentence." The barely controlled fury in my voice wasn't something he missed, but his stupid-ass expression didn't change.

"You ... holy fucking hell. I've heard it all. Never in my life." He started laughing.

The motherfucker had started *laughing*.

"You're already acting like an insane obsessed man protecting some precious jewel! At least warn the rest of us once you do the deed because I might move out. You get any more possessive of that girl, and people are going to be scared to breathe the same air as her."

"Shut up!" I snarled. I didn't need to hear this. He was making me sound fucked up.

His expression sobered, and concern flashed in his eyes. "Just remember your issues. Don't do something stupid. You've always dealt with being off a little with your addictions, but I've never seen you like this."

"I'm fine!" I growled.

"Just don't kill anyone. Right now you look ready to take out any man who gets too close to her. You can't be that way. She wants you. Hell, man, I'm pretty sure she loves you. I ain't ever seen a girl jump in front of guy trying to protect him like she did. Remind yourself that she wants you. Not someone else. Don't fucking end up doing life because someone touched her and you broke his neck."

Chapter Seventeen

BLYTHE

Although I had been late for my first class, I hadn't missed much. The professor had been late too. In my second class, Principles of Macroeconomics, we had had to listen to a lecture on fiscal policy. I had almost fallen asleep.

Grabbing my backpack, I swung it over my shoulder and started for the door as soon the professor dismissed us.

"Blythe. Right?"

I paused. Someone had said my name. I hadn't spoken to anyone in any of my classes. I turned around to see that the owner of the feminine Southern drawl was a striking redhead with breathtaking green eyes. Her hair was long, but she had it pulled over her shoulder in a low ponytail. The Bon Jovi T-shirt she was wearing looked like it was vintage.

"Uh, yeah," I replied.

Her smile was one of those that shouldn't be attractive because it was so big, but somehow it fit her and made her even more of a head-turner. Two guys had actually just walked by and looked her way. She seemed oblivious, though.

She held out her hand for me to shake. "I'm Low Hardy. Trisha and Rock are really good friends of mine. And Amanda is my sister-in-law. I saw you at Daisy May's party, but I had just walked inside when you were defending Krit and then leaving."

I shook her hand and felt a small little bubble of excitement that someone knew me. Had I made enough connections in town that people were starting to actually know who I was? The idea that I was fitting in for the first time in my life was thrilling.

"It's nice to meet you, Low. Sorry, I didn't get to meet you at the party. I wasn't, uh, well, I was learning. Friendship with Krit is a learn-as-you-go thing," I explained.

She studied me for a moment with a pleased smile on her face. "I can only imagine," she replied.

The urge to defend him rose up in me again, and I had to shove it down. She was agreeing with me, not attacking him.

"You going to lunch?" she asked. "I normally head home right after class because I hate leaving Eli with a sitter too long, but today his daddy is home with him so I have a little time."

We walked out together, and I glanced down at my phone. "I

have to be at work in twenty minutes. It's a ten-minute drive, so I can't today. I would like to sometime, though," I told her. She reminded me of Trisha. There was no judgment in her eyes, and she wasn't sizing me up. She just accepted me and wanted to get to know me.

"I'll see if Marcus can stay home one day next week. Or better yet, you can come back to my place after class and have grilled cheeses with me and Eli," she said, smiling.

Eli had to be her son. She didn't look old enough to be a mom. I started to respond, but the words fell away when my eyes locked on the tall beautiful man leaning against my car with his arms crossed over his chest and his sunglasses covering his blue eyes.

"Oh, looks like you got a visitor," Low said.

Krit dropped his arms, and I stood there and watched as he made his way over to me. His long legs were in a pair of faded jeans, but his muscular thighs could be seen through the snug fit as he walked. This was what a swagger looked like. It was something not many men could do, but when Krit walked, girls stopped and watched. I couldn't even get mad at them. He was impossible not to look at.

Krit's eyes stayed on me as he wrapped an arm around my waist, making me want to melt after that performance. "Hello, Low," he said, glancing over at her with a smile. Then he turned back to me. "Hey, love."

He called females *love*. I had heard him do it before, and he had called me that before he even knew me. But something about the way he said it to me now, the way his voice dropped when it curled around the word, meant more. Or maybe it was my wishful thinking.

"Hey," I replied, knowing that I was staring up at him like I was completely mesmerized. I couldn't help that, though. I was.

"It was nice meeting you, Blythe. We'll do that lunch next week. I'll see you later," Low said, reminding me that she was still there.

I jerked myself out of the Krit haze I was under, and turned back to her. "Oh, yes, I look forward to it. And it was nice meeting you, too."

Low's grin was one that was both pleased and knowing. She wasn't making fun of me for being so obvious about my feelings for Krit. It made me like her even more.

"See you, Krit," Low called out.

He nodded at her briefly then looked back at me. "Low's in your class?"

"Yeah," I replied a little too breathlessly.

"She'd be a good friend," he told me, then leaned down and pressed his lips to mine. I molded into him readily, letting him taste and nibble my lips before I enjoyed the feel of his tongue and the bar in it that excited me.

When he pulled back, I wanted to grab his head and force him back down.

"Missed you when I woke up. You should've woken me. I'd have helped you get dressed," he said with a naughty smirk.

I squeezed the arm that I was holding on to. "You were sleeping so sweet. I wasn't messing that up."

He cocked his pierced eyebrow. "Sweet?"

He didn't like being called sweet. Well, too bad. He was sweet. Especially right now, coming to see me because he hadn't been awake this morning. "Yes, very sweet."

"I think I lose badass points for sleeping sweet. I need to fix that," he said, then bent down and kissed me again. "But first I want to take you back home and keep you locked up in my arms all day."

Home. He was calling my apartment home a lot now. Not my home, just *home*. And he wanted to spend the day with me. And he was at the parking lot of my college campus. What was going on?

"Krit? Why are you here?" I asked.

He frowned for what seemed like a minute then ran his thumb over my lips with a soft caress. "Because I missed you."

I got that. He had told me that. But why did he miss me now? "You never missed me before?"

Something flashed in his blue eyes. They were more expressive than he realized. "I've always missed you. Don't think I didn't. I just didn't let myself act on it."

223

He had always missed me. Were we still just "going with it" like he had said when I asked him about us?

I nodded, not wanting to make him answer any more questions. When Krit had to say too much or was pushed too hard, he ran. I loved that he had come to see me today. I didn't want to ruin this. So I kept my questions to myself.

"I'm glad you came," I said instead.

He tucked his hands into the back pockets of my jeans, pressing me closer to him. "Me too," he replied.

I would have been happy standing there like that with him for eternity. However, I had a job to get to. "I have ten minutes to get to work," I told him with a sigh.

A scowl crossed his face. But he knew I had to work today. I had left him a note. Besides, he knew I worked Monday through Friday.

"Will Linc be there?" he asked in a deep gravelly voice.

Linc. Oh. *Oh.* Butterflies went off in my stomach and tried to beat their way up into my chest. Krit was jealous of Linc. I shouldn't have been excited about it, but the fact that I was capable of making Krit jealous made me giddy. I hadn't wanted to make him jealous. I just hadn't thought I ever could. It meant he cared—enough.

"He doesn't normally come to the office. He sometimes brings me sweets from the bakery, but not every day. And he never stays. He just drops them off and says hi. But I doubt he'll

224

do that anymore … after I told him …," I trailed off. I couldn't tell Krit that I'd all but told Linc that I'd kissed him. That would sound like I had been trying to make Linc jealous.

"Finish that thought, love," he said, tightening his hold on me by squeezing my bottom.

Crappity, crap, crap. I didn't want to finish that thought. But he wasn't going to let this go. "I explained to him that you were my friend, and he might have taken it as you were more than that, and so he left and hasn't been back or called or anything."

A pleased grin slowly transformed Krit's face. "You told him what, exactly?"

Oh no. I wasn't admitting all that. "I'm gonna be late. I have to go. We'll talk about this later."

Krit's mouth covered mine one more time in a harder, more intense kiss. Nothing like he'd given me before, and I wanted more of that. But he was gone too soon. "Get to work. I'll see you when you get home. And, yes, love, I want you there with me tonight. You're riding with me."

I managed to nod and not swoon into a heap on the floor. Something was very different, and if he kept this up, I wasn't going to be able to remember that friendship line anymore.

KRIT

The next week was a balance of perfection and control. I had sworn off any woman but Blythe, and I couldn't get enough of her. Just being around her was enough. Most of the time. Other times I had to watch her come for me. I was trying like hell to go slow with her, but I was at a breaking point. I wanted inside her.

For the last few nights, she hadn't gone to listen to me play because she had had to study. Not acting like a selfish brat and seducing her into coming with me was hard. Tonight she had said she could go, and although having her backstage with me messed with my head because all I wanted to do was stare at her, I was excited. I hated leaving her home at night while I went to play. She was always asleep when I got back.

Coming up with shit to do while waiting on Blythe to get off work wasn't easy either. I felt caged. I wanted to go sit up in that office with her all day, but I knew I couldn't go to her work. Not being able to get near her was eating at me.

When the door to her apartment finally opened, I stopped pacing the floor in front of the window and went directly to her. I didn't take the time to greet her. I wanted her mouth on mine. That sweet tongue exploring my mouth and making me okay again.

Blythe's hand immediately went to my shoulders as she held on and kissed me back with just as much enthusiasm. I grabbed her waist and picked her up. "Legs around me," I said against her mouth before plunging back into her warmth. Sunshine and fucking apples. I couldn't get enough.

Blythe wrapped her legs tightly around me, and I carried her to her bed. I had made it up today while I'd tried to kill time until she got home. I didn't used to have such a hard time finding ways to spend my days. But now all I wanted was her, so it made everything else seem pointless.

I sank down onto the bed, keeping her in my lap, then lay back while she moved her legs to straddle me, and her mouth was on mine again. Fuck, this was what I'd needed all day. I didn't want to go tonight. I just wanted this.

Blythe's hands were tugging at my shirt. I lifted my back up off the bed and used one hand to jerk my shirt over my head. Both of her hands were on my abs instantly. Her short perfectly manicured nails sent shivers through me as she grazed the skin there. When her thumbs began rubbing my nipples, I groaned, and my restraint broke. I had wanted to let her play, but damn, I needed her shirt off too.

I began unbuttoning her blouse, trying my best not to rip it off. Her chest was rising and falling rapidly under my touch, and I smiled against her mouth, remembering how sensitive her breasts were. She had had an orgasm several times just from my mouth on her nipples. I wanted to do that again but not today. I had gotten a taste of her pussy by licking my fingers the other night, and I wanted the whole meal now. I had eased her into sexual play this past week. But it was time I got my head between her legs.

When the last button popped free, I shoved the shirt down her arms and started working on getting rid of the bra. Blythe shrugged off both while I tore my mouth from hers and cupped both her breasts in my hands and stared at them in wonderment. "I really fucking love these," I told her.

Her eyes sparkled with pleasure like they always did when I complemented her in any way. It was as if she needed me to but didn't expect it. Which made me want to do it more.

She lowered herself until her tits pressed against me and her mouth was once again on mine. "I like the piercing in your tongue," she whispered against my lips.

"I know," I replied, unable to keep from grinning. She'd made it very obvious that she liked the piercing in my tongue. Made me wish I hadn't let my nipple piercings close up. She'd have loved them, and I would have loved letting her play. But I did have one more piercing she hadn't seen. The thrill of her being as fascinated with that piercing had my blood pulsing and patience snapping.

Grabbing her by the waist, I flipped her over onto her back and began unsnapping her jeans. "I want them off," I told her, almost afraid to give her time to say no. When she lifted her hips so I could tug her pants down, I almost wept with relief.

Simple white satin panties had never looked so damn sexy. Running my hands down her legs, I took a moment to worship her sweet untouched body. Only me. No one else had seen her like this. Just me. Fuck, I wanted to beat my chest and roar. I had never been with a virgin, and I sure as hell had never been with someone so damn pure.

"Take yours off," she whispered. Her eyes were focused on the button of my jeans. Each short fast excited breath she took did amazing things to her chest. I was torn between taking my time undressing so I could watch her like this, and covering her hard little nipples with my mouth.

I started out slow, but the heat in her eyes sent my good intentions out the window. My jeans came off with one swift movement, and then I was back on top of her. Soaking in the feel of her satin smooth skin against mine. Kissing my way down her neck, I inhaled her scent. It only made my head lighter.

"Love, if you need me to stop, then I need you to tell me now." My voice sounded like a growl. Instead of frightening her, she shivered and clung tighter to me.

"Don't stop. Please, Krit, don't stop," she begged.

That was all I needed to hear. I moved down her stomach one kiss at a time. I licked the skin pulled tight over her ribs, then circled her naval with my tongue before trailing a line of kisses along the lacey edge of her panties. She bucked her hips restlessly, and the smell of her arousal met my nose.

I couldn't think straight enough to get her panties off and enjoy seeing them slide down her legs. I ripped the mother-fuckers like an animal, and tossed them to the floor. I had one goal and, pressing her legs open with both of my hands on her inner thighs, I claimed that taste I had only had a tease of.

The first stroke of my tongue right up the center flicked at her entrance then circled her swollen nub. Blythe screamed my name, and her body bucked so hard off the bed, I had to take my hands and grab her waist to hold her down. Fuck me, I wasn't just obsessed. I was in love.

Chapter Eighteen

BLYTHE

This was ... I didn't know this was something that ... Oh *God*!
I couldn't seem to grab on to anything to keep me from spiral-
ing. I was falling, and it was exhilarating. My hands grabbed at
Krit's hair, and a groan from his mouth only added to the pleasure his mouth was already causing.

When he had touched me down there the first time, I had
been sure nothing would ever feel as good, but holy wow, I had
been so wrong. This ... was ... wow. No words. I was pulling his
hair and I didn't mean to. I tried to let go, but his mouth would
move over me and do something else, and my hands would fist
in his soft locks again. Each time I tugged, he growled, so I
decided it was fine that I was possibly pulling his hair out. He
seemed to like it.

If he was bald when this was over, I didn't care. I would love him bald. *"Oh God!"* I cried out as he slid his tongue into the tight hole I knew was meant for something else. Did people do this? A curl of his tongue as it was buried inside me sent shocks through me, and I decided I didn't care what people did. They were missing out if they didn't do this.

Then his mouth was gone, and I grabbed at him and began to whimper. I was close. It was so good. Looking up into Krit's eyes, I saw pure raw lust, and my body trembled from excitement. He wasn't done.

His boxer briefs were gone as he stood up and jerked them off. Before I could get a full view of him, he moved to my nightstand. He opened the drawer and pulled out a small foil square. I knew what that was. I wasn't a complete idiot when it came to sex. But how did it get in my nightstand?

"I put a box in there today. I didn't want this to happen and me not be prepared," he said as he rolled the condom down over himself, and I stared at him there for the first time.

Oh no … That was … It wasn't gonna go in. I hadn't realized they got that big. I mean, you couldn't see them in pants. If they were that size all the time, you would definitely see them. You wouldn't be able not to stare at them. And I saw something silver near the head just before the condom slid down over it. Was he? No … Could he have a piercing there?

His hard warmth covered me, and his mouth began kissing

along my collarbone then up my neck before he stopped and nibbled my ear.

"Trust me?" he asked gently.

Yes, I trusted him with everything. He was my only safe place. The one person who cared. I nodded and turned my head so I could see his blue eyes. "Always," I replied.

He closed his eyes tightly for a moment, then opened them again and leaned in to kiss me. His hand slipped down my stomach, and those talented fingers began teasing me. My legs fell open, and I moaned. He always made everything feel so good. I wanted to tell him I loved him. I wanted to scream it, but I knew this wasn't about love for him. He wanted me. That was it.

A pang centered in my chest, and I pushed it away. I refused to let that ruin this. I refused to let anything ruin this. I wanted my first time to be with Krit. I wanted every time to be with Krit, but I would take whatever he was willing to give. He had opened a world for me that I wasn't willing to let go of until he walked away.

"So wet," he murmured as he slid his finger inside me. "And you taste like the sweetest honey, I fucking swear. Everything about you drives me wild, Blythe. Everything."

His voice had gone deep and raspy. It sent chill bumps all over me as his hot breath tickled my skin. "I need inside you. I've got to be buried inside you. I can't wait, love. I can't fucking wait any longer."

He shifted and placed his hands on the bed beside my shoulders as he stared down at me. I lifted my gaze to meet his just as the tip of his cock touched my entrance. The stretch as he lowered himself and sank farther into me burned, but instead of being uncomfortable, there was only pleasure from it.

His slow entrance stopped as he leaned down to kiss me again. This time with a gentle stroke of his tongue. I opened for him, but just as his tongue slipped into my mouth, a sharp pain sliced through me and I cried out, grabbing his arms. I knew it was supposed to hurt. I had read enough to know what had just happened, but for a moment I forgot. Krit moved his mouth from mine and buried it in my neck as he kept his body frozen over me. He hadn't moved again.

"Tell me," he said in a tight voice as if he was also in pain. I hadn't read where it hurt the guy. Did I miss that part? Was I hurting him? Did I need to do something?

"Does it hurt you?" I asked, sliding my hand into his hair and trying to soothe him.

He moved his head and lifted it to look down at me. He didn't say anything, so I reached up to cup his face with my hands. I didn't want to hurt him. If he would just tell me what to do to ease his pain, I would.

"Blythe," he said in low whisper, and inhaled sharply through his nose. "You," he said, then stopped and let out a small laugh. "I'm never gonna be the same," he said, then lowered his mouth to mine. I clung to him, kissing him with all the love I couldn't say out loud.

His hips lowered more, and then I was full. Completely. We were joined, and nothing had ever been so right. He started to move out, and I broke the kiss to stop him from leaving me. I wanted him to stay inside me longer. "Don't go," I begged.

Krit rocked his hips until he was back inside me fully. "Nothing. Fucking *nothing* could get me to go anywhere." His voice sounded hoarse as he began to move again.

Pleasure slowly built as his hips began a steady rhythm. I lifted my legs and wrapped them around his back, wanting to hold on to him in case he ended this before I was ready. His eyes flared, and he moved a hand to grab one of my thighs and squeeze it. "I've never," he started to say, then stopped.

He had never what?

"You're so tight, love. Nothing like this." He was panting now.

The muscles in his arms flexed with each move of his hips. The friction brushed the sensitive spot just above where he was connected to me, and my body started humming. It was building again. The release I had almost had earlier when he had been kissing between my legs was coming back, but this time something was different. When he was completely inside me, he hit a spot that sent a small shock through my system.

The more he hit that spot, the more the frantic need clawed at me. I had wanted to watch him as he moved inside me, but my focus was going. The thrill was pounding in my temple, and I couldn't hold him tightly enough. Scratching. Oh no, I was scratching him, but I couldn't stop it. The clawing was inside me, and I wanted that.

"That's it, baby, come for me." His words heated my skin as his mouth latched on to my nipple. The world blew apart, and somewhere in the distance, I heard screaming, but all I could do was hold on as my body soared and floated into heaven.

Krit cried out my name, and I held on to him the best I could while my body drifted back down onto a cloud. The heaviness of Krit's hard body on top of me, pinning me to the bed, was perfect. I wrapped my body around his and inhaled oxygen again as my mind began to function once more.

We lay that way for several wonderful minutes. Krit would press kisses to my neck where his head was still tucked. His breath soothing my heated sensitive body was an added bonus. I felt like every part of me was a live wire. One touch, and it sent a zing through me.

"Blythe," Krit said as he lifted his head.

"Yeah," I replied, reaching up to brush the hair that had fallen in his eyes from his forehead.

"You need to know something."

No. Not yet. I didn't want him telling me that this was a one-time thing or about what he did with other girls. I knew that. I just ... Not yet.

"Let's not. Okay? I know it's just a thing. I'm not expecting more. Just not yet," I said, wanting to bask a few minutes longer in his arms.

His eyebrows lowered, and a frown etched his once well-sated face. Crap. I'd said the wrong thing again.

"This," he said, pressing into me again, "is not just a thing. Fuck." He leaned down until his mouth was at my forehead. "That's my fault, isn't it? You just gave me the most precious gift in the world, and you think it's just a thing for me."

I didn't respond because I wasn't sure what to say.

"Blythe, love, what I was going to say, what I need you to know," he said, moving so he was once again looking into my eyes. "I'm not sharing. You're mine. No one will touch you but me. I have an addictive personality. I always have. And you just became my number one addiction. I'm gonna want this. A lot. I'm needy and demanding, and now you're the only one who can meet that need."

KRIT

She let me take care of her. I had carried her into the bathroom and stood her in the shower under the warm spray of water and cleaned her tender skin. She'd held on to me, and a soft smile had touched her lips the whole time. She didn't argue that she was fine. She didn't laugh or push me away. She let me.

I had never had anyone to take care of. I had tried once

before, and Jess hadn't wanted me to take care of her. She'd pushed me away and let me know I wasn't who she wanted or needed. It had hurt and only been yet another slap in the face. Women wanted to fuck me. They didn't want anything more.

But Blythe, my Blythe, she let me take care of her. She seemed to glow under my attention. This was what I had been waiting for. I had thought Jess had been my answer. But she'd had a taste of this with someone else, and she knew I wasn't it for her. I felt like sending her a fucking thank-you card. What if Jason Stone hadn't come along and stolen her heart? Would I have missed this because of Jess? Would Blythe have never come into my life? The idea of not having her rocked me.

Once I had her clean, I wrapped her in a towel and carried her back to the bed. A small red bloodstain was on the sheets, and again the possessive monster inside me threw back his head and roared his pleasure. I stood there holding her and letting the proof I was the only man to be inside her wash over me.

Blythe turned her head, and I felt her stiffen in my arms. "Oh, I can clean that up," she said, starting to wiggle.

I pulled her tighter to my chest. "No. I'm going to dry you off and hold you some more. I like seeing that blood. I did that." The pleasure in my voice made Blythe smile.

"Okay," she replied. "But you have to sing tonight. What time is it?"

Shit. I'd forgotten about that again. Glancing at the clock, I had thirty minutes before I needed to be at Live Bay.

"You're going," she said with a determined look on her face.

I wasn't going to argue with her. She would be upset if I missed a show again for her, and Green would be royally pissed. "Then you're going with me. I'll go get dressed, and you get your sexy ass ready," I told her as I sat her down on the edge of the bed.

She nodded, then she bit her lip and glanced back at the blood.

"Keep looking at those sheets, baby, and we won't leave this apartment," I warned her. My need to hold her and touch her and make sure she knew just how much I cherished her was killing me.

She jerked her head back around and her eyes went big. "Sorry. Go! I will get ready."

Chuckling, I bent down and kissed her head before heading for the door.

"Oh my god! Oh, Krit! *I am so sorry!*"

I stopped and turned back around. Blythe was covering her face, and it was etched with horror. I hated seeing her upset. Two strides, and I was back in her face, pulling her hands away. "Love, what's wrong?"

"Why didn't you tell me," she moaned pitifully.

"Tell you what?" I asked as my gaze quickly ran over her, looking for something that could have upset her.

"Your back," she said, looking up at me. "I scratched it up. I didn't mean to. I really didn't. I can wash it for you and get some salve." She started to get up, but I grabbed her legs and pushed her back down.

The fact that I had scratches on my back that Blythe had put there made me insanely happy. "I'm marked," I told her, and pressed a kiss to the corner of her mouth that was currently frowning. "By you. I love being marked by you. It's sexy and it's hot, and you gave them to me while giving me a pleasure that I didn't know existed. So, don't apologize for my scratches. I fucking love them."

I kissed her tenderly on the mouth and stood up before I pushed her back onto the bed and forgot I had a gig that night.

Keeping my focus on the crowd was tough. I kept looking back to see if Blythe was there. Green and I were going to end up in a real fight this time if I didn't stop, but my need to have her near me was fucking with my head.

Trisha's familiar blond head moved through the crowd and toward the stage door. Shit. She knew what my problem was, and she was going to take my distraction away. Turning to look back at Blythe, I debated leaving the song and going to keep Trisha from taking her, when a smile lit up her face. She liked my sister.

Trisha was talking to her, and Blythe's pleased look kept me from going over there and demanding she stay near me. She would be fine with my sister. I would then have my attention focused on the crowd, especially the crowd where Blythe would be sitting. Blythe glanced over at me, and I nodded once to let her know it was fine.

She beamed a bright smile that squeezed my heart, then walked off with Trisha. We ended the song and Green walked over to me. "Thank fuck for small miracles," he muttered before taking a swig of his water. "And your back looks like the possessive monster must have just hit a new level of insane. If those claw marks are what I think they are."

I didn't even look at him. I kept my gaze locked on Blythe walking through the crowd with Trisha. She was taking her back to the table where Rock and Dewayne were. Thursday nights were date night for Rock and Trisha. Most of the time they came here, and Preston and Amanda kept the kids. The only other times Trisha and Rock were able to come were when the kids stayed the night with friends.

Blythe took a stool beside some brunette I didn't recognize, a girl who was leaning over to Dewayne a lot. He didn't do dates, so she was probably another woman trying to reel in the ever-elusive Dewayne Falco. But then, not everyone knew his story. If they did, they'd not even waste their time.

Chapter Nineteen

BLYTHE

"I was kinda hoping you'd leave her back there. Watching Green lose his shit and punch Krit in the middle of a performance woulda made tonight a helluva lot more enjoyable," the guy who Trisha had introduced as Dewayne said. He also shot me a wink before taking a drink of his beer.

Rock laughed, and Trisha shot him a warning glare. The massive muscular man she was married to immediately stopped laughing and leaned over to press a quick kiss to her lips.

"Married, kids, and he's still pussy-whipped," Dewayne said.

Rock tensed up, and his eyes zoned in on Dewayne. "Don't talk about my woman's pussy," he warned.

The girl who Trisha hadn't introduced but appeared to be flirting with Dewayne giggled beside me.

"I'm sorry, but could we not say that word since it is mine y'all are talking about. Jeez, I bring Blythe out here to rescue her from Krit's obsessive staring, and she has to listen to this crap."

"You were backstage with Krit?" the brunette beside me asked with a touch of disbelief in her tone.

I turned to her, and the wide-eyed shock on her face was enough to remind me how out of my league I was with Krit. When I was alone with him and he was telling me all those sweet things about being addicted to me, I had hope. But when someone who looked like the kind of girl Krit normally spent time with was around, I wasn't so sure of my future with Krit. "Yes," I said, hoping it didn't sound like a question.

"Krit never takes girls backstage while he sings. I mean, he did with Jess, but she was different," the girl said.

"You're looking at Krit's newest addiction," Dewayne said to the girl, then winked at me. "Got a load of those claw marks on his back. I'm impressed. You don't look like the type."

"Dewayne! *Shut up!* For tonight, please stop talking," Trisha said, glaring at Dewayne then looking at me with an apologetic frown. "Sorry about him."

"You thirsty, Blythe?" Rock asked me from across the table. "I'm gonna go get Trisha a refill if you want something."

I hadn't brought my purse because we had been running late and I'd hurried out the door. "No, thank you," I replied, and smiled at him, not wanting to be rude. It was nice of him to offer.

Rock headed off to the bar, and Trisha grinned over at me. "He's watching you like a hawk. I don't know what he thinks I'm gonna do with you."

Turning around, I looked up at Krit, and sure enough, his eyes were zeroed in on this table. He winked at me, and that giddy feeling was back. When I had first seen him performing shirtless, I had been mesmerized. Now that I knew how those muscles felt under my hands and how his arms flexed as he moved in and out of me, seeing him up there like that, I got flushed all over. The sweat shining on him made me want to go up there and feel his damp skin.

"You keep eye-fucking him, and things should get interesting," Dewayne drawled.

I spun and jerked my gaze off him, embarrassed at being caught, and turned back around.

"Stop teasing her," Trisha scolded him, which only made me blush harder. I studied the table and wished I had stayed backstage. Spending time with Trisha had sounded fun, but being under a microscope was uncomfortable.

The girl sitting next to me starting pawing at Dewayne and whispering in his ear. Thankful for that distraction, I looked back up at Trisha. She was watching the stage. "Go ahead and watch him. Ignore Dewayne. He just likes harassing people. Krit wants you watching him. He thrives off it," she said.

I didn't need any other encouragement. I turned back

around to watch him, and just like before, I found his eyes on me. Then a pair of panties hit his chest and fell to the ground at his feet. I tried hard to ignore the jealous fire that started burning in my chest. Krit's eyes dropped down when someone called his name loud enough to get his attention, and a bra was slung at him. He caught it then held it up before letting it fall to his feet.

I knew this was his world, but I wasn't doing well dealing with it tonight. Turning back around, my eyes met Trisha's. She was watching me closely. I forced a smile because I didn't want her to know how it all made me feel. She'd tell him, or worse, she'd tell me I couldn't handle it and needed to back away.

"That's his life. He's encouraged it for years. They think that's what he wants and will be their ticket into his bed. But he's never acted about anyone the way he acts about you." She leaned forward. "Please give him time to figure this out."

I nodded. I couldn't leave him. I wasn't strong enough for that. He was everything I'd never had or thought I could have. Letting him go would be impossible. He would have to push me away.

"And here he comes. Didn't take long," Dewayne said, grinning over the head of the girl who was doing something to his neck.

Trisha's smile grew, and I turned around to see that Krit was off the stage and headed my way with long determined strides.

The rest of the band was talking to fans and just now stepping down, but he was almost to me.

He invaded my personal space, but I soaked him up. His arms caged me as he rested a hand on each side of the table behind me. "You good?" he asked simply.

"Yeah," I replied a little too quickly. It hadn't even sounded real to my ears.

Krit's eyes narrowed, then he looked up at his sister. "I'm taking her," he said, then his arm was around my shoulders and we were walking back to the stage door.

"Where are we going?" I asked, confused. He was on a break.

"Back to the greenroom. I need you alone," he said as he shoved open the door and led me inside. He took us down a hallway and then opened another door. The lock clicked behind us, and I turned to look around. There were two leather sofas, and a bar with beers and a few bottles of liquor. A flat-screen television was on the far wall, and some signed posters of bands covered the other walls.

"It bothered you," he said, backing me up to the closest sofa.

"What?"

"The shit they threw at me. You turned away," he replied, and then grabbed my waist and spun me around so he was sitting on the sofa and pulling me down onto his lap. I had to straddle him in order to sit in the position he wanted me to.

"You touched it." The words fell out of my mouth before I could stop them.

His eyes slanted, and his hands came up to cup my breasts. "But these are the ones I wanna touch."

I sucked in a shaky breath and sank down onto his lap. The hard ridge from his erection touched me through only my panties and his jeans as a barrier. I couldn't stop the pleased sound that escaped me.

"Easy, love. Are you sore?"

I was, but it was a pleasant sore. "Just more sensitive," I explained.

Krit ran his hands through my hair and wrapped strands around his finger. "I love that I did that. Makes me hard just thinking about it. Being inside you, you were so tight and hot."

Okay, this naughty talk he seemed to be fond of did it for me. It wasn't just sensitive—now it was throbbing.

"What I said to you earlier wasn't because you had just shown me nirvana." He grinned, and his dimples peeked at me. "I was fucking serious. I. Am. Obsessed. With. You."

Obsessed. It wasn't love, but it was more than I had hoped for. More than I had expected. He wanted me. Someone wanted me, and it was someone I wanted more than anything else in the world.

"I'll learn to deal with the bras and panties thrown at you," I assured him. "Could you not touch them though?"

A chuckled vibrated against his chest. "I won't touch them," he replied. "Didn't mean to that time. It's a habit. I wasn't even thinking."

I leaned down and pressed a kiss to his lips. "Let's break that habit," I said teasingly.

Krit's hands had been resting on my bare thighs where my skirt had ridden up. One of his hands moved until he was cupping me. "Only panties I care about touching."

The desire to have him touch me again and feel him inside me was overwhelming. "How much time do we have?" I asked, shifting my hips so that his hand rubbed me.

His eyes lit up. "Not enough time. I can't." He swallowed hard. "I need more time with you than what I have left for that."

Disappointed, I stopped teasing myself with his hand and nodded.

"Oh, hell," he said, then slipped his hand under my panties and slid a finger inside me.

"*Ah!*" I cried, grabbing at his shoulders. I hadn't been prepared for this.

"My girl wants me to give her pleasure, then I'm gonna fucking give her pleasure," he growled, pulling my head down until his mouth captured mine. His finger began moving inside me, making me light-headed. My hips started moving with him, and I broke the kiss to gasp for air.

"That's it, ride my hand, baby. Show me how much you want it," he encouraged me in my ear as I kept my grip on his shoulders. "Fuck, you're gorgeous."

The way his voice dropped and was laced with the same need coursing through me made my frenzy for release even stronger. I loved knowing I affected him. That touching me affected him.

A banging at the door startled me, and I stopped moving as Krit swore and held me tightly to him by wrapping his free hand around my waist. "Not ready yet!" he barked, then turned back to me. "It's okay. I'm not going anywhere until you come all over my hand," he said as he flicked the one spot that seemed to need him most.

"Ah! Yes, Krit, more," I pleaded, and he pressed his thumb against the swollen area. Fireworks went off behind my eyelids as I chanted his name.

"That's it, love," he said as he held me against him, and I struggled to breathe. His hand slowly moved out of my panties. "I love watching you get off," he said, then slipped his finger into his mouth. The wicked grin on his face made me shiver. He liked tasting me down there, and it should be wrong. It sounded wrong, but it made me feel all tingly.

KRIT

"You're gonna have to get a grip, dude. This shit ain't gonna work," Green started in on me first thing the next morning. "You can't concentrate on the performance. You fuck in the damn greenroom, and sure, you've always done that, but when it was time to go back on, you dropped what you were doing to get out there. I get that you aren't gonna treat Blythe the way you treated the others. I see that this time it's different and I'm happy for you. But you're acting like she'll disappear. Save fucking her until you get her home and can finish it. When we're working, we're working." Green had been standing in the living room, apparently waiting on me to walk in.

I closed the door behind me and glared at him. "Don't refer to what I do with Blythe as fucking."

Green's eyes went wide, and he ran a hand through his hair then laughed. "Holy shit," he said, then threw up his arms in the air. "What is this with her then? You gonna tell me that you love her? Because, man, I know you. You don't do that. You don't act like this."

I wasn't that guy anymore. "I do with her," I replied, then dropped my keys on the table and walked toward the kitchen. I had made Blythe coffee and walked her to her car this morning. I made her promise to wake me up when she got up and she had. Seeing her first thing in the morning was even better than I imagined. Green was not going to ruin this for me. I had held her sleepy body against me and kissed her face.

"Not done talking," he called out after me.

"Nothing to talk about," I replied, grabbing the coffeepot to pour myself a cup. I was exhausted, but I had some things to handle today. First thing was Britt. She had called and texted me fifteen fucking times last night before I'd had to turn my phone off. I hadn't wanted Blythe to see that. Britt needed to know I was unavailable, to back the hell off and go find another booty call.

"Are you in love with her? Just answer me that. Because if that's it, I get it. But if this is some insane obsession you've got, then you need help. Because the way you're acting is whack."

"I love her. She fills the void. She's my soul."

Green leaned against the doorframe of the kitchen and stared at me. I turned back to my coffee and took a sip. He had wanted to know. Fine. Now he knew. Nothing was going to be the same. I was different, and I never wanted to go back.

"Well, I'll be goddamned," he muttered.

"Probably," I agreed, and smiled at him over my coffee cup.

He laughed. "Fucker."

Banging on our door almost caused me to spill my coffee. Green froze then glanced back at the door. "What the hell? You piss your sister off again?" he grumbled, then headed for the door. Setting my cup down, I followed him. I hadn't done anything to bring Trisha beating on my door again. That couldn't be her.

He jerked the door open, and Britt came barreling past him with a tear-streaked face and wild eyes. "*You!*" She pointed at me.

"I called you over and over, you motherfucker! I left you messages, damn you. Did you listen to any of them? Or were you too busy with your shiny new toy?"

"Oh, shit," Green said, and stepped away from Britt as she flung her arms around, yelling.

"Shoulda took the hint," I replied, annoyed that she was causing such a scene. We were never a fucking couple. She was easy and she wasn't clingy. This shit was not okay.

'Took the hint?" she spit. "Took the fucking hint? Are you kidding me?" she continued yelling.

"It's early, babe. Could you bring it down a notch or ten?" Green said from the spot across the room he had moved to.

She held her hand up as if to block him out. "Don't act like I am crazy. Don't look at me with that stupid annoyed glare. *Do not* treat me that way. I never asked anything of you. You were Krit freaking Corbin. I was lucky you fucked me more than once. I knew that, and I was pathetic enough to take what I could get. But now you think you can toss me out and ignore my calls. That's not gonna fly this time, asshole. You finally fucked up." Her yelling had turned to a cold, calculating tone. She took a step toward me then she placed a hand on her stomach. "You got me pregnant. Now it's time to grow up."

Fear was too weak of a word. Unadulterated terror was more like it. I was having a nightmare. This wasn't really happening. Not now. Not now. "*No!*" I roared, slamming my fist into the wall and glaring at the woman standing between me and the only thing I wanted in the world.

"That condom that broke two months ago? Remember that? I've not slept with anyone but you in two months. Just you. Face it. You're gonna be a daddy, Krit Corbin."The pleased tone in her voice made me want to grab her around the neck and squeeze until she couldn't breathe. She was reveling in this. I hated her.

"Get her away from me," I snarled, moving from her. I was going to snap if she didn't shut up. I didn't hit women. I never had. But the terror clawing at me had me wanting to destroy everything in my path. I picked up a lamp and slung it across the room, then turned back to look at Green. "Get. Her. *Away*. From. Me."

He moved, his eye wide. The pain I saw reflected there was more than I could handle. He knew it too. He knew what this meant. *Fuck! No!* I had to fix it. I had to save myself. If I lost her …

My legs gave out as the door behind me closed. I wrapped my arms around myself and held on. Everything was there in my hands. My world. My heart. My soul. Blythe held it all. She was all I wanted.

And I would lose her.

A sob tore from my chest, and I threw my head back and cried for the first time since I was nine years old and my mother had told me I was her biggest mistake.

Chapter Twenty

BLYTHE

The familiar white bag entered the room before Linc did. He stuck his head around the corner and held it up higher. "So, this is my peace offering for running off the other day."

Laughing, I put the phone down. I had been going to call the florist and do the orders that Pastor Keenan had laid on my desk for a funeral. "Accepted only if there's cream in that doughnut and sprinkles on top," I said.

He stepped inside and put his hand on his chest and let out a dramatic sigh. "I got one of every kind so I'm good." He set the bag in front of me and sat down on the edge of my desk like he always did. "I might have had a small attack of jealousy. I had no reason to, and I realize that. It's a guy thing, and I'm working through my male traits. Hoping I can get them under control."

He was joking. The twinkle in his eyes was enough to make this easy. "Glad you're working on those problems. Dealing with male issues can be tough. Good luck."

Linc laughed and opened the bag and pulled out a jelly doughnut. "I was a jerk. But I missed you, so here I am."

I took the doughnut, but I knew I had to be honest with him. He was funny and I liked him as a friend only. If that was what this was, then great. But I was in love with Krit. Friendship was all Linc and I would ever have. Some small talk and laughs over doughnuts on my snack break.

"You and the rocker still going strong?" he asked, trying to sound casual. The tightness when he said *rocker* gave him away.

Sighing, I set the doughnut down. "Yeah. It's an exclusive thing now."

Linc nodded. "Smart guy. Can't blame him." Then he glanced down at the doughnut. "Eat the doughnut, Blythe."

Picking it back up, I took a bite. He had brought it to me, and I needed to at least eat his gift. Even if I wasn't sure if Krit would be okay with Linc being here. Which was something I should probably talk to him about.

"He gonna be good with us being friends still?" Linc asked, keeping that easy smile that didn't really meet his eyes.

I wanted to say sure. But that would be a lie. I had no idea how he would feel. Krit was possessive. Seriously possessive. He'd shoved a guy last night when he had walked me back to Trisha's table and the guy had gotten too close to me. The guy hadn't even been looking at me. I loved feeling protected and wanted that much. I loved being special and belonging to someone. Belonging to Krit. But Linc was nice to me. He didn't deserve for me just to stop speaking to him. I wasn't sure Krit would agree, though.

"I am taking your silence as a no," Linc said.

I glanced up at him and shrugged. "I'm not sure," I replied honestly.

Linc frowned. "Is he worth that? Being controlled?"

He didn't get it. "He doesn't control me. You don't get it. But yes, he is worth that."

Linc sighed and stood up. "You're naive, Blythe. A guy like Krit isn't your prince charming. He's exciting, and I'm sure he knows all the right things to say. But he's gonna hurt you. Don't let yourself get too attached."

I was beyond attached, but that didn't matter. Linc didn't understand what I had with Krit. He hadn't seen the way Krit held me, like I was precious and breakable and all his.

After Linc left, I managed to eat two more doughnuts and finish all the typing I had been given. Tonight there was another Live Bay show, and Krit wanted me there. I was anxious to get home.

*

When I parked outside the apartment, I had wanted to run up the stairs. He would be there, waiting on me. And we would do things.

Opening my door, I scanned the room and locked my gaze on Krit as he stood by the window, looking out. He didn't turn around to see me, but I knew he had heard me. This wasn't the welcome I had been expecting. Not after last night. Not after this morning when he had kissed me at the car like he never wanted to let me go.

"Krit?" I asked, feeling fear slowly creep in. Had he decided today that he was already bored with me?

He turned slowly, and his eyes looked hollow. The light in them that I loved was gone. Something was horribly wrong. I dropped my purse to the floor and hurried over to him. "What's wrong?" I asked, grabbing his arm. My heart pounded in my chest. He was in pain. The flash in his eyes told me this wasn't about being ready to move on. "Please, you're scaring me. What happened?"

His gaze fell to my hand grabbing onto him, and he moved his hand to cover mine. The warmth helped ease my fear some, but my chest hurt because he was hurting. "Please, what can I do?" I asked, hating seeing him like this.

"Don't leave me," he said finally. His voice was hoarse.

I shook my head, confused. "I'm not planning on it. Is that what this is about?" Surely he wasn't upset over something that hadn't happened.

"If you leave me, I can't … Just please tell me you won't leave me," he pleaded. This time his eyes showed some life in them.

"I'm not. Stop this. Please, I was just at work. I'm not even late. I don't understand," I said, reaching up to cup his handsome face. It was covered in stubble today. He hadn't shaved. He rarely went without shaving. I liked the rough feel under my hands.

He closed his eyes and inhaled deeply as I touched him. There was something more. This wasn't normal.

"I messed up," he choked out.

A sick knot settled in my stomach. Oh god. Had he been with someone else today? Was this what I was up against with him? Did he still crave other women? My hands fell away, but I didn't move. I couldn't breathe just yet though.

"Before you. She … Britt … I slept with her on and off. Just when she showed up and I was in the mood. We never dated. I don't date. But Britt was comfortable."

I stepped back. He had slept with her. Oh God, I was going to be sick. "You slept with her? Today? After—"

He moved fast, cutting off my words, and grabbed me. "No! God, No! Blythe, *No*! Never. I would never touch anyone else now. I don't want to touch anyone but you. Just you, love. Just you," he said as his body trembled.

That hadn't been what he was going to say. The nausea faded, and I nodded. I had jumped to conclusions. Linc's words had gotten to me, and I hadn't realized it until just now. "Then what did you mess up?" I asked.

He closed his eyes and took a deep breath. Or at least tried to. It was shaky, and he seemed completely terrified. My instinct to protect him was back, and I wrapped my arms around his waist. "Tell me," I said.

"Britt is pregnant. She says it's mine," His jaw tensed, and his tortured gaze locked with mine.

She was pregnant. He had gotten a girl pregnant. He was going to be a father. How did I handle this? Why was he asking me not to leave him? Did he not believe her? "Are you sure it's yours?" I asked, unable to look at him.

"The condom broke about two months ago. I didn't even think about her getting pregnant. I thought she was on the fucking pill. I got myself checked to make sure I didn't get anything from her, but that was it."

I didn't have any words. I needed to think. I had to process this.

"Blythe, please, don't pull away from me. Please, don't. I can't lose you. I can't." He was begging, and I hated hearing the pain in his voice. But this time I couldn't be there to defend him and protect him. I was going to have to protect me.

"I just need some time to think," I managed to say. I was numb. I was alone again. This time it would be worse. I knew what it felt like to belong to someone. Before, I had been blissfully ignorant.

"No. No, you're closing me out. God, baby, don't do this. Don't close me out. Stay with me. Listen to me. I love you. I love you so much."

I jerked as if I had been slapped. The pain his words caused was as sharp as a knife going through my chest. Not now. I couldn't hear those words now. My entire life I had wanted nothing more than to hear someone tell me they loved me. I had been afraid to hope for it, and now, in the darkest moment of my life, those words were finally spoken. Shaking my head, I backed away from him.

"I can't. Not now. Just please leave me alone. I need time to think," I backed up until my legs hit the couch behind me.

"Blythe, you will destroy me. I love you so much. You own my soul. You are everything to me. Don't do this. Let me hold you," he was moving toward me, but I shook my head. Letting him hold me now would taint it. I felt safe in his arms. I wanted to remember that feeling. If he held me now, it would ruin that memory.

"Just leave. I need you to leave. I'm sorry, Krit. I hate that you're hurting and scared. I hate that I can't fix that for you. I want to, but if I don't have a chance to hold myself together and deal ..." I stopped. I wouldn't tell him how close I was to shattering.

"I need to hold you," he said. The thickness in his voice was getting to me.

"I need to hold myself this time," I told him, and finally lifted my gaze up to meet his. The unshed tears in his beautiful blue depths almost sent me to my knees. God, how could I do this to him? He was pleading with me. But if I caved in, I would be facing so much future pain. How much of that pain could I handle? Was I ready for that? "This is a lot for me to take in. My past ..." I swallowed. "I've never told you about my life. Not really. It made me expect certain things. You taught me not to expect those things. You made me believe I could be wanted. You wanted me when no one else ever has. I will never ever forget that. But right now I need to be alone. I owe you the world, but I don't think I am going to fit into yours any longer. Your life is about to change, and I don't see my place in it. Just give me some time."

Krit's shoulders sagged, and he reminded me of a lost defeated little boy. Nothing in the world would have kept me from going to him and taking away his pain ... except this. "You don't just fit into my world, Blythe. You are my world," he said in a haunted voice, then he walked away.

The door closed behind him, and when I was sure he was really gone, I curled up on the floor and sobbed for all I had been given and all that had been taken away.

KRIT

I sat in a chair facing the window. My eyes focused on Blythe's car. She needed to be alone and think. As long as I knew she was safely underneath me in her apartment, I could deal with it. But if she tried to leave me, I was going after her.

The more I thought about losing her, the more I realized it was impossible. I wouldn't let it happen. I wasn't going to let her leave me. Green hadn't even bitched about me not going to Live Bay tonight. Until Blythe was back in my arms, I wasn't moving from this window. If she stayed in that apartment too much longer, I was going after her though. She might think she needed to be alone, but she needed me as much as I needed her.

My phone lit up with another call from Britt. Until I knew Blythe wasn't lost to me, I couldn't deal with Britt. I wasn't going to abandon my kid. If it was mine. I knew the condom broke, but I wasn't an idiot. Girls like Britt lied. I wanted doctor's proof she was pregnant, then I wanted a paternity test the moment the kid was born. Only then would I accept that it was mine.

Blythe was my number-one concern. The devastated look on her face that had turned to acceptance had killed me. She had hinted at the past I had always wondered about. I knew someone had hurt her, but she'd said she had never felt wanted until me. Did that mean no one had wanted her? What about when she was a kid? The pastor's family that had raised her—surely they'd wanted her.

I was going to protect her. She would never feel like this again. I would make damn sure of it. If it took the rest of my life to make this up to her, I would do it. Dropping my head into my hands, I let the regret and self-loathing eat away at me. If I'd only known she would come, I would have never touched anyone else. If I had only known that Blythe would walk into my life and make everything right, I would have been ready for her. To give her the life she deserved. I wouldn't be a fucking singer in a band who had slept with more women than he could count.

The preacher's son was probably so fucking pure, it was ridiculous. He probably had a job where girls didn't throw their panties at him, and a college degree. Lifting my head, headlights pulled into the parking lot. It was almost midnight. Green would be coming in soon. He wouldn't bring the party with him. I didn't worry about that.

The car pulled up to the front of the building, but it didn't park. Then I saw her dark hair as she ran toward it. Standing up, I watched as Blythe opened the passenger door and climbed inside. I couldn't stop her. She was leaving with him. Linc's car pulled out of the parking lot and shot off. But it wasn't going toward town. It was headed for the interstate. *Motherfucker!* Grabbing my keys, I took off running. I'd find him, and when I did, I'd beat him until he couldn't breathe. He couldn't take her from me. She was mine.

Chapter Twenty-One

BLYTHE

"What did the doctor say? Did your dad talk to a doctor? Who called him?" I asked with a wide range of emotion running through me.

Linc had called me thirty minutes ago. I hadn't answered because I couldn't talk. My tears were dried up, but my body was aching from all the vomiting I had done when it had finally sunk in that another woman would carry Krit's baby inside her and she would give birth to that baby. A part of him. I had lost it.

I had curled up on the bathroom floor and whimpered after the dry heaving stopped. Linc had called four more times, and I'd realized it had been almost midnight. Something was wrong.

I had been right. Something was wrong. Pastor Williams had been admitted to the hospital. He was in ICU. He'd suffered a heart attack. Not a good one either. Apparently, they were amazed he was still alive. I had grown up in a house with the man, but I didn't know him. All I knew of him was the sermons he preached on Sunday and the times he'd stopped his wife from saying hurtful things to me. And when she had beaten me, he had stopped her when he'd caught her.

Then two months ago he had given me an apartment and a car and a chance at a life by sending me away. It had been the nicest thing anyone had ever done for me. But he hadn't hugged me when I left. He hadn't stood at the door and waved like a parent would as I drove away. He hadn't even been there the day I left. He had gotten up and gone to the church office without a goodbye.

But now he was in the hospital. I was his only living family … if that was even what I was. I was his ward, or I had been his ward for nineteen years of my life. His mother had passed away when I was ten. She had never come around or spoken to me. His father had died when Pastor Williams was a boy. I only knew that from a sermon he had given. Everything I knew about his life, the rest of his congregation did too.

"Blythe, I'll stay with you. It's okay. He made it. That's something. He is a tough guy," Linc said, reaching over to squeeze my hands.

Confused, I turned to look at him. And he frowned and touched my cheek. "You've been crying pretty hard. I shouldn't have told you over the phone. I didn't ... Dad didn't think you were very close to him. I'm so sorry."

I had washed my face after Linc had called about Pastor Williams. He had asked if I wanted to go to South Carolina, and I'd said yes. I wanted to go. Not because I needed to see Pastor Williams, but because I needed to get away. This was an excuse to clear my head. It sounded cold. But what was I supposed to feel? I didn't really know the man. Anyway, my eyes were swollen and bruised-looking from the vomiting and sobbing.

"It's okay. I'm fine. It wasn't—" I stopped myself. I wasn't ready to tell anyone about Krit. I couldn't handle it yet. Talking about it would make it worse. "I'm fine," I repeated instead.

Linc's phone lit up. He glanced down and muttered something. Then he glanced at me. "I gotta take this or she'll keep calling."

She who? I wondered, but I just shrugged.

"Hey," he said. "No, uh, I'm having to take a friend to see her father. He's in the hospital." I stiffened. I didn't refer to Pastor Williams as my father. "Yeah, I will. No, I'll be in a hospital. Let me call you." He sighed, pulled over into a shopping center parking lot, and parked behind a Starbucks. Then glanced at me. He mouthed, *Be right back,* then climbed out of the car.

I watched as he argued, or at least it looked like he was arguing, with whoever was on the phone. I laid my head back and closed my eyes. I was tired. My body was tired. This day had started out perfect. But I didn't end perfect. I shouldn't have allowed myself to think I could keep it.

Krit had been my perfect. He had marked me. Yet again. I had been molded by life. He had shown me what it felt like to belong. I would cherish that memory, and I would love him for the rest of my life. No matter what happened or where we both ended up, my heart would belong to him.

But I had been an unwanted child. I knew what that felt like. How lonely and painful it was. No kid deserved to feel that way. Every child deserved parents. If I stayed with Krit, there was a chance he wouldn't allow himself to accept his baby. And that baby deserved to have its daddy. And if I stayed with him, I would be in the way. When he went to Britt to help with the baby, I would be alone. They would be bonding over their child, and I would be something hindering them.

The car door opened, and Linc climbed back in. "Sorry about that," he said, tucking his phone into his pocket. "Want me to swing by the drive-thru and get us a coffee? I think I could use one."

"Yeah, I could use one too," I replied as I stared out the window.

*

Sometime after three in the morning Linc and I gave up trying to stay awake, and he pulled off onto an exit. We both got our own rooms, and I was asleep before my head even hit the pillow.

KRIT

The apartment was destroyed. I had even smashed the television. I'd slung the end table at it in my fit of rage. I stood among the broken pieces of furniture and felt completely numb. The blood on my knuckles was crusted over. I hadn't taken the time to wash it off after I'd put my fist through the wall three different times.

I had called her all night. Every time it went straight to her voice mail. Her phone was off. I grabbed my phone to try again, and like the other fifty times I had called, it went to voicemail. I had gone after them, but his car was gone. I didn't know if they went east or west on the interstate. I had tried going east, but after an hour and nothing, I had gone the other way. Stopping, I had called her phone and voice mail. Afraid she was back home, that he hadn't taken her out of town, I headed back to the apartment and knocked on her door and waited for over fifteen minutes. She never came. She wasn't there.

"Shiiiiit," Preston drawled as he walked into the apartment. Turning, I glanced over at Rock, Trisha, and Preston. Green must have called them. He had come home an hour ago and just stared at me.

All I'd been able to say was "She left me."

Green hadn't been able to say anything back.

"Oh, Krit," Trisha said as she walked over pieces of broken table and pulled me into her arms. I went, but I couldn't lift my arms to cling to her. Trisha was the only one who would know. The last time I had experienced a rage like this was when I'd been told my uncle Mick was dead. He had been the only adult I trusted. The one who was there when I needed him. I had torn our trailer to shreds, smashing everything I touched. My damage hadn't been this severe though. I was stronger now.

"Dude, this is fucked up. Manda left me once and I was shattered, man, but this … Hell, I never smashed up my place." Preston said.

"Shut up," Rock ordered him.

"She just needs some time to think. She'll come back, baby. You're going to hurt yourself. You can't react this way. I'll go with you to get your meds. You can get on them again. I was okay with you not taking them because you've been so good for years. Nothing ever got to you so you never lost it. But I think now, until … I think you need to take the medication again." Trisha's worried tone normally made me feel guilty. Right now I was ripped open.

"I've been so mad before, I threatened to rip shit apart. But hell … I never actually started ripping shit apart," Preston said, amazement still in his voice.

"Dude, shut up," Rock said, shoving him this time before

walking over to hand Trisha a small bag. It was from the local pharmacy.

I shook my head and stepped out of my sister's arms. I wasn't going back on the meds they gave me for my ADHD, and I wasn't going to take the damn antidepressants I knew were in that bag. I hated taking those meds. I hated how they made me feel. They changed me. I'd controlled myself for years. I could get control again. I just had to get Blythe back.

"If you don't take them, then you're going back to the house with us. Green loves you, but you're scaring him. He doesn't know what to do with you. And you've got to clean this mess up. Rock brought Preston in case we had to hold you down, but they are also here to help fix this mess. Focus on cleaning up, and we're gonna help you replace stuff. Especially Green's stuff. She will come back. She just needs time, baby. She just needs time."

"I can't lose her."

Trisha glanced over at Rock and frowned. Then she squeezed my arm. "I know. She loves you. Anyone could see that. She'll be back."

"Have you talked to Britt today?" Rock asked.

I tensed.

"Rock," Trisha warned.

"He has to be a man, Trish. He's got a girl pregnant and he has to deal with that, too."

"If that baby is really mine, then I'll take care of what's mine.

But Britt hasn't even brought me proof from the doctor yet. I'm waiting on that."

Rock nodded. "Fair enough. Don't trust her anyway. And she'll be shit for a mom. Kid's gonna need you if she is pregnant."

I hadn't even thought of that. I hadn't thought of anything but Blythe.

"Let's get this place cleaned up. We can talk about it all later," Trisha said, walking over to Rock.

I reached down and picked up some of the Sheetrock I had busted up. I had done a number on the place. I'd checked out mentally and lost it.

"Maybe you should take a picture of this place and send it to the preacher's son. Bet he runs like hell," Preston said as he tossed a piece of wood over into a pile.

"He better run fast," was all I said.

Green showed back up, and with the four of us working, it took five hours to clean the place out. Rock called a buddy of his that did Sheetrock to patch the place, and then he took Green to go replace the flat-screen and other necessary pieces of furniture we needed. I gave them my credit card and told them to put everything on there. I wasn't letting Trisha and Rock pay for my shit.

It was evening by the time we were done and Green was getting ready to head to Live Bay. I couldn't go. I wasn't sure if I'd ever be able to go again. He wasn't complaining. He said they had it under control. I let him deal with it.

Taking my seat at the window, I watched for her to come home. I called her phone again, and her recorded voice came on. I listened to her until the phone beeped, then I hung up. I'd left enough messages. So I sent her a text message instead.

PLEASE was all I could type. Then I hit send.

Chapter Twenty-Two

BLYTHE

The hospital wasn't somewhere I was familiar with. I had only been inside one once, and it had been this one. I'd had pneumonia when I was eight. I remembered more about going to the hospital than the actual visit. Pastor Williams had taken me. I had been sick for days, but Mrs. Williams was saying that I was being lazy and didn't want to do my chores.

Then one night I had heard them yelling at each other. It was the first and last time I had ever heard them fight, at least like that. Pastor Williams had come into my room, picked me up, and taken me to the hospital. They had admitted me, and then he had left. A week later he had picked me up, and I had gone home. No one had visited me that week. No one had brought me balloons like the other kids down the hall had been given. It had been just me and the television.

As I walked back through the doors of Token Memorial Hospital, that memory replayed in my head. Pastor Williams had seemed fierce that night. Like he was protecting me. But then he'd left me alone again. Maybe this was a pattern in my life.

"This way," Linc said. He had already asked where we needed to go when he'd called earlier. Pastor Williams was still in the ICU, and he needed surgery. He had a blood clot. Surgery was risky, but if he didn't have it, then there was a good chance he'd just have another heart attack due to the blockage.

We took the elevator to the third floor and made a right into a large waiting room. Linc pointed to a chair. "Go have a seat. I'll let them know we are here."

I did as I was told. I had rather he handle it anyway. I didn't want to talk to people.

"Blythe." I glanced up to see several pairs of eyes on me. Members of the congregation. Of course. They would be here. No one ever really spoke to me. I was almost surprised they knew my name. I turned to look at Sylvia Bench, the church secretary for as long as I could remember. She had been the one to call my name.

"Hello," I said, unsure what else they wanted from me. I was back in this world. The one where people ignored me or whispered about me. The one where I was an outcast and had evil inside me. Evil I had grown up wishing so hard I could get out of me.

"We wondered if you'd come," Sylvia said, studying me through her round glasses that perched on the tip of her pointy nose. She wasn't a nice person. I knew that much.

I wasn't sure what she wanted me to say to that, either. I wasn't sure if I would have come if I hadn't just had my new world snatched from underneath me, but I was here because I was running.

"Blythe." Linc was at my elbow, guiding me away from the chair I had been told to go to and out of the waiting room. What were we doing now? "I need to talk to you. It's important."

If he was about to tell me he had to leave, I wasn't sure how I would handle that. I couldn't stay here alone with these people. But now that I was here, could I just leave?

Linc pulled me around a corner and looked around to make sure no one was close enough to hear him. Then he turned to meet my curious gaze. He was acting weird. I wasn't sure I could take another man acting weird on me and then unloading something on me I couldn't handle. But then there wasn't anything Linc could tell me that would shatter me the way Krit had. I was sure Linc couldn't even hurt me.

"There's a problem. I ..." He rubbed his hand over his face and muttered a curse. I had never heard him curse before. "I shouldn't be the one who has to tell you this. I don't want to be the one. But ... I think you would want to know. I mean ... you have to know." He made a frustrated noise in his throat, then he asked. "What's your blood type?"

Was he kidding me? He was acting like this because he wanted to know my blood type? "B negative. It's rare. Why?" I only knew this because we did blood typing in high school. My teacher had made a big deal out of my blood type. Most people had been O positive.

"Wow, yeah, okay. At any time in your life did you wonder why Pastor Williams and his wife were raising you?"

I nodded. "Yeah. Because my mom was a member of the congregation, and they didn't want me to get thrown into the system and end up in foster care or something. Why are you asking me such random questions?"

Linc massaged his temples like he had a headache. "That's all you ever thought?" he asked.

"Uh, yeah."

Dropping his hand to his side, he fidgeted. Then he finally looked directly at me. "I know that this wasn't something that they ever told anyone. It was a secret. One that I only know because Pastor Williams is a close friend of my dad's. He needed to tell someone so he talked to my dad about it. I've only known since you got to Sea Breeze. My dad explained your situation before I met you that day. I was never really sure if you knew the truth or not. But... I don't see how I can't tell you now," he paused and took a deep breath. "Pastor Williams had an affair with a girl twenty years younger than him, and that girl got pregnant. Then she died in childbirth. Pastor Williams refused to let his child go into the foster care and forced his wife who couldn't have children to let the baby come live with them. Mrs. Williams agreed because she had no choice. She wasn't going to divorce her husband, but she hated what he had done. She was jealous of the child. And I'm pretty sure she never treated that little girl right."

I had been wrong.

There was something Linc could say that would once again shatter me.

I grabbed the counter for support and blinked several times. Did I just hear him correctly? Had he just said ...?

"He needs surgery now, but they don't have the blood he needs and he's gonna need it. They have sent for blood, but it could take hours, and that's too long. They need to have some now. He has B negative," he said in a hurried rush. "Look, I never wanted to be the one to tell you this. But he could die, and you are the only one right now who might be able to save him. If it was my dad, I'd want to know."

He needed my blood. That's the only reason Linc was telling me. Yet he had known the story. How many people knew this? Was I the only one?

The man I had lived in a house with my entire life and not

had any relationship with was my father. He'd watched me grow; yet he had no attachment to me at all, and he was my father. My stomach clenched, and if there had been any food in it, I was sure I would have lost it, too. But I was empty. I hadn't been able to eat.

"Talk to me," Linc urged.

I shook my head. I wasn't ready to talk to him. "Where do I go to give blood?" I asked him. That was the only thing I needed to know right now. The man had basically abandoned me while living right there in the same house as me, but I wasn't about to let him die if I could do something to help him. I'd lived my whole life thinking I had no family. When all along ... I could have had one. If he'd wanted me.

KRIT

Two weeks. That's how long it had been since I'd walked through life numb. Two weeks since I'd woken up with Blythe in my arms. Two weeks since she'd left me. I was hollow. The void I had once had was nothing compared to being hollow inside. I called her daily and left her a voice mail. Every night I sent her a text message. I kept hoping eventually she'd give in and call me. Let me know where she was and if she was all right.

I had gone to the church she worked at, demanding to know where Linc had taken her, but they'd called the cops and had me escorted out while I was yelling at them and threatening to kill

Linc. Rock had had to come pick me up at the police station. I wasn't allowed within a hundred yards of the church parking lot.

Now all I could do was wait. Trisha had said Blythe loved me. She had never told me she loved me. But I held on to the hope that I loved her enough for both of us. That she would miss me and come back.

Jackdown now had a new bass player, and Green was the lead singer. They said it was temporary until I could come back. But if Blythe didn't come back to me, I knew it was permanent. I wouldn't be able to get back on that stage again and sing.

Britt still hadn't gone to the doctor to get me any proof. Trisha had called today and asked if I'd heard anything from Britt. When I told her no, she'd said she was going to take care of that. Which meant Trisha was gonna take Britt to the doctor whether she wanted to go or not.

Someone knocked on my door, and I turned to look at it from where I sat on the sofa. It was unlocked. If it was someone I knew, they'd just open it. When they only knocked again, I got up. Blythe was the only thing running through my head. She wouldn't just open the door. She'd knock.

I took three long strides and jerked the door open. Linc Keenan didn't have much time before my fist was firmly planted in his face and I was shoving him back against the wall, my hand at his neck. I was gonna pummel him. He took her from me. He took my Blythe from me.

"Dumbass! I told you not to come here. That I'd tell him you wanted to talk to him. What part of 'he's a crazy-ass mother-fucker who wants to kill you' don't you understand?" Green's voice stopped me, and I tightened my hold on Linc's throat.

"He is here to tell you where Blythe is," Green said to me. "If you kill him, then you won't ever know. And you'll end up in jail. Again," Green said as he stared pointedly at me.

I eased my hold and turned my focus to Linc. "Where is she?"

He was holding up both of his hands in surrender "Cahn breev," he choked out.

I dropped my hand from his throat. "Where is she?" I asked again.

He rubbed his neck. "I'm gonna tell you where she is, but first I need to explain the situation."

I had my hand back at his throat instantly. "*Where is she?*" I roared, and Green was behind me, pulling me back, but I wasn't moving.

"For the love of God, tell him where she is!" Green yelled.

Linc was scratching at my hands, and I noticed he was a little blue. I dropped my hand again, and he bent over and gasped for air. I gave him five seconds then asked again.

"Where is she?"

"Token, South Carolina. Hospital with her dad, uh, Pastor Williams. He had a heart attack two weeks ago. I took her there."

He gasped again and then looked up at me. "He needed blood. He's got a rare type, and it's a small hospital. She has the same type. But she never knew he was her dad. She does now, and he's in the hospital. She's been there ever since. But"—he rubbed at his throat—"I think she needs you."

She needed me. I turned from him and walked into the apartment. I grabbed my keys then looked down at them. I needed a car. It would be faster. I had to get to her. She needed me.

"Take my car," Green said, shoving his keys into my hand. "I'll find out the specifics and text them to you. Go."

I didn't look back. I took off running.

Chapter Twenty-Three

BLYTHE

I stared at my phone. I hadn't turned it on since I left Sea Breeze. I was scared to. What if Krit had left me messages? What if he hadn't? What if he was going to doctor's appointments with Britt now? What if he had realized he missed his old life? I just couldn't face any of that.

"You look better," Malcolm said. He wasn't Pastor Williams anymore, but he also wasn't Dad. I didn't know if he would ever be Dad. That seemed like a word reserved for someone who protected you and cared for you. Malcolm had done neither.

I glanced up at him. He was less pale today. He'd been out of the ICU for three days now. "I went to the house like you suggested and took a shower. Got some sleep. Washed my clothes," I replied.

"Good. You were looking exhausted. Sorry Linc left you."

I wasn't. I had wanted him to go. He'd stayed, but I hadn't talked to him much. Then three nights after Malcolm's surgery, I'd overheard him on the phone with a girl. His fiancé. Who lived in Mississippi and who he'd been engaged to for a year. All the phone calls he had needed to take made sense now. I had known he was tense and dealing with someone, but I had never had any idea he had a fiancé.

The numbness that had taken over me since finding out about Britt's pregnancy and that Pastor Williams was my biological father had made telling Linc to leave easy. I had pointed to the door and told him to go. Then I'd walked away from him without another word. Linc was out of my life. Not because I was upset that he had a fiancé, but because I was upset he'd cheated on her with me. He should have never taken me out on those dates. There would be no friendship between us. That had been all I needed to know about Linc Keenan.

"I'm not. Glad he's gone," I replied honestly.

Malcolm nodded. He didn't ask why. Which was good because I probably wouldn't have told him. "Thought you two might be more than friends. The way he stayed near you."

"We were friends. Not anymore. There are things about him I don't like very much."

Malcolm opened his mouth to say something but stopped, and his gaze focused on something behind me. Figuring the doctor was back, I glanced over my shoulder. Krit's blue eyes were locked on me as he stood there at the door. Every emotion I had felt over the past two weeks was mirrored in his eyes.

I stood up and turned to him. "You're here," I said.

"I'd have been here sooner had someone pointed me in the right direction," he replied, his eyes not wavering from mine.

"I ..." Pausing, I turned back to Malcolm. "I need to go talk to him."

Malcolm nodded. "Yeah, I would say you do." With unease in his eyes, he glanced back at Krit.

I didn't explain Krit or introduce them. I wasn't even sure how to introduce Malcolm anymore. When he'd woken up after a successful surgery, I had been waiting on him. We hadn't said much that day or the next. But then on the third day he had been better. And he'd wanted to talk. But it really hadn't changed much. Other than I now knew the truth.

When I reached Krit, his hand shot out and grabbed mine. He laced his fingers through mine. "Hey," he said in a deep voice.

I walked down the hall toward the elevator and then I led him back outside to Malcolm's car. When I had sent Linc away I had been without a vehicle. I had walked the three miles to Malcolm's house to get his car.

Krit didn't ask questions; he just went with me. "Get in," I said, motioning to the passenger seat.

When we were both inside, I cracked the windows so we

could get some air. Then I turned to him. "You're here," I repeated. Because I wasn't sure how he was here or why.

He took my hand again and held it up to his lips. There were dark circles under his beautiful eyes and his face looked thinner. "Eight hours ago Linc showed up at my door and told me where you were."

"Eight?" It took ten hours driving time to get here.

"Eight," he repeated.

"But it's a ten-hour drive."

He ran the hand he was holding along his cheek. "Not when a man is going after his woman, it's not."

My heart squeezed. His sweet words always managed to get to me. Hearing them and knowing he really meant them would be hard to walk away from. I'd had two weeks to think. Two weeks to realize that so many things I'd thought were true weren't. But I'd also had two weeks to face the fact that I wouldn't be a hindrance to a child having their parent.

"I'm sorry I left without telling you. But I didn't expect to be gone so long. Then things happened, and I decided to stay. Me being here gave you time to adjust and for you and Britt to make plans."

He scowled. "I'm not making plans with Britt. I'll take care of the kid if it's mine. Hell, she's yet to prove to me she's actually pregnant. But the only plans I need to make are with you. I'm empty without you, love. Completely fucking empty."

God, how did I tell this man no and walk away from him? He was so determined, and I loved him so much. Not taking what I wanted when it was right there in front of me was almost impossible. "I grew up thinking I had no one. No one wanted me or loved me because I thought I had no family. I accepted the fact that I was a burden on the Williamses. They gave me a roof over my head, and I should be thankful for that. They didn't have to love me. I took verbal abuse from a hateful woman and believed every word she said. I thought I was evil and ugly. I thought I was unlovable because that's all I'd been told. But the entire time I had been living with my father. The man who helped give me life. He let this happen to me. He didn't show me love. He didn't love me. I'm marked because of that, Krit. It will be something I carry with me my entire life. I won't be the reason another child doesn't have the love of a parent." Tears were burning my eyes, and I pulled my hand out of his and held it tightly with my other hand.

"Blythe," he said quietly. "Your father is a sad son of a bitch. He had you, and he didn't love you like you deserve to be loved. I can't comprehend how anyone couldn't love you. Fuck, I can't comprehend how anyone couldn't want to cherish you and protect you. And I don't think I'll ever be able to forgive the man. So you've been warned. If you want to form a relationship with him, fine, but I don't want to be near him. I'll wait in the other room or outside in the car when you visit him." He reached over and tilted my head up so I had to look at him. One lonely tear rolled down my face, and he caught it with his thumb. "I will love my kid. I can love my kid and be a dad and not love its mom. People do it all the time. It's not a package deal. If the baby is mine, I will love it. I swear to you. I wouldn't do to that baby what was done to you. But I will be a shell of a fucking man if I have to live the rest of my life without you. So, if you're worried about me being a good dad, then know that I need you in order to be whole."

Another tear escaped, and then another. My vision got blurry as the tears filled my eyes and began streaming down my face. "I love you," I choked out, unable to say anything else.

He jerked the car door open and jumped out, then took off running around the front of my car. He opened my car door, swinging it wide, then pulled me out of the car and into his arms as his body trembled.

I clung to him as he buried his face in my neck and held me. He didn't say anything, but the slight trembling of his body was so out of place with him. "Say it again," he said against my neck after several minutes.

I reached up and ran my hand over his hair. "I love you. I've loved you for a while now."

"Fuck," he groaned, and pulled back to look at me. "I really wish you'd told me when you realized it."

"I thought it would scare you off," I admitted.

He shook his head, soaking me up as he began caressing my arms and back. "You just might be the only person on Earth who doesn't know how fucking insane I am about you. People who don't know us can take one look at me and know I'm completely owned. It's all over my face when I look at you."

"I've missed you," I told him.

He cupped my face the way he had before he kissed me the first time. "Good, because I've been lost without you," he said, then his lips touched mine and opened on a sigh. The sigh was mine.

His mouth slanted over mine as he deepened the kiss. I felt light-headed as I held on to his arms and molded myself against him. I wasn't sure if I would ever have this again. Now that I did, I knew I couldn't let it go.

"Where are you staying?" he asked against my mouth. "I need to be inside you. Soon. Now."

"The house I grew up in," I said, not wanting to go there. It was filled with bad memories, ones I didn't want to feel now. Not anymore.

"Go get in the passenger seat. We're going to get a hotel room," he said with one last kiss and a pat to my bottom.

I hurried around the car to get in, when I noticed a girl my age standing by her car watching me. I'd gone to school with her, and she'd been a member of the church. But she'd never once been nice to me. She had been one of the many to make jokes about me and make me feel even more unwanted than I already had felt. She had been watching me kiss Krit. She'd seen the way he held me, and a smile touched my lips. I guess I just gave her something to talk about. I lifted my hand and waved at her before climbing inside the car.

KRIT

Keeping my hands off Blythe long enough to get us to the nearest hotel and checked in was hard. So, the moment I closed the door to the room behind me, I picked her up and carried her to the bed. Throwing her down, I watched as she giggled and smiled up at me. Jerking my shirt off, I tossed it aside, and then I made quick work of my jeans and boots. She sat there watching me as if mesmerized.

"Naked, love. I want you naked," I told her.

She snapped out of her trance and started undressing, and this time it was me who watched with complete fascination.

When her bra dropped to the floor and she tugged her shorts and panties down, I wanted to take time to appreciate how fucking beautiful she was. But that would have to wait until next time because I needed inside her more than I needed to breathe. "Please tell me you take birth control." I wanted in her without a barrier so bad, I could taste it.

She shook her head. "I've never needed it," she said, looking crestfallen.

"Soon as we get home, you're going to the doctor. I want you bare. Nothing between us," I told her, then kissed her lips as I leaned back to put the condom on.

"Wait," she said, reaching out to stop me. I started to ask why, when she touched the piercing she'd only stared at before with wonder. I hadn't given her a chance to explore it the other times. I had been too ready to get inside her, and she'd been nervous.

"Love," I said through my teeth, then followed it with a hiss as she wrapped her hand around my cock. "Oh, hell." I fisted both my hands and watched as she ran her thumb over the metal that I'd gotten one drunken night after a dare.

"Does it hurt?" she asked when my body jerked in response to her touch.

"Not the way you're thinking," I said. "But we might need to do this show and tell another time, love. I'm real close and you touching me ain't helping."

A sneaky smile tugged at her lips as she lowered her head and ran her tongue over the tip of my swollen head. "*Fuck!*" I grabbed her by the waist and tossed her back down on the bed. Her legs fell open, and my cock slipped right inside her wet slit. It had its own suction as it pulled me in and squeezed.

Blythe cried out, and her hips came up off the bed. It was hot, and holy hell, she was soaking wet. The sensation as I began to move was different than anything I had ever felt. Something was different. It was better and, motherfuck, I didn't think it could get any better with her.

"Ohgod, ohgod, ohgod, I can feel it." Blythe panted. "I can, Krit, I can feel it. It's touching something I can't …" She cried out my name again and began to shiver, trying to get me deeper. It was different for her, too. "There! *Oh God! Krit! Oh God!*" She clawed at my back as she wrapped herself around me like she couldn't get close enough. Her body began shaking and small cries escaped her.

Just before I found my release, I realized what she felt. With one hard jerk backward, I shot my release all over her stomach. I'd forgotten the condom. I stared down at my cock and her juices coated it as it lay on her stomach. She'd marked me this time.

Her gaze lifted from my cum all over her stomach and on the tips of her breasts to look at me. "Oops," she said, her eyes wide.

A laugh erupted out of me, and I watched her press her lips together to keep from laughing too. Then she dropped her gaze back to my dick. "I need to get birth control because that piercing was definitely my very favorite."

"Is that so?" I asked, thinking that being buried in her with nothing between us was my very favorite.

She nodded. "Oh yeah."

She wasn't leaving me. I hadn't lost her. She was mine. "Let me go get a towel and clean up my mess," I said, standing up.

"You kinda did make a big one."

"Couldn't help it, love. Your tight little pussy milking me like it couldn't get me deep enough kinda sent me over the edge."

Her eyes flared, and the heat was back. Hell yes. My girl liked sex.

"Blythe."

"Yes?"

"You're perfect. I wouldn't change a thing. Know that," I told her, then turned to go get a towel. Now that I knew she'd lived a life of being put down, I intended to make sure she spent the rest of her life being reminded how wonderful she was.

Chapter Twenty-Four

BLYTHE

Krit was outside the door. He wasn't ready to face Malcolm, and I wondered if he ever would be. I walked into the room and sat down in the chair beside Malcolm. They said he could go home tomorrow. The church was supplying him with a nurse, and I didn't want to stay. Not any longer. I had to get back to my new life. The one where I had something worth living for.

"You're leaving," he said as he opened his eyes and looked at me.

"Yeah. It's time I went home," I told him. Krit was my home now. I had a home to go to, and that felt good. No, it felt amazing.

"The pierced tattooed guy?" he asked.

I nodded. "His name is Krit," I told him.

Malcolm glanced at the door. "He out there?"

"Yes, but he doesn't like you. He, uh, he isn't sure he should be around you. He doesn't forgive you for ..." I didn't finish that. Malcolm understood.

"So he loves you then," Malcolm said.

"Yeah, he does."

"Do you love him?"

"More than life. He's my home. He's healed me. Fixed all that was broken," I told the man who had played a part in breaking me.

Malcolm didn't say anything. He turned his head and looked out the window. "Go be happy, Blythe. Go live the life you deserved all along. Let him love you the way you deserve to be loved."

He didn't say he loved me. But he did tell me to go. So I stood up and did as I was told. When I stepped out of the door, Krit's arms were right there holding me close to his hard safe body. "You're my home too," he said against my head.

"Let's go home," I told him.

Krit slid his arm over my shoulders and we walked through the waiting room where church members sat waiting to visit Malcolm. They all looked at me and then at the sexy rocker whose arm was possessively wrapped around me. I smiled at them and walked away. Away from the life that hadn't wanted me and toward the life that I was meant for.

KRIT

Blythe was sleeping in my arms when the knocking on her apartment door started. We had gotten home late, and she was exhausted. I slipped out of bed, jerked on my discarded jeans, and headed for the door before Blythe was disturbed.

Trisha stood outside Blythe's door with Britt and Jedrick Owens. I'd gone to school with Jedrick. Last I heard, he was playing football at Oklahoma State. Dude was a monster on the field. "What's this?" I asked, rubbing the sleep from my eyes.

"Inside!" Trisha barked, and strutted in. She had her "don't mess with me" look on her face. Britt and Jedrick followed her, and Jedrick's eyes met mine.

"Your sister scares the shit out me, man," he muttered as he sauntered into the apartment.

I managed a grin and turned to look at Trisha, who looked like she was ready to lay the smackdown on anyone who interrupted her. "I took Britt to the doctor. I was tired of her not going, so I made the appointment and took her myself. She fought me on it a little, but then she decided it was in her best interest to do as I said," Trisha said, shooting a glare at Britt, who stiffened. "She's pregnant, all right. Four months pregnant to be specific. Four months ago Britt wasn't even in Sea Breeze. She had gone to see her aunt in Oklahoma. It was summer break, and she and Jedrick had hooked up during spring break and had been talking on the phone.

"Problem was, Britt's daddy is a redneck and a racist. Britt knew her daddy would never let her date Jedrick. Didn't matter that he was already being drafted into the NFL. He was the wrong color. So, Britt ran off to spend time with him." Trisha stopped and looked at Jedrick.

"Now you tell us all about the protection you used with Britt," Trisha told Jedrick.

The guy stifled a yawn. Apparently, my sister had woken him up too. "We didn't. Britt said she was clean and on birth control."

"How often did you have sex with Britt that month?" Trisha asked.

"Fuck, I don't know. A couple of times a day, every day. She's a fucking machine." He paused and grinned. "Fucking machine," he repeated, and laughed at his own joke.

"And why did you want to slap Krit with Jedrick's baby?" Trisha asked Britt, who let out a loud annoyed sigh and shot daggers at my sister.

"Because I love Krit," she replied.

"Wrong answer. Try again," Trisha repeated in a sharp tone.

"Because the condom broke that one time. When it happened, I knew I could say it was his and he'd believe me."

Trisha motioned toward Jedrick. "Hate to point out the obvious, but when the baby was born, it was gonna be obvious it wasn't Krit's. He and Jedrick do not share the same color skin."

Britt threw her hands up in the air. "I didn't know what I was gonna do! I was desperate. I was starting to show, and my dad noticed. He demanded I tell him whose baby it was. He was yelling and calling me a slut. I couldn't tell him it was Jederick's. He would have killed me. So, I said it was Krit's."

My relief was turning into rage as I realized what Britt had almost taken from me. That Blythe had dealt with a life-changing bomb without me there to hold her because of Britt's lie. I took a step toward her, when Jedrick stepped in front of me.

"Dat's my baby mama, man," he said.

"Krit." Blythe's sweet voice called out, and I turned around to see her standing there in my T-shirt. "It's okay. It's really better than okay," she said, a smile lighting up her face. She'd heard everything. She was right. "Let them go." Her eyes shifted to Trisha's. "Except Trisha. I can make coffee if she wants to stay."

"She wants to leave too," I answered without looking back at my sister. I was thankful for her hand in figuring this out, but I wanted my morning alone with Blythe.

"Day-um," Jedrick said, reminding me there was another man in the room.

"Go back to the room," I told her, stepping in his line of view.

Jedrick laughed. "Don' blame you at all."

"Go," I said, pointing to the door.

Jedrick looked more than happy to leave, and Britt scurried out behind him. I turned to look at Trisha. "Thanks."

She reached over and patted my cheek like I was ten. "That's what big sisters are for. Fixing shit," she said with a smile. "Now, go be happy. She came back, didn't she? Even when she thought you were gonna be someone else's baby daddy," she pointed out.

"If I run off to Vegas and get hitched, you'll forgive me for not having a wedding right?" I asked her.

"You run off to Vegas and I'll kill you," she said with a smile, then turned and walked to the door. "Bye, Blythe!" she called out.

Blythe's head peeked around the corner. "Bye! I'd say again that you could stay, but he doesn't seem to like that idea," she said, grinning as she looked at me.

"I can see that. I'll let y'all enjoy your morning," she said, then left us alone.

Blythe stepped out of her hidden spot behind the door and walked toward me. "I would have stayed by your side through it all. But I'm very glad that the only babies you'll be having will be mine."

Grabbing her and carrying her over to the sofa while she squealed, I sank down with her in my lap. "If you don't go get birth control fast, we'll be having those babies a lot sooner than planned," I told her.

"I'm going to the clinic today," she assured me, then kissed my nose. "I love you this morning."

"I love you more this morning," I replied, then slid my hands under my shirt that was covering her up. "I had intended to wake you up by kissing these beauties," I told her as I held her breasts in my hands.

"I hate that I missed that, but we can go back in there and I can pretend to be asleep," she said with a little sexy smirk.

"Can you pretend to be asleep naked? That way I can wake you up by sliding my tongue up that hot little slit between your legs."

Blythe's eyes flared, and she wiggled off my lap and stood up.

"Where are you going?" I asked, reaching for her to bring her back.

She dodged me and grinned. "No way. I'm going to go pretend I'm asleep." She ran for the room then glanced back over her shoulder. "Naked," she called out.

Jumping up, I followed behind, giving her just enough time to strip down and get back in our bed.

Chapter Twenty-Five

Two months later

BLYTHE

I had almost finished writing my first complete novel. It was a romance. And an epic one at that. I was thrilled with how it had come together, and even if no one else ever read it, I had it to reread and remember. Because it was our story. It was a story of healing, redemption, passion, forgiveness, and love.

I wanted to have it edited and at least bound before Christmas. The one person I did want to read it was Krit. I would have never guessed that the beautiful man who had stood watching me twirl around my apartment with an amused grin would be the one to make me whole. Our story was beautiful, and having it all written down in words meant it was a story that would never be forgotten. When we are long gone, our great-

grandchildren would have this story to read and know that they came from love.

Krit opened the door and stepped inside. I closed my MacBook so he couldn't peek at the words.

"Put it there." I pointed at the spot I'd cleared out in our living room.

Krit picked up the Virginia pine tree we had picked out together at the Christmas tree farm, carried it over to the corner, and stood it up.

It was going to be my first real Christmas. I had never been given a Christmas present or I'd never decorated a tree. Those were things I'd watched happen in the house I'd grown up in, but I'd never been invited to participate.

"How's that?" Krit asked, standing back to survey his work.

"Perfect," I told him, throwing my arms around his neck. "Now we get to decorate." The excitement was almost too much. I had always wanted to decorate a tree.

"Love, I'll do whatever the hell you want me to as long as it makes you smile like that," he said, turning around and kissing me firmly on the mouth.

"Good. Because we're decorating cookies tonight, and that will make me smile," I told him.

He smirked. "Icing and you and a kitchen counter. Yeah, sounds like my kind of fun."

"The icing goes on the cookies," I told him.

He nodded. "Sure it does. And then it goes on your nipples, and if you're really good, between your thighs."

The catch in my breath made him grin. "That's what I thought. My girl likes to play."

"Okay, we'll play, but only if I get to put some icing on my favorite piercing." I said.

His eyes lit up, and he tugged my hand, pulling me toward the kitchen.

"What are you doing? We have a tree to decorate," I said, giggling as I followed him.

"No, love. We are going to get that icing and let you put it on your favorite piercing. Play first, decorate the tree later."

"Krit," I said, and he stopped and looked back at me.

"Yeah, sweetheart?"

"I love you."

He towered over me, and his blue eyes smoldered as he gazed down at me. "I love you more," he whispered against my lips, then he made me forget about decorations and cookies. I was lost in the one man who had been made just for me.

Lyrics

BAD FOR YOU

Verse 1
I've always had an addictive personality—
Take a little then want a little more.
Being told no isn't okay with me.
They call it obsession, but I know it's more.

Pre-Chorus
I know they tell you to stay away from the devil,
But, baby, come a little closer, open my door.

Chorus
They say I'm bad for you.
They say I'm wrong for the innocent, I'll only burn you up.

But I'm addicted now, and there's no changing that.

I just may be bad for you, but this lesson you're gonna learn.

Verse 2

Accuse me of insanity or desire to possess.

I've heard it before but never like this.

I'd tell you not to fear this, but then I'd be a liar.

You lost your free will right after our first kiss.

Pre-Chorus

I know they tell you to stay away from the devil.

But, baby, come a little closer. Open my door.

Chorus

They say I'm bad for you.

They say I'm wrong for an angel, I'll only burn you up.

But I'm addicted now, and there's no changing that.

I just may be bad for you, but this lesson you're gonna learn.

Bridge

Good girls should stay away from the dark corners.

Temptation will always lurk within the turn.

Keeping you pure may be the only thing that redeems me.

But I never asked not to burn.

SHE'S TO BLAME

Verse 1
Just another night, baby, and you're just another girl.
I don't do mornings and I never will.
You wanted a taste and I wanted a distraction.
Don't go begging for more because I like the chase, not the kill.

Pre-Chorus
It wasn't all-consuming, girl—you gave it too easily.
You know what you got into, but you still begged me.
Don't leave your phone number—I'm not gonna call.
Say it, baby. Scream it all you want. I've heard it all.

Chorus
They all want to save me. They all want to own me.
But I've been owned before. That ship has sailed.
She took my soul a long time ago when she walked out that
*   door.*

So don't think you're gonna win me.

I'm not a prize and you won't score.

Nothing left inside to gain. I'm empty there, and she's to blame.

Verse 2

I've broken hearts and left them in a trail behind me. But they only had me one night.

She owned my heart for years, then took it with her in her flight.

I liked the escape you give me, and I'll take it without remorse.

I don't even care if you fake it. I'm using you more, no reason for force.

Pre-Chorus

It wasn't all-consuming, girl—you gave it too easily.

You know what you got into, but you still begged me.

Walking away is my favorite part because I know I didn't lose my heart.

You want more than I can give. Someday you might see.

Chorus

They all want to save me. They all want to own me.

But I've been owned before. That ship has sailed.

She took my soul a long time ago when she walked out that
   door.
So don't think you're gonna win me.
I'm not a prize and you won't score.
Nothing left inside to gain. I'm empty there, and she's to
   blame.

Bridge
Walk away now if you want to keep your innocence.
Run like hell girl if you're not ready for me.
Everybody is the same and no matter how sweet you look ...
There will always be only one face I see.
You've been warned and that's all I can do.
Let's forget the talking and the wasting of my time.
This is all about me, babe. I'm not worried about you.
Just another night, babe and you're just another girl.

Chorus
They all want to save me. They all want to own me.
But I've been owned before. That ship has sailed.
She took my soul a long time ago when she walked out that
   door.
So don't think you're gonna win me.
I'm not a prize and you won't score.
Nothing left inside to gain. I'm empty there, and she's to blame.

About the Author

Abbi Glines is the New York Times, USA Today, and Wall Street Journal bestselling author of the Sea Breeze, Vincent Boys, Existence, and Rosemary Beach series. A devoted booklover, Abbi lives with her family in Alabama. She maintains a Twitter addiction at @AbbiGlines and can also be found at facebook.com/AbbiGlinesAuthor and AbbiGlines.com.

Can't get enough of Abbi Glines?

Here's a sneak peek of . . .

hold on tight

Chapter One

SIENNA

I never expected to step foot in Sea Breeze, Alabama, again. When my parents had packed my bags and shipped me off to live in Fort Worth, Texas, with my mom's sister, who I hardly knew, I had been told I would return to Sea Breeze after the baby was born. What I hadn't been told was that they weren't planning on my baby returning with me.

I glanced back at Micah, asleep in his car seat with his Darth Vader action figure clenched tightly in his hand. Our life hadn't been easy, but we had each other. I wouldn't go back and do it any other way. Micah was my life. He had healed me when I was sure nothing ever could.

Keeping Micah meant being disowned by my strict religious parents. My aunt wasn't the most affectionate person in the world, but she'd disagreed with my parents' decision. I had been expected to work and pay my own way, but at least she'd given us a roof over our heads.

Giving up on high school and getting my GED was my only option. My aunt Cathy was the principal at the local high school and helped me get a trade school grant, so when Micah was eighteen months old, I enrolled in beauty school. Before his third birthday I had a degree in cosmetology.

I owed my aunt more than I could ever repay her.

Micah and I moved out just last year and finally got an apartment of our own. I didn't date because I didn't trust anyone around my son. I also felt guilty paying for a sitter when we needed that money for more important things, like rent, day care, and food. It didn't keep men from flirting, though, and trying to get me to go out with them. Janell, the owner of the salon where I worked, said that the men all thought I was playing hard to get. It just made them more persistent.

The truth was, I was lonely sometimes, but then Micah would smile and I'd see his father in him and I'd remember that for ten years of my life I'd had someone. A very special someone. And now I had Micah. I didn't need anything more.

When the call had come two months ago from my mother to tell me about my father's heart attack, I hadn't known what to feel. He had never met Micah, and now he never would. My mother had used Dad's life insurance money to move to a retirement community in central Florida. She'd given her house to Micah and me.

Not one time did she apologize for deserting me when I'd needed her most, or for turning her back on her only grandchild. But the fact that she had given the house to us meant something. I only hoped one day she would realize what she was missing by not knowing him.

Janell had helped me by giving me a glowing reference, and I had managed to get a job in Sea Breeze working at one of the most elite salons in town. I would be making more money, and I wouldn't be paying rent any longer. Our life would be better in Sea Breeze. Micah would get to grow up in the small coastal town that I loved.

My only fear, and the one reason I almost didn't come back home, was the idea of the Falcos seeing Micah. Once I'd realized that my parents hadn't been planning on me keeping my son, I sent a letter to Tabby Falco, Dustin's mother.

She never replied.

The first year of Micah's life I wrote them countless letters and included pictures of him. He looked so much like his father. I wanted them to see that Dustin wasn't completely lost to us. He had left a part of himself behind.

Not once did she respond.

A few times I'd almost worked up the nerve to call them, but if they weren't replying to my letters, then they didn't want to talk to me. They didn't want Micah. It had hurt even worse than my parents not wanting him. I had hated the Falcos for their desertion. But then I'd learned to let go. Move on. Be happy with my life. With my beautiful little boy.

"Momma? Where are we?" a sleepy little voice asked from the backseat of my twelve-year-old Honda Civic.

"We're home. Our new home," I replied, pulling into the driveway of the house that had once been my home and would soon be again.

"Our new house?" he asked with excitement in his voice as he wiggled in his seat to see better.

"Yep, baby. Our new house. Ready to go inside and see it?" I asked him, opening my car door and getting out. It was a two-door, so I had to lean my seat forward to reach him in the backseat. He unbuckled himself, then scrambled out of his seat and jumped out of the car.

"Do other people live in there too?" he asked, staring up at the two-bedroom wood-frame house with wide eyes.

"Just us, kiddo. You'll have your own bedroom here. Mine is right across the hall from yours."

"Whoa," he said, his eyes shining with amazement. Even when we had lived with my aunt Cathy, Micah and I had shared a room. Once we'd moved into an apartment, a studio was all I could afford with day care costs. This house was only twelve hundred square feet, but it was the biggest living space he and I had ever had all to ourselves. The studio apartment had been a third of this size.

"Let's go see your new room. We might need to paint it. Not sure what color the walls are," I told him. The last time I'd been in my old bedroom, it had been pink. Micah was determined that pink was for girls and wanted nothing to do with it.

From my purse I pulled out the key that my mother had mailed me along with the letter and the deed to the house. I took a deep breath before unlocking the door. Stepping back, I motioned for Micah to go inside. "Check it out."

His grin spread across his face as he took off running into the house, whooping as he saw the size of the living room. Then he turned and headed down the short hallway. I paused at the door, unable to ignore the house across the street any longer, and turned around to look at it. I didn't recognize the truck in the driveway, but then again, it had been six years. I was sure the Falcos were still there. Mother hadn't mentioned that they'd moved.

I wondered if they would speak to Micah when he played in the yard. Or would they ignore him like they had since his birth? I wouldn't tell him who they were. I hadn't told him about my parents. He didn't know this had once been my home. He didn't know he had grandparents. In preschool he had been asked to tell the class about his grandparents, and when he'd told them about Aunt Cathy, he had called her Aunt Cathy. The kids in his class had teased him, telling him that his aunt wasn't his grandparent. He'd come home confused and upset that he didn't know who his grandparents were.

I had just told him he didn't have any.

When he'd asked about his father, I had explained that God had wanted his father because he was such an awesome man, so he had brought him to heaven to live there with him before Micah was born.

That had been enough for Micah. He hadn't asked any more questions. He was happy with the knowledge that his mother loved him unconditionally and that we were a family. It had been hard for him when he saw that other kids had large families, but once he'd understood that each family was different, he was okay with that.

"Momma! Momma!" Micah called out in excitement. "There's a blue room. It's a really cool blue room too! It's even got toys in it already!"

Toys? I closed the front door behind me and headed down the hall. Stepping into the bedroom that had once been mine, I stopped and looked around me in awe. It was blue. A bright, happy blue. It had a full-size bed and a matching wooden dresser. There was a blue quilt on the bed with orange basketballs all over it, and in the center sat a basketball-shaped pillow. A toy box under the window was open, with pirate swords, a baseball bat and glove, a large red fire truck, and what looked like a big bag of Legos sticking out of it. An indoor basketball hoop sat in the opposite corner, with a ball lying on the floor beside it.

Above his bed was painted MICAH.

"Do you think the people who used to live here left it for me? Or do we gotta give it back?" he asked, a hopeful expression on his face. "And look, Momma, my name is already on the wall."

Tears stung my eyes, and I had to swallow hard as I stood there taking in the room. I didn't know what to think. This was not what I had expected, but then again, I hadn't expected to be given this house, either. A white envelope caught my attention. It was leaning against the wall on top of the dresser, with my name and Micah's name written on it.

Walking over to it, I wiped at the tear that had escaped, and I tried to hide my face from my very observant five-year-old. The envelope was sealed, so I slid my finger underneath and opened it up.

Sienna,

This is your home now. It doesn't make up for the past or for the years I wasn't there when you needed me. But it is all I have to give you. I don't expect to buy your forgiveness. This room is as much for me as it is for Micah. I've always wanted to buy him things. Christmas presents and birthday presents and gifts just because he is my grandson. I couldn't do that, though. Not while I lived with your father.

I won't speak ill of your father—that is not what this is

about. I loved him. He was a good man, but he was a proud man and I had to respect that. I believe in my heart that if he had it to do over, he would have done things differently. I hate that he never got to meet our grandson.

Please tell Micah that the room is his with love from someone who hopes she can meet him one day. When you are ready, of course. If you are ever ready. I just ask that you can find it in your heart to forgive me. I want to be a part of your lives.

My address and phone number are listed below. If you want to send me a letter or give me a call, I would love that. Or maybe send me some photos of Micah. I have a photo album full thanks to your aunt Cathy. He's a beautiful one, but then, so is his mother.

Love always,

Mom

"Momma, why're you crying?" Micah asked as he tugged on the bottom of my shorts.

I folded the letter and tucked it in my back pocket before bending down and looking at him.

He reached out and wiped my face with his little hands. "It's okay if we can't stay here. Just so I'm with you," he said. The sadness in his eyes hurt my heart.

This house was too good for him to believe. I grabbed his

hands and squeezed them tightly. "This is our home. The person who gave it to us did all this just for you. These are happy tears, not sad ones," I told him. I wasn't ready to explain about his grandmother. I didn't know how I felt about introducing him to her. There was too much pain for me to deal with right now. But her words and this room meant a lot. It didn't make up for her abandonment, but knowing she loved Micah enough to do this did help me consider letting her into our life.

"So I get to keep this? All of it?" he asked, looking around at the room again, his eyes wide with wonder. We had even shared a bed up until now.

"Yes. All of this is yours. Just yours. You have your own space now. Your own bed. Even your own closet."

Micah walked over to his bed and ran his little hand over the quilt. He knew what a basketball was. I had bought him one with my first paycheck. It was a part of his father I wanted him to have. "Did the person who did this for me know my daddy was the best basketball player in the world?" he asked, glancing back at me.

I nodded, biting back a smile.

"We're gonna be happy here, Momma," he said, then turned to go back to his toy box. I watched him for a few minutes I watched him as he dug through the things my mother had left him. Then I slipped out of the room to check out the rest of the house.

In the letter she'd sent with the house key and the deed, she'd told me she was leaving the furniture behind. The place where she was living now was furnished. I wasn't sure how I felt about sleeping on my parents' bed, but all I'd had was a mattress, and we'd left that behind in Texas.

Opening the door to the master bedroom, I froze before relief washed over me. It was my old bed, dresser, and vanity. Even my old desk. She had moved it all into here, knowing I wouldn't want their things. The quilt on the bed was the same one that had been on my bed when I'd left six years ago. It was pale pink with big daisies all over it.

I was home.

PRESENT DAY ...

DEWAYNE

I pulled my truck into my parents' driveway and parked beside my dad's truck. Normally, I tried to come over and visit once a week. The past two weeks, however, I just hadn't been in the mood. Momma had broken down and cried the last time I was here, reminding us all that it was the six-year anniversary of my little brother's death.

The only way I knew how to deal with that was to get my ass drunk every damn night until I was numb again. Until I was past the pain, and the empty space in my chest didn't ache so damn bad. After managing to stay sober for the past two nights, I decided I had better get back over here to see my momma before she came looking for me.

That woman had a temper on her, and I didn't need her coming after me. I wasn't scared of much, but Tabby Falco was someone I feared. Loved all five feet three inches of her, but I was terrified of her.

Glancing across the street, I noticed a beat-up white Honda Civic. It had seen better days. Nina Roy had moved out about a month ago, just a few weeks after her husband's death. Momma said she'd gone to Florida. The place had sat empty for the past month. Was someone moving in? If so, that car didn't make it look like it was the good kind of neighbors. I might have to stop by and make sure my parents were safe.

They didn't need to be dealing with wild parties or a meth house from some trashy new neighbors. I took a step closer and checked out the license plate. Texas. Now I was as curious as I was concerned. Who the hell did Nina Roy sell her house to? I never even saw a For Sale sign in the yard. If she'd rented it, we might really have a problem. Just last week three rented houses just an hour north of here were busted for meth.

"What you gawking at our new neighbor's car for? Get in here and see your momma!" I turned to see my dad standing at the door with it wide open, an annoyed look on his face. Once upon a time I wouldn't have felt the need to protect the man. I wouldn't have thought anything could touch him. But then he'd had the stroke. Things had changed. I had officially taken over my dad's construction company, Falco Construction. Dad just couldn't handle it anymore. He had always seemed larger than life, but nothing had been the same since Dustin's death.

"You met them?" I asked him, nodding toward the house across the street.

He shook his head. "Car showed up. Haven't seen who was in it. No moving van or U-Haul. Just the car. Sometime around noon yesterday. Car was gone at two today when I glanced outside, but then it was back when I went to water the flowers at four."

This was just getting worse. Someone had moved in without stuff. This wasn't the best subdivision in Sea Breeze, but so far it had been safe from things like meth houses. I wasn't about to let that shit find its way into my parents' neighborhood.

"I'll be right back," I told him, and started across the street before he could stop me. Not that he could stop me.

"Get back over here, boy," he called, but I held a hand up.

"Just a sec. I need to check this out," I replied, and kept my eyes focused on the door and the windows. I didn't want to spook whoever was inside and end up getting shot if they were in there setting up shop.

Nina Roy should've thought about who she was letting move into this place. But then, I wasn't sure that woman had much of a heart, anyway. Her daughter had been shipped off shortly after my brother's death, never to return. They'd been best friends for most of their lives, and it had progressed to the relationship stage. Word was, sweet little Sienna had suffered a mental breakdown and they had sent her off to a facility. No one had ever seen her again. It wasn't easy for me to accept for a long time. Much as I hated to admit it, I'd taken her leaving harder than I should have. Especially knowing what Dustin's death had done to her. That was one more thing to add to my list of fuck-ups.

I knocked on the door and waited. I kept my eyes on the doorknob in case it slowly turned. If the fucker had a gun, I was ready to disarm him. Before I could think about just how I would do that, the door swung open and a pair of brown eyes were looking up at me with keen interest.

"Hi," the little boy said, staring at me as if he wasn't sure he had done the right thing by opening the door.

This was not what I had been expecting. I hadn't imagined a family had moved in across the street, not from the looks of that vehicle. It didn't look like a family car—it wasn't safe for adults, much less kids.

"Hi, your folks home?" I asked him, and he stared at me a moment longer before frowning.

"I don't have folks. I have a momma, but she's in the bathroom. She had to go pee. I probably shouldn't have answered the door."

The kid was cute. And he was right. He didn't need to be opening the door. And giving a complete stranger that kind of information. If he had just a mother, then the car in the driveway concerned me for other reasons. If that was all she had, how the hell had she afforded this house? It wasn't an expensive house or anything, but I'd think a used rental trailer would have been more in her price range.

"Maybe in the future you should wait for her to open the door. You got lucky this time." I pointed at my parents' house. My dad was standing on the front porch watching us. "That's my parents' house. I was coming to meet the new neighbors."

The kid peeked around my legs and looked at the house and my dad, then turned his attention back to me. "You live with your parents? My momma ain't got no parents."

Again, more info than he needed to be sharing. Hell, did this woman not teach her kid not to talk to strangers and spill her life story? It wasn't safe.

"Probably shouldn't tell strangers that, either, little man," I told him.

He frowned and held out his hand as if to shake mine. "My name is Micah. What's yours?"

Although he shouldn't have been telling me his name, I couldn't help but grin. The kid was a charmer. I clasped his hand in mine and gave it a shake. "Nice to meet you, Micah. My name's Dewayne."

His grin got huge. "Like Dwyane Wade? You know, from the Miami Heat?"

I didn't keep up with basketball much, but I knew who Dwyane Wade was. I nodded.

"I wish I had a name that cool. But I would want to be named LeBron."

"I take it you're a Heat fan," I said.

He nodded vigorously. "Oh yeah. I'll be the best one day. My dad was the world's best basketball player. I will be too."

I thought he'd said he didn't have a dad. Just a mom.

"Micah?" a soft, feminine voice called.

The kid's eyes got big and he spun around. "Yeah, Momma. I'm at the door with our neighbor. He came to visit."

I lifted my eyes from the kid just in time to see legs. Lots of fucking legs, all smooth and creamy and encased in tiny little cutoff blue jean shorts. Holy hell. My eyes continued their upward track, taking in the tiny waist and generous breasts barely covered up by a tank top before reaching her face.

Mary, Mother of Jesus. No. Fucking. Way.

I knew that face. It was older. She was a woman now, but I knew that face. Those bright blue eyes, all that long, silky red hair, and those pink lips that made men, young and old, fantasize. But this ... She couldn't—I stopped and stepped back, and then my eyes went back to the boy in front of me ...

Jax Stone 🖤 Sadie
breathe

Krit 🖤 Blythe
bad for you

Jason Stone 🖤 Jess
misbehaving

the
Sea Breeze
series
Abbi Glines

just for now
Preston 🖤 Amanda

hold on tight
Dewayne 🖤 Sienna

because of low
Marcus 🖤 Willow

while it lasts

sometimes it last
Cage 🖤 Eva